Shilo
A Sweet, Quirky, Romantic Muddle
Jennifer Lynn Cary

Tandem Services Press

What Readers Are Saying

The Crockett Chronicles trilogy

"I love historical novels and this one did not disappoint. I was caught up from the first sentence and completely in love with the Crocketts by the end. Can't wait to follow along their next journey. Well done!" –Virginia Denise

"I love this book! The story is soooooo engaging! I can hardly put it down!"—DeNage

Tales of the Hob Nob Annex Café

"This is a well written book that hooks you on the first page. It's a very enjoyable read that makes you forget about all your troubles and step back in time. I loved this book and look forward to what this author writes next." –Ann Ferri

"I loved reading this book! It had me intrigued from the first page, and as the stories began, I could hardly wait to turn the page to see what happened next! Love the mix of true facts mixed with some good, clean, fun fiction! Easy, quick read. I highly recommend this book!" –CatSmit

The Relentless Series

"I lost my heart in this book, caught up in the lives of each character. I remember these times, which made it more real to me. I had tears of joy, tears of sorrow, grief, and smiles in the unexpected. Great story and hard to put down. Keep reading.... You won't regret it."—Novabelle

"I enjoyed another book by Jennifer Cary! As with all her books the story held your attention from the beginning to the end and I look forward to reading all her future books!"—Mary Rima

"I live in Indiana so I know of the places this book talks about. I so absolutely LOVED this story. It's the first one in this series I've read. I'm glad because I feel it should be the first book as it tells of the 2 families & how they connect. It so touched my heart that at times I cried. I couldn't put it down after starting it so anxious to know how things would turn out with all the difficulties Val & Jimmy had. I'm sure the other books in this series are equally as great."—Pat

The Traveling Prayer Shawl

"When her sister's inheritance depends on it, Cami must do the thing she resolved she'd never do, the thing which will break her heart as well as add one more tough task to her already overstuffed calendar. She must fulfill her grandmother's last request - and what's more, there's a deadline that puts in jeopardy her major project at work. As she begins working on the request, she finds even more complications. The inheritance may raise a conflict of interests. How Cami negotiates these and other potential pitfalls made for an interesting and warmhearted story.

Recommended to those who enjoy Christian Women's Fiction and readers who enjoy Debbie Macomber's stories."—Dana McNeely

"I loved this book so much I hated for it to end!"—Cindy

The Weather Girls trilogy

"I just finished all three of the Weather Girls books on my Kindle Fire! I found that once I started, I couldn't stop - and went from one to two to three - in a matter of 4 days! I work so had to leave my evenings to reading - but oh I hated to quit and go to bed! And then I'd run the story through in my mind again!" —Novabelle

"What a fun series! I'm loving spending time in the past with this family and learning more about the girls and their unique personalities." —Erin S

The Forgotten Gratitude Journal

"This incredible book is written in split time. I don't want to give any more away about the story. It's so enjoyable and I couldn't put it down, needing to know what happened to Molly and RJ!" —Annmarie K

"Jennifer Lynn Cary has written a beautiful split time story about love, love lost and love found again! Throw a mystery villain in the mix and you have a romance with suspense and drama! Such a good read for any romance lover!" —Anita Stafford

Cheryl's Going Home

"This book will touch your heart and soul. Cheryl and Aaron's heart-warming story is full of emotions, and you can feel every one of them. This book will make you laugh, cry and feel every emotion in between. I loved it and highly recommend this book and the entire series." —Ann Ferri

"The book is Christian fiction, but it is not heavy handed and fits the characters and the early 1970ties. The book is Cheryl's story, but also her estranged husband, Aaron's story as well. Their two stories, expertly woven together, share the experience of the rebuilding of their relationship from each of their POVs. It's a lovely journey evoking the time and place with musical and celebrity references from the era." —MLRumph

Judy in Disguise

"Wow. I usually don't read strictly romance but this book captured my attention from the back cover and did not disappoint." —Cheri Swalwell

"I love how this author can transport readers back to the 1970's and brings the past to life." —Connie Hill

Sylvia's Mother

"Sylvia's Mother of The Weather Girls Wedding Shoppe and Venue series will take you on a journey like no other and transporting you in the 1970s and showing you the lessons of God's Redemption, overcoming major obstacles, and showing what it means to be a Child of God." —lesliejune

"I was captivated by the storyline from the very first page." —familymgrkendra

Runaround Sue

"You'll find yourself laughing and crying along with Sue as she navigates the path to forgiveness. It's a book you don't want to miss." —author Jodie Wolfe

"One of the many things author Jennifer Lynn Cary excels at is plunking a reader firmly into a believable setting, one that can walk right off the page and into their hearts." —author Jenny Knipfer

Cracklin' Rosie

"I enjoy the humor and heart this romantic comedy delivers." Cheryl @ Hartfiction

"I love this series and hope there are more books to come." —author Cheri Stalwell

Ronnie

"This 70s rom-com, Ronnie, by Jennifer Lynn Cary, is truly a blast from the past." — Babbling Becky L

"WOW, this just might be my favorite book of the series." —familymgrkendra

Tracy

"I love the emotions, the feelings, the reality that comes out in this story." —Novabelle

"I love it when I get to travel back to Kokomo, Indiana in a Jennifer Lynn Cary book–it's like I'm catching up with old friends and getting reacquainted with new friends..." —Lesleijune

In memory of
Heather Farrah
who was, like Shilo, compassionate and brave.
A true friend.

A friend loves at all times, And a brother is born for adversity.

Proverbs 17:17

Contents

The Cardinal in the Sycamore

Once upon a time, a legend grew from the native people living in Central Indiana.

If a couple really loved each other and they kissed beneath a certain sycamore tree *and* a cardinal landed on the branch above them, they would have a long life together.

In the late nineteenth century, a gas boom hit the sleepy farming town of Kokomo.

A family named Ferguson made their wealth with the event and built an impressive mansion on the grounds of the old sycamore tree. When they did, word of the legend came to them, and they passed it down their generations.

Finally, in 1970 the last member of the family sold Ferguson House to Sunny Day Whitcomb who, along with her sisters Stormy Day Crawford and Windy Day Norman, opened the *Weather Girls Wedding Shoppe and Venue* in the old mansion.

Now when couples come, they have their photos taken beneath the shade of the old sycamore and hope for a cardinal sighting to add spice to their kiss.

Welcome to the stories of the *Weather Girls Wedding Shoppe and Venue* series.

Shilo:
A Sweet, Quirky, Romantic Muddle

Chapter 1
Wednesday, May 23, 1973 Kokomo, Indiana

S creeching brakes jerked Shilo Anderson as she leaned against the window frame, rousing her from the familiar dream. A dream so comforting and longed for, but on hold until she reached Heaven's streets of gold.

As her dream disintegrated, through cracked lids she noted the eastern horizon glittering with the sun's rays peeking over in greeting. They must be close to her destination.

The semi's air brakes screeched again, and she straightened in the passenger seat.

"Hey, I was about to wake you. This here's Kokomo, or what you can see from the 31." Right. Mr. Campbell gave her the ride for this last leg. Her brain woke up.

Shilo recognized landmarks she hadn't seen in a decade. "I'd know it anywhere, Mr. Campbell." She yawned and blinked the final bit of her sleepiness away.

"Remember, it's Ben?" He kept his eyes on the stoplight dangling above. "I was thinking. I'm doing good for time. How's about I take you a little closer? I can do Markland and Washington, then let you out so you won't have so much walking to do. Plenty of places for me to circle back to the highway."

"That's kind of you, Mr. .... ah, Ben. You don't have to, but I appreciate it." She stretched her legs and wiggled her toes. Shilo's primary mode of transport was her feet, so she wasn't worried. But at least if he drove her that close, she might have time to find a place to make herself more presentable. It'd been a long journey from Southern California.

"Then it's settled." Ben started humming "Kiss an Angel Good Morning" and focused on his driving, turning west when they reached the light where Markland Avenue crossed US 31. Ben Campbell looked to be in his mid-forties with a touch of a bulge around his middle and graying hair at his temples beneath his red ballcap. They'd chatted off and on since he picked her up at a Tri-County Truckstop in Villa Ridge near St. Louis. He was married with two daughters of his own. Maybe that's why he let her hitch a ride, to offer protection that he'd want for his own girls. One genuinely nice guy.

Shilo could only guess his reasons. At least he hadn't lectured. And he made no unwanted moves. Now that she thought of it, all the rides proved to be kind-hearted, even the woman trucker, Bess. She said girls needed to stick together.

However, Shilo knew who protected her, and she sent up a silent word of thanks and blessing over Ben and the other truckers.

He stayed in the right lane so that when they reached the drop-off point, Shilo could climb out fast. And now that they hit that spot, she gathered her backpack and slipped the strap over her shoulder while the semi came to a complete stop. She cracked open the door. "Thank you so much, Ben."

"Listen, I realize I'm not your dad, but I gotta say something. Hitch-hiking ain't no thing for a girl, especially one as pretty as you. You need to stay safe, ya hear?"

"I hear." She smiled. More than nice, Ben was kind. So, he should understand. "I am safe. God's been riding with me the entire trip. He takes good care of me." The trust and peace she'd experienced this whole week as each need was met and every move fell into place could only be from the hand of her Heavenly Father. She flashed the guy a parting smile. "God bless you with safe travels, Ben Campbell." Then, with a little wave, she hopped out and closed the door. A single pat on the handle before she oriented herself.

Foster Park would be a few blocks north. Maybe she'd spot a cafe opened up for the early morning breakfast crowd. She'd clean up in their restroom and order something cheap from the menu. The money she'd scraped together to make this trip had dwindled. But with how God provided so far, she had no doubt He would again. She'd been able to trust Him ever since He saved her life.

She spun around in a slow three-sixty to get the lay of the land. Wolfcale's on the corner of Waugh and Markland looked to be open even though it was barely five in the morning. Shilo hitched her backpack strap higher on her shoulder and headed inside. Bells jangled announcing her presence while the scent of fresh coffee filled the air. The place looked clean too. It all called welcome to her.

A waitress who already appeared weary wiped the counter.

"May I use your restroom?" Shilo flashed her friendliest smile.

"Sure, dearie, but you'll need to order something." The woman's nameplate read Myrtle.

"I plan to, Myrtle. I want to clean up a bit first."

Myrtle handed her a key with an elaborate foot-long fob. "Yeah, we get all kinds through here, so management is cautious."

"Ah-ha." Shilo accepted the conglomeration. "I'll be out in a few and will check your menu then. Thanks."

The restroom gleamed with cleanliness, probably from a combination of the guardian of the lock and Shilo being the first to enter for the day.

Whatever the reason, she had one more thing to be grateful for. "Thank You, Father."

Now to get presentable. She pulled out her long denim skirt she'd made from an old pair of jeans before she left home and shook the fabric to get rid of the wrinkles. It was the best she could do with what she had. And she did want to look appropriate at the meeting.

God even orchestrated for her to arrive on the day of her appointment. He was so good to her.

After brushing her teeth and washing her face, she dabbed on a touch of make-up. These days she rarely wore any, but a little mascara and gloss would be proper for today.

She also rinsed off her body as best she could before rolling on her Secret deodorant and pulling on fresh panties and a bra. Her white peasant blouse with the cotton lace didn't fare as well as her skirt, wrinkle-wise, but maybe they'd relax as her body warmed the material. She'd leave her tennies on while she still had walking to do but switch them out when she got closer to the office building.

One last glance in the mirror. The strawberry blonde with her hair in a heavy braid over her shoulder looked to be as good as she was going to get. Besides, her stomach chose that moment to rumble. "Okay, okay, I'll feed you." Another silent thank You sent winging heavenward, and she returned to the counter with the key. "That feels a lot better."

"I can tell, hon. Now what should I getcha?" Myrtle snapped her gum. Must be a fresh stick with the flavor scent hanging on the waitress's words. Doublemint?

Shilo took a seat on a bar stool and checked out the menu. What she wanted was some good ol' biscuits and gravy. But with the sum total of her finances in the front pocket of her backpack, she needed to conserve. "How about a cup of coffee and ..." She had to make the most food out of the least amount of cost. "A donut. I'd like a glazed, please." She tucked the plastic trifold back into the holder.

"Are you sure that's all you want?"

It wasn't, but Shilo couldn't say that. She wouldn't lie either. "It's enough."

Myrtle scribbled on her pad, ripped off the top page, and tucked it on the chrome wheel that hung in the window between the front and the kitchen. Then she brought over the biggest glazed donut Shilo'd ever seen and poured her a cup of coffee. "Need cream?"

"Yes, please."

A tiny silver pitcher, still cold from its place in the cooler, appeared next to Shilo's mug.

"Thank you." She bowed her head and said grace over her meal before doctoring her coffee and tucking into the beautiful donut that tasted even better than it looked. Someone knew how to make donuts.

"Here ya go, hon." Myrtle slid a plate of biscuits and gravy with a side of bacon toward her.

"Oh, no, that's not mine."

"Doncha want it? Food's just gonna go to waste if you won't eat it."

Shilo glanced about the place. She was their first and only customer. Why'd Myrtle put in that order? "Are you sure? I don't understand."

"Someone told me you needed this." Myrtle sort of motioned with her eyes toward the ceiling.

But Shilo understood what she meant. "Thank you so much." Her heart squeezed with gratitude. If she'd toyed with even the remotest of doubts, this dispelled them all. God was with her on this trip, and He took good care of her. Just as she told Ben. Yep, he'd been a godsend too, like everyone she'd encountered to arrive here.

Shilo savored each bite. She hadn't enjoyed biscuits and gravy in close to a decade. It comforted her like a blanket on the inside.

When it was time to go, she pulled out an extra dollar bill. Freely you've received, freely give. It left her with a few coins, but with Aunt Sarah's words ringing in her heart, Shilo waved to Myrtle and continued on her way.

Foster Park wasn't much more than a half a mile down Washington Street. She'd hang out until her appointment. There hadn't been an exact time given in the message, strictly speaking. Maybe they'd figured she would call first. But that would take more money. Besides, since she'd hitched from San Diego, she'd had no way of knowing when she started off if she'd arrive on the right day. Still, she had faith and trust.

The walk felt great to her long legs that had been curled up more often than not on the passenger seat of a semi's cab. Her jean skirt made a soft swish-swosh with her stride.

Soon Foster Park came into view. Shilo crossed the street and wandered to the nearest bench to take in her surroundings. She'd missed this—the early morning dew, the small wild violets sprinkled among the hardy dandelions. Even the sky above seemed a bit bluer, the clouds puffier. The rosebushes in the yards across the way offered their scent as a companion as she sat.

There was something special about being from a town like this. Even if San Diego was home now, Kokomo would always own a place in her heart. Another gift from her Heavenly Father, allowing this town to have a part in her.

The flowers gave her an idea. She pulled out her hairbrush and undid her long braid, brushing until the strands crackled with static. Then she gathered some of the tiny violets and re-braided her hair, sticking the miniature blooms between the plaits. Jesse always liked flowers. When she finished, she put the brush away and held out a compact mirror to double-check her work. Not bad.

The day warmed, though, and it was still too early to head downtown to the office building. Here she'd rest, get some green in her soul, and enjoy an extended quiet time communing with Jesus.

That reminded her of what she tucked into the side pocket of her backpack right before she left. A new-to-her harmonica. She'd picked out a few worship songs to learn back home. Maybe she ought to practice them. Nothing like music to usher her into the presence of God.

"Jesus Loves Me" was the first song she conquered and had been the easiest to figure out. She started that one now, singing the words in her mind while she blew out the tune.

But in the middle of the second chorus, someone tapped her shoulder.

Shilo lowered the harmonica and squinted up to a tall figure in a blue uniform topped off with a hat. "Hello. Beautiful day, isn't it?" She put her hand up to shield her eyes for a better view.

The officer didn't smile. He didn't look mean either. Just all business. "Do you realize what time it is?"

"No, sir. I'm sorry, but I haven't got a watch. I just arrived in town."

"You don't live here?"

"No, sir."

"Do you have a place to stay?"

Shilo shook her head. "Not at the moment."

"We've got ordinances around here. I'm afraid I need to take you in for vagrancy and disturbing the peace." He pulled out a set of handcuffs.

"I'll come peaceably, sir. I didn't realize I broke any rules."

She saw in his eyes that he wavered before he put his cuffs back on his belt. "Okay, no bracelets, but I still need to take you in. It's not safe to be out by yourself so early in the morning."

Shilo smiled. Another person concerned for her safety. If only they understood.

She walked with him to his patrol car and sat in the back, where she wondered if her clothes would get messed up before her appointment. This minor detour hadn't even been a blip in her thoughts about the trip.

As she walked into the station with the officer, he turned her over to a matron. First, she was fingerprinted and processed before someone asked if she needed to make a phone call.

She did.

At least they'd burned up enough time putting her through the paces that there was a chance of someone answering her call now. A well-used edition of the Yellow Pages, the lawyer section full of dog-eared pages, sat on a shelf beneath the wall telephone. Shilo hunted up her number and dialed.

"Hamilton, Franklin, and Reynolds. How may I direct your call?"

"I need to speak with Jesse Franklin, please." *Lord, let him be in.*

"I can connect you with his secretary. One moment, please."

The Muzak recording had just started, her short nails tapping to the beat on the graffitied wall, when the call picked up again. "Jesse Franklin's office. How may I help you?"

"Hello. This is Shilo Anderson. May I speak with him?"

"He's in conference. I'm happy to take a message."

"I have an appointment with him for today." She paused. Shilo didn't want the entire world to know. But apparently, she'd need to inform Jesse's secretary. "I won't be able to make it. I've been arrested."

"Hey, Jesse, got a minute?"

Jesse Franklin slowed his steps and turned to the voice, the one that made him cringe each time he heard it. "Sure, what's up?"

"I hoped you'd cover for me at the lunch meeting with the Drurys. I sort of double booked myself and—"

"And you don't want to deal with Mrs. Drury's tears anymore. I get it." He didn't want to deal with the weepy woman, either. That was the main reason he'd handed off the file to Eli Shanahan, so he wouldn't have to. In his head Jesse said no, firm and clear, telling Eli to just do his job. But then he opened his mouth. "Fine. But only this once. What time is the meeting?"

"Twelve fifteen at the Elks Lodge. Thanks, man." With a slap to Jesse's back, he hustled away. Probably out of fear that Jesse'd changed his mind. Which he ought to do, and fast. Why? Why did he let himself get pulled into these situations? He didn't want to be Eli's mentor any more than Eli wanted him to be. No love lost between them, that was for sure.

Besides, the bomb Grandfather dropped on him right before their seven a.m. meeting continued to ring in his ears. The old man had pushed his way through Jesse's life for as long as he could remember, but this was the worst.

Still, he stopped by his secretary's desk to have her add the lunch appointment to his calendar and to help keep him from forgetting.

Vivian Watters worked for the firm before Jesse finished grade school. Short and matronly with salt and pepper hair, she hadn't been hired for her beauty. She was to make him look good, and she did an excellent job of that.

"Viv, I need to add a lunch meeting to today's schedule. Twelve fifteen at the Elk's Lodge. The Drurys."

As she wrote that down, he rounded past her and strode into his office, slipping out of his jacket and loosening his tie.

"Don't get too comfortable. You had a phone call. Here's the message." Vivian tore off a sheet from the official memo pad bearing the name of his grandfather's firm, *Hamilton, Franklin, and Reynolds,* before she left his office, closing the door behind her.

Jesse watched her leave, grateful for her efficiency, before checking the paper in his hand.

Shilo Anderson will not make her meeting today. She has been arrest—

"Viv!" He jumped to his feet and hollered again as she opened his door.

"Yes, boss?"

"When did she call? Where did she call from? Where is she now?" He'd already put his jacket back on.

"She's here in town at the jail. I called and checked. They have her for vagrancy and disturbing the peace."

"No way. I can't believe it."

"Believe it. I don't think she's been arraigned yet. This is fresh on the books." Vivian adjusted his tie. "Want me to reschedule the Drurys?"

He couldn't even guess how long this would take. Besides, he had a meeting with Shilo already scheduled for some time today—when was it? "What time was I to meet with Ms. Anderson?"

"You'd said to keep it open, that you'd see her whenever she arrived." Her brows rose noting again without words that this was unusual.

"Good, good. I'll be bringing her back here." A shiver got trapped between his shoulder blades. "How do I look?"

"Handsome as always. Why? What are you worried about?"

"Worried? I'm not worried. It's just, well, I haven't seen her in a long time. A decade." What if she didn't recognize him? What if she'd changed and he didn't recognize her?

"Bet you pick up right where you left off. Now, go rescue her. I'll handle things here." She pointed toward the elevator and motioned him on his way.

He punched the buttons for the basement parking garage while Vivian's words echoed around him. Pick up where they left off? He wasn't sure that was possible. Rescue her? Absolutely. She was the one who'd gotten away. If she needed him, he'd be there. Too bad it took ten years for him to get the chance to play Sir Galahad.

His steed wasn't white, either. Instead, his mode of transportation was blue, Ferrari Blu. It would have to do, he guessed.

Jesse pulled from the lot and headed for the police department. If he convinced the chief to have the officer drop his charges, that would solve everything. Vagrancy? Disturbing the peace? None of that sounded like Shilo. Even though it'd been a long time, he couldn't imagine that she'd changed that much.

He pulled open the police station door, he stepped into organized chaos. The clatter of typewriters, the smell of stale cigarette smoke, and people—the washed and the unwashed—busy moving to where they needed to be.

He stopped at the front desk to learn the chief wasn't in, but Captain Bob Sargent covered the position, so Jesse asked to speak with him.

"Hey, Franklin, come on in." Bob, in his short-sleeved shirt with his tie askew, waved Jesse back. "What brings you here today? I thought you didn't mess with criminal cases."

"I don't. But my secretary got a call from a client who came from California to meet with me. Said she'd been arrested for vagrancy and disturbing the peace. Just want to understand what's going on." He took a chair in the chief's office while Bob closed the door.

"Happened today? This morning?"

"Yeah." Jesse started to drum his fingers but caught himself. *Settle down, boy.*

Bob opened the door again and called for someone.

A few seconds later, a woman entered with a clipboard and a sheaf of papers.

"What's your client's name?"

"Shilo. Shilo Anderson."

Jesse hopped up to read over the woman's shoulder.

She pulled her pencil out and used the eraser end to scan the paper. Then she flipped a page. "Anderson, Anderson. Here you go. Shilo Anderson. Picked up for vagrancy and dis—"

"We got that part. Who's the arresting officer?" Bob said it, though Jesse thought it.

"Nucum. Bryan Nucum." She slid her pencil back behind her ear, all business.

"Is he here? Or on patrol?" Bob handled the situation, allowing Jesse to just watch.

"I'll go see." The woman left.

"Isn't Nucum that new guy who's so gung-ho?" Jesse'd heard the name before, maybe from Eli who'd just finished with a traffic case where the client got a ticket but swore he wasn't speeding. He had to hand it to Eli, it was a stroke of genius. He asked the officer to demonstrate how he calibrated his speed gun with the tuning fork. Nucum showed that he tapped the tuning fork against his shoe to get the tone. That was all

Eli needed. Enough evidence had shown that tapping against the shoe in that manner could put nicks into the tuning fork that caused the tone to be off, thus making the calibrations of the speed gun wrong. Everyone in the gallery waiting to be seen about a speeding ticket that day got dismissed.

If it was the same guy, Jesse hoped for the same luck and returned to his chair.

A knock sounded at the jamb before the door cracked open. "You wanted to see me?"

Bob stood. "Yeah, come on in, Nucum. Wanted to ask you about that girl you brought in today."

"Oh, she was hanging out at Foster Park around quarter-after-six this morning, playing her harmonica. I asked her if she lived here, and she said no."

Now Jesse stood and shoved his hands in his pockets for everyone's protection. "Did you ask about her plans?"

"No, sir."

"So, you didn't check if maybe she was waiting for someplace to open before she found a place to stay?"

"Huh?" This genius would fall apart on a witness stand.

Bob stepped in. "Never mind, Nucum. We can let this one go. She doesn't seem like a hardened criminal."

"That harmonica, though—"

"It's fine. Franklin, why don't you have Shirley take you over to get your client. I'll take care of the rest here." Bob motioned the officer to the desk.

Jesse slipped out. He didn't want to hear any more anyway. Besides, the sooner he got to Shilo, the better.

Just as Bob said, Shirley took him to where they held Shilo as she waited for her arraignment, their footsteps making an echo on the way upstairs.

Other women filled the cells, but only one stood out to him. A little older, a bit thinner, but he had no doubt which one was Shilo. Especially when she spotted him and smiled with that tiny gap between her front teeth and her advertisement-worthy hair in a braid over her shoulder.

Shirley unlocked the cell and Shilo stepped out, wrapping him in one enormous hug.

He wanted to melt into the floor almost as much as he longed to return her embrace. Only he was a professional, and he needed to maintain a respectable image, especially with the police department.

"Oh, Jesse, it's so good to see you." She didn't seem to notice he'd held back. Maybe that was good and didn't hurt her feelings.

"Hey, Shilo. Let's get you out of here."

"Thank you." Shilo turned to the women in the cell. "Bye, girls, I'll be praying for you."

Guess some things do change.

She linked her arm with his. "Jesse, I can't believe it's you. I'm so glad to see you."

"Did anything happen?"

"Oh, no, just another arrest. It's fine."

This isn't the first time? But he couldn't say that out loud, not with Shirley walking out with them.

"Let's get your things, and I'll take you back to the office."

She squeezed his arm. "Thank you, Jesse. I appreciate that." She leaned her head against his shoulder.

With most men, she'd be putting her head on their shoulders because of her height. But with his six-foot-three stature, she only leaned against him.

And he liked it. Even if it was more of a public display of affection than he was comfortable with. This was Shilo.

Shirley slipped behind a counter and into the back room.

"How many suitcases did you bring?" Could he fit them all into his trunk?

"Just my backpack. I travel light these days." She grinned that grin. The one that made his knees weak. How could she still have this effect on him?

Shirley returned with a khaki green backpack sporting an off-white trim, holding it out as if it might be contagious. True, the bag had seen better days. Was Shilo that bad off? Jesse rubbed his chin. What waited back in his office could be just what she needed.

Shilo signed her receipt, and Jesse walked her to his car. She stalled. "This is yours?" Her gray eyes grew nearly twice their size.

His ears warmed. She was the last person he wanted to think he was pretentious. "It makes Grandfather crazy. Calls it flashy."

Her grin teased her lips. "Bet that cinched the deal."

"You're right." He winked and unlocked her door, holding it until she was safely inside. Then he rounded the car to his side and climbed in.

He started the ignition and out of habit punched the button for his eight-track, *The Temptations* filling the vehicle with "My Girl." He couldn't have picked a better song, only it was a decade too late for them. Maybe. He was afraid to hope.

"You still listen to Motown."

"Of course. When something is good, it's good." Jesse backed from the spot and eased into traffic. "I'll take you to the office. We'll get business out of the way."

"That's cool." Shilo leaned back and closed her eyes with a sigh.

She must not have gotten much sleep, especially if she was in the park that early in the morning. *Wonder what time her bus got in?*

"So, Jesse, how've you been? Tell me what you've been up to these past ten years." She turned her head his way and opened her right eye. Man, she looked tired.

"Hmm. I went to college, Ball State, and then finished my law degree at IU. Grandfather took me into the firm, and as soon as I passed the bar, I became an associate. Now I'm a junior partner." He wouldn't mention the next step since he couldn't see it happening. No way would that old man push him like that, even if he did dangle the full partnership. It bordered on creepy.

"You've done well. Are you happy?"

"What's happy?" He shrugged. "I do what's required. Sometimes I meet great people and get to help those who really need it, but pretty much I do as I'm told."

She turned in her seat, giving him her full attention. "Oh Jesse, that's got to be one of the saddest things ever."

"What's sad about it? It just is. That's reality." He tossed her a half-smile.

The weight of her stare pressed on him. "You didn't used to be such a cynic."

He turned the car into the parking garage. "You've been gone a long time, Shilo. Things change."

"No way you'd change your character that much." She shook her head, and he felt her disappointment.

Maybe you never knew the real me. No, he couldn't say that out loud. Instead, he parked and, then came around to get her door. They remained quiet all the way up the elevator to the second floor.

Jesse introduced her to Vivian before ushering her into his office and closing the door.

"Make yourself comfortable. Can I get you something to drink?" Maybe if he played the friendly host, this awkwardness would go away.

She shook her head. "No, let's get on with this."

Okey-dokey. He pulled out the file marked with her grandfather's name and opened to the will. "I can read it to you or give you a copy after explaining the main points."

"Do that. Just the main points. I'll read it later."

Jesse cleared his throat and shuffled the pages to the summation, trying to keep his hands busy. "Okay. Your grandfather left everything to you. His entire estate, which, since all the debts have been covered, comes to around $2.4 million. That's apart from his house and possessions."

She stared at him as if she were flash-frozen.

"Shilo, are you okay?"

Silence.

"Shilo?" He came around his desk, knelt in front of her, and sort of waved his hand. "Are you okay? Let me get you a drink of water." So not the reaction he'd expected.

He poured a glass from the pitcher he kept in his small refrigerator and molded her hands around the cup.

She glanced up at him as she grasped the tumbler, blinked, and took a sip. "Oh, I had no idea."

He paused long enough to make sure she was okay, then returned to his chair. "He made one stipulation, though. You must either be married at the time of this reading or be willing to be married within thirty days after."

Her mouth opened and closed as if she wanted to form words before something squeaked out. "Married? I have to get married to receive the inheritance?" It took a moment, but she sighed, and a smile emerged. "Then that's easy." She stood and set her glass on his desk. "Thanks anyway, Jesse. I'm sorry you got stuck with this, but no thanks. I don't marry for money."

She slung her backpack over her shoulder and left his office.

All at once he was eighteen again watching his world walk away.

Chapter 2

"Shilo, wait a sec."

She turned to Jesse, who'd followed her out. He handed her a fat envelope that she slid into an outside pocket of her backpack. None of this played out how she'd imagined.

He paused and did that thing with his toe and the floor, sort of twisting his foot like he used to when he wanted to say something but struggled with the words. "Um, where will you go? Do you need a place to stay?"

He might think he'd changed, but she could tell deep down he remained the same sweet boy. "I'm heading for Aunt Sarah's. She's not far from here, right?"

"Straight up Taylor Street. Want me to give you a ride?"

"No thanks. I'll enjoy the walk. So good to see you again. And thank you for coming to get me. Bet you've had less embarrassing rescues." She grinned as he blushed.

"Happy to, for you, Shy."

Shilo wrapped him in a hug and kissed his cheek before catching his secretary watching the whole exchange. "Take good care of him, Vivian. He's someone special."

Vivian smiled. "Will do, Ms. Anderson. I agree."

And with that, Shilo waved goodbye to Jesse, probably for the last time. That little notion squeezed her heart, and she hurried toward the elevator before she lost her cool.

She'd punched the button for the first floor when someone called, "Hold the elevator," and a hand shoved between the doors before they closed, prying them open.

Shilo glanced away to get her emotions under control before offering the stranger a smile.

"Good golly, Miss Molly. It can't be, but lo-and-behold. Shilo Anderson, the girl of my dreams. Where in the world have you been?"

If she hadn't recognized the confident voice first, that grin gave him away. "Eli Shanahan. What are you doing here?"

"Hey, I work here. The actual question is what are you doing here? I can't believe it's you." He beat her to the hug. "Yep, you're real alright. I coulda sworn I was trippin'."

That was so Eli that she had to smile. "Jesse and I discussed my grandfather's will. So, you work here? With Jesse and his grandfather?"

"Uh-huh. A full-fledged lawyer. Didn't see that coming, did ya?"

"Nope, I sure didn't."

"Tell you what. I'm on my way to grab a cup of coffee off the premises. Want to join me?" He glanced over his shoulder even though the elevator doors opened to no one waiting.

"Sounds like fun." She slipped her arm around his and let him guide her out.

"Kresge's is only a couple blocks away. How's that?"

"I'm with ya. Lead on."

As they walked sidewalks poured decades ago by the WPA and passed businesses that seemed to have jumped from her recollections with a little more wear, a little less fresh paint, and a whole lot more reality, they chatted about the weather. A part of Shilo's brain filtered through her memories of Eli, how he always used those puppy dog eyes to break down defenses.

He and Jesse never got along. Neither understood the reason she cared for them both. Eli, fun-loving, boundary-pushing, a wink and a prayer from trouble, stood in stark contrast to rule-following, soft-hearted Jesse. Even Eli's Nordic blond verses Jesse's tall and dark stood in extreme opposite with each other, though both were now very handsome men. However, the truth? She didn't picture either of them as lawyers. What happened?

"Here we go." Eli held the door for her and then headed to the lunch counter. "How do you take your coffee?" Registers up front rang up sundry purchases while the scent of freshly brewed java mingled with hot dogs, eggs, and hamburgers cooking on the grill filled the air around the small luncheonette counter.

"Cream and sugar, please." She smiled and grabbed a table while he ordered.

Soon they were seated, and all she could do was shake her head while watching him grin. He was born to charm his way through life, especially since he no longer cut those blond curls into a crew cut, and his dimples made his blue eyes twinkle. The mustache was new, but it looked good on him.

"What's going through that beautiful brain of yours?" He posted his elbow on the tabletop and leaned his chin on his fist.

Truth was, looking at him took her back to their high school years, especially the last one. So much happened. And it all seemed to start in the fall. If anyone told her then that she'd be sitting here having a coffee with him after what he did, well ... She shook her head at the craziness of life. "Just recalling homecoming our senior year."

He straightened up. "No, please don't go there. That so wasn't my finest hour."

"I've forgiven you. I did back then, remember? Even let you take me to the Stardust Ball. It's just that I'm still, oh, I don't know, in awe of the gall it took?"

He hung his head. "I was a cruel and callow fellow in my youth."

"Not cruel. Thoughtless. Definitely self-centered. You only asked me because I was up for homecoming queen, and you weren't about to let Jesse ask me first. You should've gone with Sondra, and none of that would've happened."

"Yeah. Jesse's always been a thorn in my side, even back then. Maybe my whole life."

She moved her cup out of the way and leaned forward on her forearms. "Why? You two are nothing alike. You had different friends and preferences. I've never understood that."

"It's too long a story to go into, but our grandfathers are to blame. However, let me apologize once more for homecoming 1962." He captured her hand and kissed the back like some romance hero.

She yanked it away and giggled. "Oh stop, silly. I told you I forgave you a long time ago. I only hope you never tried that same stunt with anyone while in college."

"Um, are you referring to my claim of not feeling well and taking my date home early in order to go back and leave with the homecoming queen? That stunt? No. Once was enough. I felt bad from the moment I did it."

Now she took his hand. "Sounds like it's not my forgiveness you need. Maybe you ought to forgive yourself."

He chuckled. "New topic. How long are you in town for, and when can I see you again?"

"I'm here until I leave. Not sure when that will be, but right now, I've no plans for any specific length of time. Just want to check on Aunt Sarah, maybe walk around the old neighborhood before heading home. Nothing much here to keep me."

"Hope that changes. I'd love to get together again. Oh, hey, there's always the class reunion. Got a letter about it just yesterday." He rose.

Shilo got the message. He needed to leave. She stood as well, pushing in her chair. "That's a possibility. Maybe. Eli, it's so good to catch up with you." She placed a kiss against his cheek. "And thank you for the coffee." Time she headed for Aunt Sarah's anyway.

"C'mon, I'll walk you to your car."

"I didn't drive. What do I need a car for here? I can walk to about anywhere in town."

Eli studied her a minute. "Still down-to-earth Shilo. Man, I've missed you. Let me at least escort you over to Taylor Street before I head back to the office."

"I'd like that." She walked with him outside and the couple blocks to where she'd turn west to her aunt's place.

"By the way, I need to ask you something." He'd grown so serious, she couldn't imagine what the problem might be.

"Lay it on me."

He paused, turning her to look at him. "Is it true that it never rains in Southern California?"

Shilo snorted. Same ol' Eli. "Oh man, it pours." She tossed him a wink, and they both cracked up.

Another hug and kiss on the cheek—though she caught him trying to make it more and giggled—and she waved goodbye and headed to Aunt Sarah's alone.

Usually one to enjoy another's company, Shilo had to admit this time she craved the solitude. She had tons to ponder. So much had happened since Ben dropped her off, and she needed that quiet to discuss things with Jesus.

"None of this surprised You, did it, Jesus? Did I miss hearing You on something? Maybe I didn't need to come here. Did You want me to stay in California?"

That's when her traveling companion paraded through her mind all the wonderful reminders of His loving providence—the kind and respectful truckers, the food, and other provisions provided when she needed it, even having Jesse rescue her from jail. No arraignment or sentencing this time. At least she didn't have a record in her hometown.

So why was she here? "I trust You, Jesus, and if You've led me to Kokomo, You've got a reason. Please, if it won't mess with Your plans, would You give me a glimpse of where we're headed?"

Peace enfolded her, and she almost felt Jesus's arm around her as He kissed the top of her head. Everything would be fine. Whatever He planned.

Aunt Sarah's place came into view—a gable-front house painted white with red trim around the windows. Though it appeared in need of a fresh coat. That struck Shilo, as her aunt always took meticulous care of her home.

But standing on the sidewalk gawking wouldn't get her inside. She mounted the two steps to the walkway and the five leading to the slab porch buffeted on either side by white rail fencing. Just as she raised her fist to knock, the crimson door yanked open.

"Oh, my stars. You're here. I can't believe it." Aunt Sarah pulled Shilo into an Olympic-worthy bear hug that wouldn't let go. "You've come home, sweet girl. You've come home."

Tears fell from Shilo's eyes as her own shoulder grew damp. She hugged back and thanked God. Oh, how she'd missed this dear woman. Who else could've softened the edges of Grandpa's sternness by teaching her to use makeup, taking her shopping for school clothes, and comforting her when Eli pulled his stunt. Their "Girls' Night" slumber parties filled the void left by the death of her mother.

Aunt Sarah pulled away but grabbed Shilo's hand, dragging her across the threshold. "You get in here and let me look at you." She twirled Shilo as if in a dance, scanning her from head to toe. "You're too thin. I've always thought that, but hoped you'd fill out once you got a little older. Are you eating enough?"

Shilo laughed and dropped a kiss on the soft cheek of the sweetest woman alive. "I get plenty. Trust me. But let me look at you. How are you?"

Aunt Sarah's bottom lip trembled for a moment. If Shilo hadn't been studying her face, she'd have missed it. "What's wrong?"

Her aunt shook her head and led her to the couch. "It's nothing, child. Sit. I'd rather hear all about you. Your letters don't tell me enough."

"Let's see. I'm living with friends down by the beach. I've learned to sew—we picked up an old Singer that I've made pals with, and together we turn out all sorts of things to sell to the tourists. Covers my share of the rent and groceries. Sundays we go to church at the shoreline. Someone shares what God's put on their heart, and we sing—'Seek Ye First,' 'I Love You, Lord,' or 'Spirit Song,' or whatever God puts on someone's heart. Maybe even 'Rock of Ages.'" Aunt Sarah smiled at that. "If someone needs baptizing, we dunk 'em in the ocean." Shilo winked, sure her aunt would laugh at that one.

She did. So good, some things hadn't changed.

"Have you been to see Jesse yet?"

Shilo nodded, having decided she didn't need to share about the little run-in this morning. "Yeah, he must've learned how to reach me from you."

"He called a couple weeks ago, and I invited him over for dinner. We had a lovely chat. He's still sweet on you."

"Oh, ancient history, Aunt Sarah." Shilo dismissed this with a wave of her hand, though a flash of the man who rescued her this morning did make her pulse jump. "We've both grown up and moved on." Or at least she ought to encourage herself to do that before anything got started.

"Maybe you did, but I don't think he has. You were all he talked about that evening. He apologized for it having been such a while since we spoke. He's become a wonderful young man. You'd make a beautiful couple." Aunt Sarah had been the only one to know back in the day that Shilo's feelings for Jesse went beyond friendship. One of those late-night confessions that her aunt respected and didn't try to mess with.

But life happens despite the best laid intentions. What did the Bible say? A man makes his plans, but God directs his steps.

"Let's talk about you. How've you been? You almost never share about yourself, just what's going on in town."

Aunt Sarah's lip quivered again, and this time Shilo wouldn't let her off the hook. "You need to tell me something, don't you?"

Her aunt nodded. "Oh, dearheart, I hate to bring up anything bad on your first night. You are staying here with me, right?"

"I'd hoped to crash here for a quick visit, though I ought to get home to San Diego before too long. But you're not gonna dissuade me from learning what's bothering you." She grasped her aunt's hand and stroked the back of it with her thumb. "Tell me, please."

With a sigh, Aunt Sarah smiled. "You'll find out soon enough, anyway. I've got cancer. Breast cancer."

An icy fist latched hold of Shilo's insides, but she turned her thoughts heavenward, lifting a silent prayer before responding. "When did you learn?"

"About a week ago. I saw the specialist this morning. They want to do surgery right away." Aunt Sarah reached for a tissue from the box on the end table and proceeded to wad it in her hands while she spoke. "Then follow up with what they call chemotherapy. Says it's something new to breast cancer protocol, and that my insurance won't cover it. Radiation is covered, just not the chemo—that's what he calls it. He says it should give me a better outcome. But I haven't got the money. You'd not believe how astronomical the cost, and I'm only getting your Uncle Arthur's social security and pension. Still two more years before I qualify for Medicare, but right now they wouldn't cover it either. I've been on the phone since I walked through the door, and the bottom line is, no chemotherapy. I have to take my chances."

This was why she came. Now Shilo understood why God orchestrated the inheritance. Shilo might not need it, but her aunt sure did. She squeezed Aunt Sarah's hand. "I might be able to help."

Jesse and Eli both flashed through her mind.

Now, who did she ask to marry her?

"You didn't make the Drury's meeting?"

Jesse raised his head to see Eli standing in his doorway. "Something came up. Viv rescheduled."

"Oh." Eli shoved away from the doorframe and took a seat on the corner of Jesse's desk. "So, what's your take on Shilo Anderson being back in town? Looks pretty good, huh?"

"How did you find out?"

Jesse made certain that nobody besides Vivian had that information. Maybe out of selfishness, but he was in no mood to share the woman he still dreamed about with his arch nemesis. Even seeing her in person didn't change one iota of how he imagined her.

"Ran into her at the elevator. We went for coffee to catch up. She said she was in town for a short time, so I'm hoping to ask her out. You don't have her aunt's phone number, do you?" The smile Eli produced had nothing to do with friendly. Instead, it shouted "check," making Jesse aware his queen was in danger.

It would never do for Eli to realize just how close to a win he'd come. Jesse attempted to school his expression by rubbing his chin. "I'm sure Sarah's number's here somewhere. I'll get it to you later." *Like when Antarctica turns into the Sahara.* He returned his attention to the contract. "Anything else?"

"No. I won't keep you."

"Close the door on your way out." *And maybe don't open doors without permission.*

Jesse started the next section of the contract, and his phone rang. Could he not catch a break today? An in-house call. "Franklin, here."

"Jesse, I want to see you in my office. I've got the feeling I haven't made myself clear."

If someone took a sledgehammer to his brain, his head couldn't hurt this bad. Jesse pinched the bridge of his nose. "Yes, Grandfather. On my way."

He knew what the conversation, or rather lecture, would be about. He'd heard what the old man said this morning before the meeting. Just because he kept his mouth shut didn't mean he'd become deaf. Or agreed to obey.

Every demand from the head of this firm crossed the line between professional and personal. Grandfather had no qualms about butting into both. And though the old man's wisdom concerning the law remained legendary, his demands on Jesse's private life had fast become that too, but for different reasons.

It started when Jesse could not major in art at Ball State. Grandfather held the purse strings with the final say. All the way through law school and joining the firm. Okay, so Jesse grew to appreciate the law. And maybe, given time, he'd have considered it for a career. But that's not what happened. Grandfather told him what to do.

And when one gives up their backbone at an early age to please the one in power, it's mighty difficult to grow another.

Which explained why Jesse never argued. Rather, he kept silent, and even that Grandfather considered mutinous. He wouldn't let up on this until Jesse agreed to kowtow to the old man's whims. A tenuous high-wire act without a net to save him when the tightrope gave way.

"Viv, I need to go see Grandfather. I'll be in his office." *Please interrupt for anything. Any. Thing.*

His wonderful secretary nodded with a wink. She understood. Too bad he hated public displays of affection. Otherwise, he'd have kissed her motherly cheek. Maybe he'd order her some flowers. Yep, that's what he'd do.

He headed to the elevator and up to the third floor to the executive suites. Grandfather was now the sole surviving founder of *Hamilton, Franklin, and Reynolds.* Joshua Hamilton's kids all married and moved out of state, and none of the grandkids showed an interest. Abner Reynolds died childless but treated his sister's daughters and their children as his own. One of them being Eli Shanahan. What hold had Abner Reynolds on Jesse's grandfather that made him do so much for Eli and make Jesse's life so miserable?

Jesse reached Grandfather's office. Mrs. Watson typed away as he approached. "Go on in. He's waiting for you." She flashed him a quick smile and kept her fingers moving on the keys.

Go on in. Right. Jesse stared the doorknob down until he finally grasped it and turned.

"Get in here, boy. We need to get this all straight." No sitting, no pleasantries. All business with Jesse's personal business.

The old man with the height and girth of John Wayne and the thick white mane that never allowed a hair out of place stood behind his desk as if he were a supreme court judge.

"I heard what you said this morning, Grandfather. I listened." Jesse jammed his hands in his pockets. *Slow down, heart. No need to pound out of my chest and give him more fodder for his assessment of me.*

"Then what are you going to do?"

Oh, so he needed to produce a plan for what he ultimately planned to avoid. Got it. "I'm considering what you said. I have to meet the right person first. She'll need to fit in, so not just anyone."

"You're correct about that. The Forresters are hosting a party at the country club on Saturday. I suggest you be there. That will be a good place to start your search for a wife." Grandfather returned to the paperwork on his desk as if it held more importance to him than the man he was slowly eviscerating.

Jesse did his best not to wince. He couldn't imagine any woman wanting to settle for a spineless worm like him. After all, wouldn't this be a great issue for him to make his stand? Tell the old man where to get off? But no. He didn't possess the pride to say he'd find Miss Right when he was good and ready. And not a second before. He steadied himself with a glance out the window toward freedom. If only he were a bird ...

"If you want that full partnership, you will do this. No arguments."

"I'm not arguing with you, Grandfather."

"Your voice might not be, but your face is. You need to work on that too. How you ever win a case is beyond me." Now he raised his steely gaze to lock with Jesse's, and a subtle shake of his wooly head expressed his contempt more than mere words could.

Jesse hadn't lost but two cases in his entire career, and both should've never been brought into court. He blamed the clients for pressing him against his better judgment. One would think, with the number of patrons he'd added to the firm plus the cases he'd won, that would be enough to consider him for full partnership. Only Grandfather pulled the strings and insisted on his way. Jesse's sympathies already went to the poor unsuspecting girl to be lured into the old man's trap.

"If that's all, Grandfather, I need to get back. I'm prepping for my next client." He took a step backward toward the door.

Grandfather waved his hand as if shooing away a gnat.

Jesse took the cue and split for his office before the old man changed his mind.

All the way to the elevator and down to his floor, the scene in his office this morning repeated itself. Shilo had to be living pretty much hand-to-mouth. No, she didn't seem upset. In fact, she appeared relieved to have a reason to turn the inheritance down. Over two million dollars. And she hadn't blinked or stuttered once. "I won't marry for money."

If only he had a bit of her gumption.

Back when they were friends, she'd gotten him to do the right thing more than once, making Grandfather angry at her interference. He missed those good times.

What would his grandfather say if he'd answered the same way? "I won't marry for money or promotion?"

He'd fall over with a coronary.

Well, he didn't want to kill the grump, only put up boundaries.

"You're back." Viv stood from her desk.

"I am. All in one piece."

"I called, but you'd just left. You have a visitor."

"Who?"

"Miss Anderson."

Jesse straightened. "Where? Is she still here?"

"She's inside."

He didn't wait for more but charged into his office.

Shilo sat in the same chair as this morning.

He brushed his hair from his forehead. "Hello, again."

"Hello. I hope you don't mind. I've come up with a question or two."

Jesse took his seat behind his desk. "Not at all. What questions?" He tried to present a professional front, but his heart pounded in his ears as his brain jumped ahead with more hope than anyone should possess.

"That get married clause. How soon afterward would I get access to the cash?"

That threw him. She'd said she wouldn't marry for money, but now she'd changed her mind? Why?

"You should receive a check within a week. Everything is in order, so there's just the matter of transferring the funds once you present proof of marriage." He paused but couldn't help himself. "This morning you said you wouldn't marry for money. What changed?"

Shilo's face pinkened, and her eyes grew moist. "Um, I just talked with Aunt Sarah. She ...um, she's been diagnosed with cancer, and the treatment is beyond what she can afford. I'd pay for her, but I don't have that kind of income. Unless I can get married quick." The corners of her lips rose a tad, though it looked more sad than happy.

She wouldn't marry for money for herself, but she'd do anything for her aunt. Jesse got the message loud and clear.

"Okay. Who do you plan to marry? You don't mind my asking, right?" Oh, he hoped she didn't care, but he needed to know.

"I ran into Eli today. He took me for coffee, and we laughed at old memories. I'm considering asking him."

Eli? Breath froze in his lungs. *No, not Eli. Please, no.*

She stared at him. "You look like you've been sucking on a persimmon. Do you two still have that much trouble getting along?"

Grandfather had been right. He needed more control over his face. "It's a long story."

"That's what he said too."

Jesse's heart thudded to a halt with those words. "You've already asked him?"

But Shilo laughed, a soft chuckle. "No. I wanted to make sure of things with you first."

"What things? Oh, right. Your questions." Then his mouth took over. "Shilo, would this be an honest-to-goodness marriage?"

"What do you mean?"

"Would you plan something to meet the letter of the law, or do you want a genuine commitment?" He had to stop talking.

"I'd make it a real commitment. If that's what he wanted in order to marry me."

"Then don't ask him." He'd gotten that much out. Could he say the rest? If he took a second to picture Shy married to Eli, oh, yeah.

"Why?"

"Marry me. I won't force you into anything. In fact, you'd be helping me out as well. We'd work together. We've always been friends. We'd get along fine. What do you say?" His heart thundered in his chest. He said it. Got it all out. But as the silence hung in the air, his tongue started to sweat. And why didn't she answer?

Chapter 3

What just happened, Lord?

W Shilo stood statue still, weighing Jesse's gaze for how earnest he was. This was the last thing she expected. "Can we go to a justice of the peace?"

Jesse nodded. "Sure, no, wait." He glanced away, and his cheeks gained color. "We'd need the whole shebang for the wedding. Social things and all. What's the problem?"

"Oh. I won't do a church wedding, because I can't make those promises before God for a marriage of convenience. How soon can we get the whole shebang, like you said, finished?" Time for Aunt Sarah ticked away.

Jesse stared at her, then his desk, then her. He appeared stumped and at a loss. Then he flashed a nervous grin. "Let me call my secretary." He jumped to open the door. "Viv, would you come in a sec?"

She bustled in, eyes huge behind her glasses. "What's the matter, boss?"

He closed the door after her. "I, we could use your help. Uh, you met Miss Anderson this morning." Jesse's nerves seemed to be getting the better of him. Poor guy. Should she say thanks anyway and go find Eli? Only, there was something about thinking of Jesse as her future husband that set her soul to dancing in a way thoughts of Eli couldn't.

"Yes, I did." Viv flashed a smile at Shilo but returned her stare at Jess as if he'd lost his ever-lovin' mind.

"We're getting married." He let the words out all in one whoosh. Did he already regret his impulsive proposal?

Now Vivian grinned. "Congratulations! This is wonderful news."

"Yeah, but we need to know how to make this work. Shilo doesn't want a church wedding, and you know Grandfather would die just to turn in his grave over stopping by City Hall." Couldn't he just explain?

"You don't want a church wedding?" Viv now stared at Shilo like she was the mindless one.

The truth needed to come out. "My aunt—"

Jesse waved his hand in the air cutting her off. "Long story, but I'm hoping you have an idea."

They stared at each other.

Jesse cleared his throat. "How about we all have a seat?" He motioned toward his chairs like some car show model. "Maybe then we can figure this out. Viv, we want to get married as soon as possible without it causing problems for Grandfather."

"May I say something before I share my idea?" Viv took the other chair, then focused on Jesse.

"Of course."

"You need to start doing what is right for you and stop living for that old man's crumbs." She held up her hand. "I know, I won't say more. You now know how I feel about it."

Jesse sighed, though Shilo thought that was excellent advice. "What is your idea?"

"At my church, there's a family of sisters who own a bridal place. It's called The Weather Girls Wedding Shoppe and Venue. They have everything you need there plus places to host the wedding and reception.

It wouldn't be at a church, but the pastor has been known to marry couples there on site. I heard recently that Sunny, she's one of the sisters, her husband Pat has become a justice of the peace and can marry couples if that's what they prefer." Vivian shrugged.

Jesse turned Shilo's way. "Would this work for you?"

Stunned that he finally included her, she blinked and then coughed into her fist. "Would they be willing to wait until after I get my inheritance for me to pay them?"

Now Vivian really stared at Jesse, who twitched and blinked.

"It's not what you're thinking, Viv. You gotta trust me on this. I'll explain, but right now we need to get this figured out since we're on a time frame." He turned back to Shilo. "If they won't, I'll cover it. No problem. You choose the wedding you want. And Viv, would you get us the number for those sisters, please?"

Shilo followed Vivian as she pulled out the Yellow Pages from a nook behind Jesse's desk. She normally didn't worry about what others thought of her, only what God did. But it bothered her for Jesse's secretary to consider her a gold digger.

And Jesse. *That's another thing, Lord.* It suddenly occurred to her that maybe he only volunteered to marry her because he needed to beat Eli. The stabbing to her heart with that thought hurt as much as it surprised her. She never should've told him her plan.

If this had occurred back ten years ago, she'd have chosen Jesse, no question. But somehow the tender hearted boy had grown into an uptight, competitive man. What happened? And was it too late to change her answer?

Vivian came back and handed her a slip of paper. "Here's the phone number and address for The Weather Girls. I'm sure they can help."

"Thank you." Shilo flashed her friendliest smile. If she and Jesse were to be married, she wanted a good relationship with his secretary. "You mentioned your church. I'll need one if I'm staying."

Vivian's expression mellowed from professional to friendly, and she sat again. "Sure. I'd love for you to be my guest. We have two services. The earlier is more traditional, and the later has more young families. The Day sisters attend then."

"Day sisters?"

"Their maiden name is Day, but they are all married now. Sunny, Stormy, and Windy. That's why they named their business The Weather Girls."

Shilo grinned, though she caught Jesse rolling his eyes and shaking his head as he leaned over his desk to be part of the conversation. She returned her focus to Vivian. "I'll call them as soon as I get to Aunt Sarah's. What time is your second service?"

"At 10:45. Here, let me write down the address for you." Vivian scribbled something on her clipboard before handing Shilo another slip of paper.

Jesse snatched the note. "I'll take you. You don't have a car anyway."

Hey, wait a sec. "Aunt Sarah does. Maybe she'd like to go."

Vivian ignored Jesse and focused on Shilo. "You've mentioned your aunt. Is her last name Flanders?"

"Yes. Do you know her?"

"Oh, my, yes. She's one of the dearest people at my church."

"Small world, huh?" The lone male voice seemed out of place.

Shilo and Vivian stared at Jesse.

"I mean, Kokomo's not that huge, but there are several churches. Who'd have guessed ..." He trailed off, glancing back and forth between both women.

Shilo felt a nudge for the guy trying to normalize the abnormal in his office and tossed him a smile. Okay, maybe the dweeb was just nervous. To be honest, she was too. She'd had to fold her hands in her lap to keep them from shaking. She turned to Vivian. "I guess you haven't heard, and I shouldn't say anything since you and Aunt Sarah are friends, but I'm not doing this for myself. I promise."

Vivian patted her knee. "You explain when it's right. In the meantime, whatever I can do to help, let me know. I'm excited for you two. You make a great couple." She stood and headed for the outer office.

Now Jesse tracked Vivian as if she were nuts.

"I caught that look, boss, but Miss Anderson is exactly what you need in your life. I'll be at my desk." Vivian closed the door after her.

"I like her." Shilo could imagine Viv becoming a close friend.

"Of course you do." Jesse shook his head. "Listen, Shilo, we ought to talk more about this, but if I don't finish what I'm working on, I won't be ready for mediation tomorrow. What if you call the number Viv gave you, and I can check in with you tonight. Better yet, maybe I can even get away and take you and Sarah to dinner. Will that work?"

He tried so hard: She read it in his eyes. "Yeah, that's cool. I'll head on home now and let Aunt Sarah know our plans."

"Would you rather wait for tonight so we can tell her together?" There's that sweet boy she knew. Only Jesse wasn't a boy anymore. Man, was that apparent.

"I'd like that. Thank you." She stood. Time to get moving.

"How are you getting back? Did you borrow Sarah's car?"

Shilo shook her head. "No, I hoofed it, like usual. Second nature anymore."

"Let me call you a cab." He raised the receiver before he finished his sentence.

"No, really, Jesse. It gives me time to think. But I appreciate the thought." She kissed his cheek. "I'm allowed to do that now, right?"

His neck reddened, and the color splashed up to his cheeks. "I suppose so."

"I noticed you aren't comfortable with hugs. Hope you'll get used to mine." She winked and waved as she left his office.

Vivian glanced up. "I'm so happy for you both. Congratulations."

"Thanks, Vivian. I'll see you on Sunday."

No one took the elevator with her, and the lobby stood empty. Just as well. A replay of the last time she left Jesse's office zipped through her brain. *Eli. Oh, man.* Somehow, she needed to make him aware she was no longer available.

That is, unless Jesse didn't mind her seeing old friends.

The second that notion occurred, a question about her intelligence followed. Jesse cool with her seeing Eli? Ha! Who was she kidding?

But the important thing was that Aunt Sarah would have every advantage now to beat her cancer.

What about prayer?

Yes, Lord. She needed to remember God was the Healer. He'd healed Shilo. He could heal Aunt Sarah. Chemotherapy or no chemotherapy.

Shilo spent the rest of the walk talking with Jesus and getting her priorities set. She found a peace finally about supplying the price for the chemo, but also understood, any healing that came out of this, all glory went to God.

Aunt Sarah must've been peeking through her curtains because she opened her door before Shilo mounted the steps. "'Bout time you got back. That was some walk, especially with the temperature getting warmer outside."

"I needed to stretch my legs. How about we go out to dinner tonight?"

"Oh, hon, we don't need to be spending needlessly." Aunt Sarah shook her head and led back into the house.

"Not a problem. I've got it on good authority that someone plans to take us out. He's supposed to phone to say when he'll be by. But if you want us to drive and meet him there, wherever there is ..." Shilo wished she'd asked more questions. She changed tactics. "May I make a phone call? It's local."

"Of course, dearheart. And if you want to surprise me about the dinner, go right ahead." Aunt Sarah patted Shilo's shoulder. "Maybe I oughta get myself a little gussied up." With a smile, she headed to her bedroom.

Giving Shilo the privacy to make her call.

"Good afternoon, you've reached The Weather Girls. This is Stormy. How may I help you?"

"Stormy, my name is Shilo. I'm calling to learn more about your services." She began to pace, one-two-three-four, then back one-two-three-four while twirling the curly phone cord between her fingers.

Shilo heard a slight rustle of paper. "We're here to help brides plan their big day and tailor a design specific for each couple. Have you set a date?"

"No, not yet, but we need to make it soon. Is it possible to meet with you in person?" Her teeth captured her bottom lip. This had grown into something far more complicated than she'd anticipated.

"Of course. Is it just you or will your fiancé join us?"

"Oh, hmm. Let me think. Maybe I should get the appointment and bring him if he's available." That's what she'd do. Breathing came easier. Talking things out with herself always helped.

"Okeydoke. Now, what time of day?"

Oh, no, another one? Her hand lifted her bangs from her forehead. "When do you have openings?" Maybe that would help make the decision.

Stormy rustled more paper. "Actually, we're getting into our busy season. Would you be okay with coming next week? Got an opening on Monday at eleven."

Shilo thanked her and got the address. Thank God there were no more decisions to make, at least for now. She hung up just in time for Aunt Sarah to come back into the room.

"Did you want to change your clothes too?"

What Shilo wanted was a shower and nap, but her jean skirt and peasant blouse combo was the best outfit she'd brought, though if she said anything to her aunt, that might start a problem. "I'll wear this. I look okay, right?" Too late if she didn't.

"You're lovely as always, sweetie." Aunt Sarah pinched her cheek for good measure.

That's when the phone rang. Aunt Sarah picked up. "Hello? Well, nice to hear your voice, Jesse." She paused and glanced over at Shilo. "I see. That would be lovely. We'll be ready. Thank you. Yes, we'll expect you then." She hung up and gave Shilo's face a search. "So Jesse's the one taking us out. Hmm. Did you go back to talk with him more?"

Shilo chose her words with care. "Yes. His office isn't far."

"A busy lawyer and you went and interrupted his day?" Aunt Sarah tipped her head, a dare tossed out.

"He had a minute, and we chatted." Shilo forced herself to not just watch her laced fingers and meet her aunt's gaze.

"And now he wants to take us to dinner?"

"Well, we didn't have a whole lot of time to talk, so he suggested we go out tonight." That was true, and Shilo did everything in her power to only speak the truth.

Aunt Sarah shook her head. "Why am I coming?"

"I wasn't about to leave you here alone."

"Oh, child, I'm aware there's more to this, but I'll play along. Just don't do something crazy." Aunt Sarah headed down the hall muttering to herself.

Don't do something crazy? What about getting engaged? Does that count? It should. The further Shilo got from her meeting with Jesse today, the more she couldn't wrap her mind around what was happening. Yes, she'd do anything for Aunt Sarah. And when she realized the inheritance allowed her to pay for the chemotherapy if she agreed to get married, it seemed so simple. But now? This might be the craziest thing she'd ever done, and she'd done some super crazy things in her time.

She plopped on the nearest chair for fear her legs would give out. What had she agreed to? She was too worn out to be making decisions. Then she stood and paced before she sat again. Over and over.

What had she been thinking?

Shilo repeated that routine for who knew how long. A knock at the door snapped her out of it.

Jesse stood on the other side of the screen. One glance at his face and doubts disintegrated.

She let him in. "We're about ready. I ne—"

"Good, you're here. I'm all set." Aunt Sarah's appearance took away the opportunity to ask if Jesse had misgivings.

If he did, he didn't show it.

They piled into his Ferrari, which, fortunately, happened to be a hatchback, so it included rear seating. Shilo insisted Aunt Sarah sit in the front, but that woman's stubborn streak countered with Shilo's long legs wouldn't fit back there. Though probably right, Shilo still felt disrespectful not giving her aunt the better seat.

"So where are you taking us tonight, Jesse? Shilo said she didn't know."

Jesse teased with a grin, which he flashed Shilo's way. "How does Monte's sound? I'm in the mood for steak."

"Me too," piped from the back seat.

Shilo leaned into the leather upholstery. She needed that sweet voice to keep piping up for a long time to come. That meant marrying Jesse, so she'd be able to pay for the chemotherapy. No more worries.

Jesse parked and came around to get the door for them. Shilo climbed out and pulled the seat forward as Jesse lent her aunt a hand. Then, after locking up, he tucked Aunt Sarah's fingers at his elbow and escorted her inside the restaurant.

It was the cutest thing Shilo had seen in a long time. Sort of Mutt and Jeff like.

The hostess showed them to their table—Jesse had made reservations—and their orders were taken right away, leaving a wide gap in the conversation.

Jesse glanced at Shilo and took her hand. "Now?"

Shilo nodded.

"Now what?" Aunt Sarah's eyes were as sharp as ever, and there was no doubt she'd noted their hand clasp.

"Jesse asked me to marry him today, and I said yes. Other than his secretary—who, by the way, knows you—you are the first to be told. Vivian only found out because we had a question, and she helped us." Shilo paused as her aunt stared at them. "Aren't you going to say anything, Aunt Sarah?"

Jesse had taken Shilo's hand to give her confidence, but now he was glad to clutch hers for his own shot of courage as he awaited Sarah's reaction.

"After one day? This is sudden. What happened?" Sarah glanced from Shilo to Jesse and back.

Just as he inhaled in order to spin things to make sense, Shilo provided the unvarnished truth, or what she knew of it. "Grandpa's will said I have to be married or get married right away if I wanted to inherit. Jesse volunteered when I asked him questions about the money. This way, you'll be able to get your chemotherapy."

"You are marrying each other for money?" Sarah's stare made Jesse want to slide under the table.

"Jesse isn't. He's helping me. And if you didn't need it, I'd have said no thank you. In fact, I did say that, but changed my mind after our talk."

Sarah crossed her arms and sat back in her chair. "No. I won't stand for it. You do not get married for anything less than love."

"I do love Jesse. He's one of my oldest and dearest friends." Her words halted the breath in his chest. It was the closest he'd come to anyone telling him that.

But it didn't pacify Sarah. "That's not what I mean, and you know that, Shilo. I raised you better than this."

Shilo squeezed his hand. "It's all set. You might as well get used to the idea of having Jesse for a nephew. You like him, don't you? That's what you said."

"Of course I like him. Jesse, I've enjoyed watching you grow up and become a good man. I think you're making a sacrifice that you don't comprehend."

It was time he spoke up. "Sarah, I'm aware of what we're doing. Shilo will be cared for and appreciated. I don't want any of her money, so what she does with it is solely at her discretion. And to be honest, she's an asset for me." Since he hadn't told Shilo about his grandfather's demand, he'd leave things at that.

"How?" Now Sarah nailed him with her gaze.

"Um, having a beautiful, intelligent woman with me when I deal with the social ends of my job can only be a bonus. And the brightness and playfulness that's so much a part of Shilo makes my life less dark. I'm there for her, whatever her needs, and we'll be a good team."

Sarah's gaze grew tender, and she leaned forward, placing her forearms on the table. "What about love?"

That he didn't know how to answer.

But Shilo squeezed his hand again. "Who's to say if our friendship won't grow into that? And before you tell us to wait and see, we don't have the luxury of time. You need the treatments now."

Sarah's sigh came close to breaking Jesse's heart. Filled with defeat and resignation, she acted as if this was harder than having to go without her treatment. "There's no talking you out of this, I can see it. I'm just worried that maybe you'll meet the person you are supposed to spend the rest of your life with and won't be able to, or worse yet, you'll both suffer through a divorce. I don't want that pain for either of you."

"What if I told you I've prayed about this? And I believe this is what God is telling me to do?"

Shilo prayed about it? Jesse didn't remember her being so spiritual. But she asked Viv about a church. Maybe that's who she was now.

"Then I'm gonna trust the Lord for this." Sarah glanced up. "And right on time. Here comes dinner." She smiled, though still a little sad.

"Who wants to say the blessing?" Shilo peeked from him to her aunt, making Jesse set aside his fork and knife.

"Why don't you pray, dearheart?" Sarah folded her hands and bowed her head after a nod to Shilo.

"I will. Thanks." She closed her eyes and bowed her head, clasping her hands together. "Oh, Father, I had no idea what all You had in store with this trip when we started off. But You did. Now You've brought me here with two of my very favorite people in the world. What a blast! For that and for this delicious food, thank You. And please show Aunt Sarah how You are in this, so she's cool with everything. Love You, Father. Amen."

Whoa. Jesse didn't understand a lot about God, wasn't even sure he believed in Him, though he was open. Sort of. But Shilo, wow. And the way she prayed, like she knew God listened to her. Talk about blowing his mind.

It'd been a decade since they'd seen each other. He had yet to learn what all she'd experienced over the years. Did she get mixed up in the drug culture, and if so, had it messed with her brain? If that's the case, she might not be the best person to satisfy Grandfather's edict.

Now, what did he do?

Sarah's potato-laden fork hovered in front of her. "I take it from what you said that your grandfather doesn't know about your plans yet. When will you tell him?"

Another thing he needed to discuss with Shilo. "We've been invited to a party at the country club this Saturday." He turned to her. "We could make an announcement then, if that's okay with you?" He hoped she caught all the unspoken importance.

"Oh. Well, sure, yeah. I'd better figure out what to wear, I guess."

"What if I take you ring shopping on Saturday? You can pick something while we're out." She'd understood. Good.

"I don't want you to be spending money on me."

"You've got to have a ring. That's required. And I'm fine helping you choose something. Isn't a husband supposed to follow his wife around and carry everything? It'll be good practice." He flashed her a grin.

"Well, I'm not big on shopping but, sure. However, once I get the money, I'll pay you back."

"There's no need. It's an investment. For us both." It seemed he needed to claim a stronger motivation, because the expression on Shilo's face broadcast loud and clear that she wasn't buying it.

"Just plan on repayment."

"Your first argument. I hope all of them will be as civilized as this one." Sarah snickered before popping a piece of steak in her mouth.

"Do you agree I need to repay Jesse, Aunt Sarah?"

"Oh, you aren't dragging me into your discussion. Make this practice. You'll be working things out together for a long time once you're married."

Shilo loaded up her spoon with mashed potatoes, gravy, and baby peas with pearl onions and aimed the gooey mess at him. "Jesse, I will repay you, now or later."

"You wouldn't." Oh, but he knew she would. Shilo had no qualms about flinging her dinner at him despite any social norms. "Fine. You can reimburse me once you receive your inheritance." No way would he let her start a food fight here in the restaurant.

Shilo lowered her weaponized utensil.

Would she have done it? How could he even doubt? Of course she would've. Which begged the question, how would she fit in with the country club set? At one time, she knew how to do that. Having taken those special débutante classes—what'd they call them? Oh, right, charm school. And when she got picked to be a Breck Girl with her gorgeous hair, she must've moved in the higher society circles.

However, today revealed another side. Something not in sync with a social butterfly. Maybe that was good. Those unmarried daughters of his grandfather's friends bored him to tears. If he wanted a wife who would check all those boxes, he had his pick. But if he desired one who would make life a treat—the very thing it hadn't been in a very long time, if ever—he needed Shilo.

Was that what Viv saw?

Sarah chose not to order dessert, but somehow Shilo convinced him to share some sugar cream pie. "I haven't had any since I left, and my cravings are overpowering me now that I've seen it on the menu, but I'm too full to eat more than a couple bites." Just like that. All in one breath. Her exuberance over pie made him grin and give in. Already he knew he'd have a hard time ever telling her no.

And that knowledge stretched his grin bigger.

After paying the tab and driving the women home, he paused Shilo at the door. "Could we talk a little? Just us?"

"Sure. Let's go out back. Aunt Sarah has a swing. We can share the stars." Her smile summoned him to follow her.

They sat together on the swing and before he was aware, she'd curled up next to him, and his arm encircled her. It was so natural and right, he couldn't question how it occurred.

"I called The Weather Girls today. They gave me an appointment for eleven Monday morning. Think you might be available? I guessed when would work best for you, and Stormy said this is their busy season."

He'd need to double check with Viv, but he might manage that. "I should be. I'll take you to lunch after." It was time he shared the rest.

"I realize you're under the impression that I'm helping you, but you're helping me too."

"You've already told me that. I don't see how, but I'm so grateful I'd do about anything for you, Jesse." She peered up at him, completely guileless.

How could he confess that he was marrying her so he'd land a big promotion?

"Jesse?"

"Hmm?"

"Do you need me to keep this a secret until Saturday?" She sat up.

"It would help so Grandfather doesn't get wind of things beforehand." Talk about a peck of trouble.

"Oh. I was thinking. Eli said he might call so we could go out, and that's not right now that we're engaged. So, what do I tell him?"

Eli. Of course. He'd be a fly in the ointment. "Tell him to leave you alone."

"Oh, Jesse, I can't do that. Look, I respect that there's no love lost between you two. I won't try to interfere though, if you'll get along for my sake, please. Because, whether you like it or not, Eli is a friend of mine."

"What about—"

"I've forgiven him. A long time ago. I wouldn't have considered asking him if I hadn't."

Jesse knew better than to say anything, but the words slipped out before he stopped them. "So why not ask me first?"

"You didn't seem to show any interest aside from taking care of my legal needs."

Just like always, he'd been too slow, too timid to reveal his feelings. And he'd almost lost out again. He had to stop holding back. She sat here next to him. He had the perfect opportunity. Jesse turned toward Shilo, tucking escaped strands behind her ear, then tracing the delicate shell before letting his fingers glide down her cheek to her jaw.

Her gray eyes grew luminous in the moonlight, her pink lips parting in a gentle invitation.

Jesse had prayed for this moment throughout high school and now here they were, ten years later. Maybe there was a God and He offered what Jesse had always wanted. Dreamed of. Desired.

Because, yes, that desire roared to the surface, and he needed to kiss her. Slowly, fearing she'd change her mind, sure he'd combust if she did, he leaned closer.

"Shilo, are you out here?"

He jumped back at her aunt's voice.

Shilo, though, looked disappointed as she answered. "Yeah, Aunt Sarah."

"Someone's here to see you. Want me to send him out?"

Someone? Him? Jesse knew of only one person it could be and at once understood the old adage about no atheists in foxholes.

Because the first thing he did was pray.

The second was to pull Shilo to him while yelling at her aunt. "No, we're busy."

Chapter 4

"There you two are."

Shilo pulled herself from Jesse and stood to say hello to Eli, who apparently recognized Jesse's voice and charged ahead. These two were still as bad as they were in high school.

"Hey Eli. What brings you by?"

"Oh, I was headed out to grab a drink at Woody's and figured I'd run by and see if you'd like to come."

Jesse stood too. "So, seeing my car parked at the curb had nothing to do with you stopping by?"

Eli's slow grin grew. "It might've been an incentive. But really, how about the two of you joining me? We'll have fun like in the old days."

"We didn't drink back then, or at least I didn't. And I still don't, Eli. Jesse and I were just hanging out, sharing the stars. Want to join—"

"No." Jesse's response turned all eyes on him. "Er, well, I'm sure Eli has other things to do. Maybe someone waiting for him at Woody's?"

Eli shook his head. "Nope, I'm free as a bird. So, what were you doing? Sharing the stars? What's that mean?"

"A private thing. You wouldn't understand." Jesse put his arm around her waist and pulled her closer. For someone who balked at hugs in public, he touched her a lot more this evening.

This would go on indefinitely if they didn't let Eli in on things. And if they did, there'd be no way to control the information so that Mr.

Franklin didn't discover their plans before Saturday night. Shilo turned to Jesse. "Do you think ..." Shilo hoped he'd fill in the rest and give her an answer.

"Do you think what?" Eli stared at each of them in turn.

Jesse's face revealed the thoughts running through his mind as his pressed lips worked from side to side. Finally, he shrugged. "Look, we're not ready to let others know yet, but Shilo and I have been in communication. That's why she's here. We're getting serious."

"Why didn't you tell me that earlier today?" Eli's eyes flashed hurt for an instant. Jesse wouldn't have noticed, but Shilo did.

Jesse's guarded message protected Saturday's announcement and also took a bit of liberty with the truth. Yes, they'd been in communication. He'd contacted her that she needed to come back about her inheritance. And that's why she came. Plus, they'd gotten serious, if one considered planning to marry to get the money for Aunt Sarah's medical bills serious. Jesse'd spoken all truth, but the unspoken part was full of less than honesty.

Shilo recognized the trait as something she'd put behind her. No more trying to hype herself for jobs, no more pretty spins on things so Aunt Sarah wouldn't worry. God showed her how to walk in Truth. This felt all wrong, even dirty. "Jesse?"

He squeezed her tighter for a moment.

Okay, they'd have to talk about this, but after Eli left.

If he left. He still stared at the two of them as if weighing all the words against what he saw and knew to be true. "You only had to let me know, Shilo."

"We didn't make our decision until this afternoon. I'm sorry, Eli." And she was. With all Eli's faults, there was someone special inside him, someone she'd spotted glimpses of over the years. How would she share Jesus with him if they couldn't even tell the guy the truth?

All his bravado evaporated. He shoved his hands in his pockets. "Clearly, I'm interrupting something, so I'll go. Hope things work out, but if it doesn't, you know where to find me."

She moved to give him a hug, but Jesse's arm pulled her tight, holding her to him until Eli left alongside the house and out toward the street. She faced her captor. "He's hurt, Jesse, and doesn't understand."

"Had you given him any encouragement?"

"I said I didn't think I had a reason to stay here—which at the time I didn't—so he told me he hoped that changed, and that he wanted to see me. I simply answered I'd like that. No promises made." Shilo chewed at her lip. She'd never planned to hurt Eli in all this.

But Jesse shook his head and put his hands on her shoulders, rubbing them before moving on to her arms and back. "No, but he took that as an opening, and we closed that door. The guy bugs the bejeebers out of me, but to be fair, I see his point. Saturday's not that far away. Then everyone can know."

Did possessiveness encourage his touch? She hoped not. However, she did hope that he'd try to kiss her again. She was drawn to him, though he'd changed. This new Jesse, who grew embarrassed at public hugging but hadn't stopped touching her since they sat on the swing, was an enigma. Would she scare him if she kissed him? Was it more important to him to make the first move?

And if their marriage was to be one of simple friendship with separate bedrooms, why was she reveling in his touch so much? She needed to sort her feelings out.

"I'd better get going. Do you have plans for tomorrow?" His hand slid down her arm to find hers and gave it a little squeeze.

She had to roll her thoughts to a stop before finding the correct route to answer his question. "Yeah. Aunt Sarah has a doctor's appointment with her surgeon. She's supposed to find out when they've scheduled her surgery."

"I see. That will be good for us to know too. You'll want her to be at the wedding."

Shilo nodded her head. "Most definitely."

"Suppose I call tomorrow afternoon?"

"I should be able to tell you everything then." She rose on tiptoe and brushed a kiss on his cheek. "Thank you for dinner and for helping me explain to Aunt Sarah. And thank you for wanting to marry me, Jesse."

He grew quiet, and with his arm over her shoulders, walked her to the back door. "Sweet dreams, Shilo. It's all going to work out. I promise."

She understood his unspoken "or I'll die trying" and knew he'd give this his all. That was the Jesse she remembered. "Night, Jess." Shilo trailed her fingers along his jaw before climbing the steps to the back door. But before going in, she turned.

He still stood at the base, watching, waiting for her.

She flashed him a smile and opened the door. By the time she got inside the kitchen and peeked out the window, he'd gone. "Sweet dreams, Jesse."

Thursday, May 24, 1973

Morning came hard and fast. Shilo longed to stay curled up on the clean sheets, hugging the goose-down pillow to her. She hadn't realized how bone-weary she'd become from the trip. And her bed at home wasn't as comfortable as this one in Aunt Sarah's guest room. She squeezed her eyes tight, waiting to go back to sleep when she heard humming coming down the hall. Aunt Sarah was up. She should be too. After a stretch and yawn, she was.

"Good morning, Aunt Sarah. You sound chipper." Shilo planted a kiss on the woman's cheek, stepping up behind her as she worked at the sink.

"I hope I didn't wake you. It's still early your time."

"Nope, I needed to be up, though that bed is amazing. What can I help with?"

"Nothing, sweetie. Just brought in a few veggies from my garden and figured we could add them to lunch after we get back from the doctor. Do you still want to go with me?" She ran water over the carrots and then dumped the sliced-off greens into the trash.

"Don't throw all that away. You can use those carrot tops."

"You can?"

"Oh yes. They work in salads and soups like parsley. And if you replant them as houseplants, they'll look so pretty. Here, let me show you." Shilo pulled out several of the tops that were still attached to a little orange disk at the base. "Plant these and you won't get new carrots, but you'll have plenty of greens to cook with and they'll brighten things on your windowsill. Got any empty pots and some soil?"

"Out in the shed. But you still didn't answer my question. Are you coming with me?"

"Yes. Yes, I am. What time do you want to go?"

"I hope to leave here in an hour."

"I'll be ready. Let me get these little babies planted, and then I'll clean up before I grab some coffee and toast."

Shilo went out the back way in her bare feet, wiggling her toes in the lush green grass before entering the tiny shed where Aunt Sarah kept her planting tools. She found a couple of pots and a bag of soil, making quick work of starting the carrot greens in their new lives. Just like God did for her. No longer who she'd been, but given new life to grow and thrive. Every time something reminded her of His goodness, she had to say thank you all over again.

Then she headed off to the shower and her clean clothes. Maybe going shopping with Jesse was a good thing. She would need more than what she had now.

And how would she get the rest of her things in San Diego? Should she write to her roommates and ask them to send her stuff? She'd have to pay them, and she didn't have the cash for that, at least not yet. One more thing to wait on until after she and Jesse got married.

Married. Wow. It wasn't just some dream. She and Jesse were really doing this. Well, not *really.* But legally. What would her parents say about that?

With three minutes to spare, she finished the last sip of her coffee and bite of her toast. Her well-worn jeans with patches of lace and her plain white T-shirt were all that was left of her clean clothes. She'd better do laundry when they came back home.

Aunt Sarah still drove the 1959 Rambler that Uncle Arthur surprised her with on their thirtieth wedding anniversary. He'd given her the brand-new car and she'd babied it all these years. Even now it looked like it could be in an auto showroom. Something about that not changing while she'd been gone soothed Shilo.

They pulled into the parking lot of a strip mall across the street from St Joe's hospital where several doctors housed their practices. They were to meet Dr. J. Gordan Rakkar, surgical oncologist.

The waiting room, painted in a neutral beige with framed abstract art on the walls, neither invited nor stood unfriendly. In fact, she'd barely call the room utilitarian. Shilo chose a seat where her aunt could sit next to her after she checked in and picked up a *McCall's* magazine. When she flipped to the back, a Breck Girl greeted her. That had been Shilo, once upon a time. She sent up a little prayer that the girl found good and not the same traps she'd fallen prey to.

Aunt Sarah only sat for under thirty seconds before the nurse opened the door to the back rooms and called her name.

Shilo returned the magazine to the end table and followed her aunt.

Instead of going to an exam room, the nurse led her to an office done in dark mahogany with an enormous desk fit for a president and two matching armchairs. She let Aunt Sarah choose the one she wanted before taking the other.

Moments later the doctor entered, pulling his glasses from his balding head and onto the bridge of his nose as he perused the papers in the file he held. "Good morning. I have here the final tests we were waiting for. Surgery is required as soon as we can schedule the OR. I've looked at tomorrow for St. Joe's and they have an opening. You'll need to check in at seven in the morning. Any questions?"

"That soon?" Aunt Sarah's voice trembled.

Dr. Rakkar nodded.

Shilo raised her hand as if back in school. "Doctor, how long will she have to stay?"

"At least a week. Are you going to be her caretaker when she comes home?"

"Yes." She got her answer in before Aunt Sarah stopped her.

"I'll be fine."

"I know, but I still plan to be there." Shilo patted her aunt's knee and turned back to the doctor. "How soon after she comes home will she start her treatments?"

"You've come to a decision regarding chemotherapy?" Dr. Rakkar finally made eye contact with Aunt Sarah.

But Shilo spoke up. "Yes. We'll be paying for that. How do I set that up?"

"We can discuss that after the surgery. Plan for a one-week stay. By then we'll be able to talk about the therapy schedule. Any other questions?"

Shilo had more than she could count but none that the doctor would be able to answer.

Jesse thumbed through the Yellow Pages in his office with the door closed. No need of Viv walking in while he planned her surprise. Moments later he pulled his finger down the page of florists to land on Rose's Blooms and committed the phone number to his short-term memory before dialing.

"I'd like to order three separate bouquets to be delivered. One of a dozen yellow roses, next a mix of daisies, forget-me-nots, and pink carnations, and then ..." what did he want for Sarah? "How about a mix of flowers with the dominant color being yellow?"

The girl at the other end seemed to get his drift, and by the time they finished, she had the addresses and his credit card number.

Viv more than earned her favorite yellow roses. She said they represented friendship and appreciation. Two things he hoped she realized he extended to her.

Actually, it wasn't only Viv who'd shared what flowers meant. One of the few instances his mother took time with him while on sabbatical from their dig in the Middle East, she'd told him about the blooms neighbors grew in their gardens and what it said about the people who lived in the houses. Glimpses into their souls and a little into his mother's too. Maybe that's why he appreciated flowers of all sizes and shapes, something she'd shared with him. So now, when words were hard to get out, expressing his thoughts through bouquets came easier.

Shilo had worked little violets into her braid yesterday morning when he picked her up from jail. Of course, by then the tiny flowers looked withered, but he'd noticed. Had she done that for him?

Well, anyway, she liked the simpler flowers, so he told her how he saw her with the daisies represented purity and innocence. The forget-me-nots expressed faithful love, memories, and undying hope. The pink carnations explained he felt grateful to her for agreeing to marry him. All words he would choke on if forced to confess. Shilo'd been the only girl for him back in the day, and her appearance now only confirmed what an idiot he'd been to let her get away.

He had no idea what he wanted to say to Sarah except that he appreciated her and hoped she'd come through this health challenge just fine.

The knock on his door brought him out of his floral daydream. "Yes?"

Eli stepped in. "Hey, got a minute?"

He did, but he didn't want to give it to this guy. But mentoring Eli according to Grandfather's plan meant he should be available to help.

As if this visit had anything to do with the firm. He needed to turn off his inner cynic.

"What do you need?"

"Wanted to say I didn't mean to step on any toes last night. But way to go on working fast."

"What are you saying?"

"You know exactly what I mean. Playing it so cool yesterday when I mentioned her, and then by eight o'clock you two were a thing. Gotta hand it to you, you're smooth, dude."

Jesse stood and shuffled a few files around. "Look, I'm busy. If you need help with something connected to the firm, I'll work you in, but if you're jealous about last night, I haven't got the time."

"Jealous? Seriously? Shilo is amazing, and I doubt you understand how incredible she is. But take your shot. When you're out of the picture, I'll pick up the pieces." He spun on his heel and left before Jesse could manufacture a comeback.

Just one more instance of why he made the deal with Shilo. If they got married, he might get brave enough to express himself. Plus, she'd never cheat if they were married—not Shilo—no matter what the deal, so there wouldn't be any pieces for Eli to pick up.

However, now that he got that bit of business accomplished, he'd focus on what to take to the courthouse and head out.

It looked to be a long day of negotiation. He'd amended the contracts at least four times now, but both sides seemed to look for that loophole to win it all. That would never happen. At this point, he only racked up billable hours, and they'd be buying his next car. Or his honeymoon.

Nah. Shilo would want something simple. And to be honest, so did he. They could stay at the family cabin up on Mississinewa Lake. This time of year, they'd swim and boat and take walks in the woods. That sounded more like Shilo, and it would be a welcome relief from the stress of work.

Work.

He better drag his mind back on that, or he'd never get his clients to accept this latest contract.

Three hours later, he'd done it. Most likely because everyone's stomach disharmoniously growled. But now the contract lay signed, sealed, and notarized, ready for Viv to file. A case he was glad to be rid of. It'd dogged him for six months.

Time to grab a late lunch and check in with Shilo.

But as he entered the second floor of the firm, three or four of the secretaries stood in the doorway to his outer office where Viv held down the fort. What in the world?

Then Karen Miner, Bill Youst's secretary, glanced over her shoulder. "He's here, girls."

All eyes turned on him. Not menacing, like he'd done something wrong, but weird.

"They're gorgeous, Mr. Franklin."

"Can you get my boss to send some to me?"

"Wow, Vivian is so lucky!"

The crowd parted enough to let him into the office where Viv stood, tears rolling down her cheeks. Oh, no, what happened?

But she rushed around the desk and hugged him. Hugged him. No, no, no.

"You shouldn't have, but they made my day. More like my month or year. They're incredible." She released him, and that's when he saw the giant bouquet of yellow roses.

There had to be at least three dozen. He'd only ordered one. One dozen. If that girl messed up this part of his order, what happened to Shilo's and Sarah's?

Everyone continued to stare at him. Like they expected him to say something.

This wasn't a summation before a jury. That he could rehearse and do. These were women who worked here in the firm. What would they say if they realized he got tongue-tied just thinking of talking to them?

"Um, well, Viv works hard. She deserves it. Excuse me." He made it to his inner sanctum and closed the door, leaning against it until he made sense of his world.

Viv knew he was getting married. She also realized the reason, in part at least. So, there's no way she'd be making more of this. Right? He staggered to his desk, setting his briefcase on the floor beside him as his phone rang. The inner office line.

"Franklin here."

"Why are you trying to make the rest of us look bad?" Tom Hamer. "I'm sure today's not Secretaries' Day. Is it her birthday?"

"No, nothing like that." Jesse ran his hand through his hair. "Viv went over and above helping me yesterday, and I wanted to say thank you. Only the florist got the order wrong and what was a simple arrangement turned into—"

"A big deal. Right. That'll teach you to use your words like any self-respecting lawyer. Well, I'll tell Bill and Ed. But you've set a precedent. Anytime I do anything to say thanks to Evelyn, it's gonna get measured against this. You plan to tell Vivian that the florist goofed?"

"Are you kidding? I'm staying hidden in my office until everyone goes home. Not sticking my head out there." Just the idea of confessing scared him to pieces.

Tom chuckled. "Serves you right. Okay, get back to work. See you eventually."

Jesse hung up the phone. So not only were the women all thinking things—what were they thinking? No, it couldn't be that. Viv held a good fifteen years on him. Not old enough to be his mother, but maybe a big sister. And the men, did they wonder about that too? Or did they figure he was an idiot? If that's it, they were right.

His intercom buzzed. He wanted to ignore it with everything in his being. But he flipped the switch. "Yes?"

"Boss, Rose's Blooms called. Um, may I come in a moment?"

What could he do? Keep his secretary locked out? "Sure."

Viv peeked around the door before slipping inside, standing with her back glued to the jam and her hands behind her, probably keeping the knob handy. "You never meant to send that arrangement, did you?"

He shook his head, too humiliated to catch her gaze or speak.

"The girl said that they'd received two orders for yellow roses and the driver just switched them. The cards got put on the wrong arrangements, so it didn't come to light at first. But the other customer was livid and wants his order back."

"What? They're coming here to take your flowers? No, that's not happening. I'll pay for the company to make another one."

"You don't have to."

"Yes, I do. I'm not going to let them walk out of here with those roses after all that hullabaloo."

"Boss, I talked with the girl. They'd already offered that to the customer, and he calmed down. It's all good. Thank you for thinking of me and for wanting to protect me from misunderstandings."

"Nah, you deserve them. I figured a dozen was enough, though they wouldn't have drawn quite the crowd." He tried to picture that and chuckled.

"You're right. Maybe." She paused. "So, we're good?"

He nodded. "Always were."

She smiled and left without trying to hug him again. For which he was grateful.

Guess he ought to call Shilo. He couldn't imagine the company messing up the rest of his order like that. Well, maybe, but he doubted they did.

Sarah picked up and when she recognized his voice, she gushed. "Oh, Jesse, the flowers are lovely. The perfect thing to set on the dining room table. But I'm sure you didn't call to talk to me. Let me get Shilo."

It took a moment, but soon he heard the voice that still made his insides go all jiggly. He'd hoped that was only a high school response and would fade with age, but apparently not. Though other women might intimidate him, no one ever gave him such a visceral reaction, and the more time he spent around her, the stronger it became. So strong now that he needed to force himself to focus on her words and not just the sound that brought on this response.

"... and so, we have to be at the hospital by seven in the morning. He said the surgery shouldn't take too long, but she's got to stay a week. Before she leaves, we'll know more about her therapy schedules."

"How is she doing with all that?"

"She's stoic. She's Aunt Sarah."

"What about you? Will you be alone waiting for her?"

"Jesse, I'm never alone. God is with me. But it'll be just the two of us in the waiting room."

"Make that the three of us."

"You're coming?"

"Try to keep me away." *Big talk. Can you back it up?* "I'll have Viv rearrange my schedule. Oh, what about Saturday? Will you be okay to be gone for a while during the day and in the evening?" What would he do if she wasn't?

"I'll figure out something. We should shop close to home so I can get to the hospital fast if needed. Aunt Sarah said her friend Delores Burke volunteered to come by if she wanted, so that's an option."

His brain started problem-solving and came up with a plan. Hopefully, Viv won't feel obligated and will just want to.

Chapter 5

S hilo glanced about for the clock as she entered the room. They'd let her stay with Aunt Sarah until time to wheel her into surgery, but now they'd relegated her to wait with the others who had loved ones having operations. A TV played the *Today Show* with the volume lowered in the background. Barbara Walters and Frank McGee discussed the Senate's Watergate hearings. Not something that interested her.

Then she spotted him.

Jesse must've been watching for her as he stood and headed her way. Whether he liked it or not, she hugged him. He didn't resist.

"How are you holding up?" Jesse guided her toward a set of chairs in the corner.

"Until they wheeled her away, I held onto knowing God's got this. Then I walked down the corridor to here more alone than I've been in a while. So glad you came."

He threaded his fingers between hers and kissed her hand.

The tenderness overwhelmed her, and she couldn't stop the single tear.

Jesse drew her close. "She's going to come through just fine, Shy. You'll see." He rubbed her back while she cried on his shoulder.

Shilo pulled away, wiping her eyes. "I'm sorry. Where is my faith? I know God's got it all under control."

"The doctors are fantastic here, and the care staff goes out of their way to help. Don't worry."

She stared at him. Not so much because he glossed over her mini crisis of belief, but more out of the surety of his convictions. "How do you know?"

"Grandfather had an episode last year. If you think he's a bear when he's healthy, you should see him when he isn't. It was his gall bladder, and they gave him emergency surgery. He threatened to call for some New York doctor, but he wouldn't have lived until the guy arrived. Grandfather came through just fine, though the nursing staff sure seemed glad to get rid of him. I will say, though, no matter how rude and privileged he behaved, they never sank to his level. They were kind and thoughtful."

Shilo's musing wandered out her mouth. "Did you send them flowers?"

He grinned. "Of course. And a giant box of chocolates for the floor staff. I mean, if I ever end up in here, I hope they give me the benefit of the doubt if I'm in too much pain to be polite."

That made her laugh.

Jesse linked hands with her again. "Want to get some coffee? We can let the volunteer at the desk know where we are."

She nodded and stood with him.

There was something so comforting in letting Jesse take control. All she had to do was walk beside him and allow him to manage things. Maybe with Jesse becoming her husband, God wanted to work through him for her. At this point, though, she'd gladly hand off all decisions because her brain now did its Porky Pig impersonation. "Th-th-that's all, folks!"

Jesse walked her to the cafeteria where he grabbed them both cups of coffee and brought back packets of Coffee Mate and sugar. "Thought I remembered you preferring yours sweet and creamy."

"Yep. Thanks. And thank you for taking care of me. I don't understand why I'm reacting this way." She was all for God working through Jesse, but not to where she couldn't feel His presence anymore.

"I'd have been shocked if you weren't a bit out of it. Up to now, it has just been appointments and plans, but you've arrived at the crucial moment. And nothing is in your control." He sipped his black coffee but kept his gaze on her.

She could tell even when she looked away. Laser-focused, taking in every nuance of movement and expression. She might as well be under a microscope. "Let's talk about something else."

"Okay." He paused and turned his attention to some sugar granules on the tabletop that he pushed around with this forefinger before glancing up at her face again. "Tell me what life has been like for you these past ten years."

Whew! A decade worth of stories packed into under an hour in St. Joe's cafeteria, huh? Talk about a *Reader's Digest* version. "Hmm. You knew about the Breck Girl ad I did."

He nodded.

"Well, I figured I'd use that foothold to get in the door with the Ford Modeling Agency. Eileen was sweet but told me I needed more than great hair. And then said if I got my gap closed, she might take me on."

"Wait. She wanted you to have dental work on your front teeth? I always liked that about your smile." He blushed and stammered. "Sorry, go on."

So, he liked her smile the way it was. That was almost as good as a hug. "I auditioned for some off-Broadway productions while picking up classes and waitressing. Got put into some crowd scenes a few times, never any actual parts. But I had friends heading for California, so I hitched a ride with them. Had a little better luck in LA. Appeared on the *Dating Game* once. Didn't win, but the guy tried to dump the girl he chose to pick me up. Not a smooth move. I slipped out while she ruined their big prize.

"Let's see. I danced at the Whiskey-A-Go-Go for a while." She noted his eyes grew a bit bigger.

"In a cage?"

Shilo nodded and glanced away before she watched that play out in his expression. "Some friends mentioned this big music festival, so we all rode together up to Monterrey."

"You went to the Monterrey Music Festival? Who did you see?" He sounded as if this was all groovy galore.

Of course, Shilo glossed over the not so groovy parts. "The Mamas and the Papas, Jimi Hendrix, Scott MacKenzie, Janice Joplin—"

"Seriously?"

She'd never seen his eyes so huge. "Yeah. Cass Elliot was kindhearted. At least to me. Janice, I couldn't help but pity her. She put on this big kinda mask to look happy and mellow, but when she didn't realize I was looking, a sadness dropped like some curtain over her eyes. I wasn't shocked to learn she'd OD'd." The conversation grew solemn and if she kept going, it would become a whole lot worse before it got better.

Maybe she ought to skip to where the good stuff started. "Ya know, I ended up in St. Vincent's once, not too healthy, when this dude and his wife came into my room. Funny, he said God sent him to the hospital but didn't tell him why. So, he and his wife cruised around on the floors where they were allowed and when they found my room, the door stood open, so they wandered in. Started rapping about God and Jesus. Before long, I wanted what they had, a relationship with the Creator of the world. So, they prayed with me. Then they prayed for me. By the next morning, the doctors' minds were blown. I mean, ka-blooey." She waved her hands on either side of her head like her brain just exploded.

"The day after that, they released me. I found that guy and his wife. Lonnie and Connie Frisbee. He'd been preaching out by the ocean and asked if I wanted to be baptized. I did, so he dunked me right there in the Pacific." She chuckled at the memory. "I lived in his House of Miracles for a short time before God led me to San Diego. Lonnie closed up all his House of Miracles locations and a bunch of them moved up to Oregon to start their Shilo Youth Revival Centers."

"Named for you?"

She shrugged. "No idea. I miss them, but I've made more friends in San Diego."

"Have you told them you won't be back?"

"No, not yet. I sort of wish I could tell them in person, but it'd be hard to leave again." She glanced around the room for a clock and a change of topic. "We've been gone awhile. Should we go back?"

Jesse stood and took her empty cup along with his and their other trash and dumped it while she walked beside him. But then he held her hand to lead her to the waiting room.

She'd shared a lot. More than she intended to in one sitting. Not that she planned to keep secrets, but so much history might overwhelm him if she told him all at once. Still she'd laid the groundwork. Set the stage. Now when she confessed the other things, maybe he'd have some context for understanding. At least, she hoped.

They claimed the same chairs they'd deserted earlier.

A certain question had gnawed at her almost from the time she first got the call from Jesse, though she'd figured it was water under the bridge, and she should let it go. But now, with everything that'd happened, she really wanted to know. "Jesse, why didn't you ever answer any of my letters?"

He stared, confusion in his eyes. "What letters? I kept waiting to hear from you, so I knew where to write, but I never got any."

Shilo sat straighter. *What in the world happened?* "I sent you at least ten because every time I moved in the first two years, I wanted to let you know where I was. By the time I left for LA, I'd given up and figured you'd moved on with your life."

"Oh Shy, I never got them. Not a one. I thought you'd decided you weren't coming home and just severed ties."

"Must've seemed like I'd never return, but the truth was I didn't have the bread to make that kind of trip."

"How did you handle getting here?"

She held up her fist with her thumb pointed out.

"You hitched? All the way from California? That's so dangerous! Shy, I would've sent you a plane ticket. All you had to do was ask." Now he looked hurt, his eyes reflecting pain. Or fear? She wasn't sure.

"It's no big deal. I only do it when the destination is too much to hoof it. Don't worry. God's got this. He took such great care of me to get me here. Besides, you're too young to sound so much like the establishment." She chuckled, hoping to get him to chill. When had he gotten so square?

Jesse shook his head. "Promise me you'll never hitchhike again."

He needed to give her a break and mellow. "Let's just say I have no plans of it. I hate to make promises I might end up breaking."

"I'm getting you a car."

"No, you're not. I don't need one, and if I did, I'd buy it with my inheritance. So, save your money." She hoped he wasn't going to get overprotective, though having someone look out for her was sort of nice. It'd been a long time since that had been a part of her life. A very long time.

Jesse stared at the floor. "Another reason we should get married as soon as possible. I won't feel safe if I have to worry about someone picking you up."

Time to change the subject before he ended up like a dog with his bone over the situation. "I'm hoping we can do something between when Aunt Sarah gets out of the hospital and before she starts her treatments. Only we can't know when that is until next Friday. Or around then. How long an engagement will your Grandfather expect?"

Jesse chuckled. "About six months."

She gasped and wanted to say something, but he cut her off.

"Don't worry about it. We're doing this for us, er, for you." His neck grew rosy and sent splotches of red to his cheeks. "Let's try to pull things together in two to three weeks. That'll give Sarah at least a week at home to recuperate. And that way you should have your money in time for her treatments. I'm sure they'll want her incision to heal some first."

That made sense. Shilo nodded agreement but remained silent. This was all too real. Too ... real.

Jesse joined her quiet retreat and leaned back in his chair. But then, his fingers laced with hers and the unspoken grew louder.

She was falling in love with Jesse. All over again.

She'd hitchhiked here from San Diego. If Jesse had known that ahead of time, he'd have been terrified. True, he sounded more like the middle-aged guys at the firm, but that case he followed last summer with the parents who suffered through not knowing where their daughter ended up aged him. Calling him square or part of the establishment wasn't enough to shake that memory.

But Shilo had no fear. Another thing that scared him.

So much happened in her life during the past ten years. She'd been part of so many iconic moments of the last decade. Did she go to Woodstock? He was too afraid of her answer to ask. He'd seen the movie and knew about the massive drug use and sex. Imagining her as part of that counterculture messed with his angelic version of her that he kept on a pedestal.

However, those things that had made him build the pedestal in the first place remained. She still cared for others with her whole heart. Maybe more than in the past. Simple things still gave her joy. Her joining the Jesus People movement in California shouldn't have surprised him, but her fervor did. She lived her faith.

"Oh, do you still plan to go to church on Sunday?"

She popped her eyes open and turned a smile on him. Did the sun just come out? "Oh, yeah. Do you still want to go with me?"

"Of course. I'll pick you up."

"Thanks." She leaned back and closed her lids again.

Was she trying to sleep or praying? He had no clue but decided not to interrupt her anymore. It was enough to just experience her hand in his.

To be honest, it'd shocked him how quickly his former feelings for her returned. Gushed through a breached dam was more like it.

Creating problems.

First, he'd made a deal with her and needed to stick to his word. However, if she seemed willing to take their relationship further, he wouldn't be upset. At all.

Second, he realized he didn't really know her, or the woman she'd become after leaving Kokomo. He needed to know her, to assure himself that his feelings were for Shilo and not her memory.

Okay, he'd organized that in his head. Now to slog through the rest of the week. Saturday night would be a subversive battle of wills. Grandfather wouldn't be pleased even though Jesse was technically obeying. No, the man would steam but try to put on a civil face in public.

He should prepare Shilo.

But how did he do that without explaining about Grandfather's edict?

It wasn't a matter of not telling her, he knew he would. However, when and how? One more thing to figure out.

He could practice at home, like he practiced his openings and summations. There now, that was a great idea. He'd do that tonight.

Unless he talked Shilo into dinner and stopping by his house. She ought to check out where she'll be living. And maybe that would help him share more of his past ten years with her as well.

"Miss Anderson?"

Shilo bolted straight in her chair, glancing around for whoever called her name.

Jesse pointed toward the hospital volunteer at the desk and then walked over with her.

"I'm Shilo Anderson."

"Just got off the phone with surgery. Your aunt is being taken to recovery now. Dr. Rakkar will be down to speak with you in a few minutes."

"Thank you."

Her fingers took hold of his hand, so he gave her a little squeeze. She thanked him with one of her amazing smiles.

Then they returned to their seats to stare at the door, willing the doctor to come in.

Finally, he did and spotted them right off, coming to sit beside Shilo.

"Everything went according to plan. No surprises, and I believe we got it all. She'll be in recovery for a few hours before we take her to her room. You ought to go get some fresh air and a bite before you come back. Your aunt will be sleeping for a while as well, so you don't need to rush."

"Thank you, doctor." Shilo relaxed, her shoulders lowering and tension draining from her face.

Dr. Rakkar patted her shoulder and left.

"He's right. What would you like to do?"

Shilo shook her head. "I can't make any decisions now. I trust you to choose something." She squeezed his hand that she'd never let go of.

Jesse thought for a moment before lighting on an idea. "I realize we're going shopping tomorrow, but what about we hunt for the ring today? We can go downtown to Lord's Jewelers. Maybe they'll have something you'll like that won't need to be sized."

"Please, nothing expensive or flashy." Concern shoved Shilo's pale eyebrows closer together.

"It's whatever you choose. So don't worry about it. Getting the engagement ring is part of the future husband's job, though maybe I'm supposed to get you something and surprise you? No, that's if I surprise you by proposing. Right? Just want to follow the rules." He chuckled to cover his nerves and headed her toward the exit.

"I won't fight you today. I'm out of fight. Doing better, I guess, since Aunt Sarah is out of surgery and the doctor is optimistic, but it's so heavy, like too much weight to think through." She leaned her head against his shoulder. "I trust you, Jesse. Always have."

And that warmed his heart the same as it churned his gut with fear, fear that he'd let her down somehow. Now would be a good time to be a praying man and ask for help.

"Okay, let's get out of here. You drove Sarah's car today, right?"

She nodded.

"Then we'll leave it here until I come up with a plan for that. In the meantime, let's go downtown. Unless you want a bite to eat first?"

Now she shook her head, making her braid bounce.

"Okay, downtown to Lord's Jewelers. I'm parked over that way." He pointed and led her to his ride, holding her door and getting her situated before rounding the car to his side.

Music. They needed some. He popped in *The Best of the Four Tops*. "Baby, I Need Your Loving" came through his speakers. He hadn't planned the message, but the more they spent time together, the greater the words spoke to him.

Besides, with the music, there was no urge for talk.

Ten minutes later, he parked in front of the jewelry shop on Main Street while "Sugar Pie, Honey Bunch" played. He almost hated to turn the thing off. However, he shut the engine down, locked up his side, and came around to help her from his Ferrari.

"I love that your taste in music hasn't changed. That familiarity is comforting, Jesse." She kissed his cheek, leaving him floundering.

What was he doing?

Oh, right. Buying an engagement ring.

As his fingers laced with hers, he realized that that amount of public display didn't bother him half as much as it should. How she felt about his music was how he received her touch. Familiar comfort.

He held the door for her while small silver bells on the inside handle jingled, drawing out another smile from her. It was the little things. He needed to keep that forefront in his mind. She appreciated what others considered insignificant. Endearing her even more to him.

At the counter she looked through the glass at all the sparkling gems.

That gave him an idea, though he wondered if it could be done before tomorrow evening. Her birthstone was opal. Could they add something around the diamond with that?

Oh, yeah, he recalled her birthday. October twentieth. He didn't require anything to help him remember, either.

"What about this one?" Shilo pointed to a modest ring with a single tiny chip.

He shook his head. "You deserve something more than that."

"No, I don't. It's a symbol. It shouldn't be gaudy."

"I'm not talking gaudy. We can do tasteful and still go with a bigger diamond. Tell you what. I'll pick out your engagement ring, and you choose the wedding bands. Deal?"

She shrugged. "Okay, just don't go overboard. Should we get my ring size? I haven't a clue what it is."

That only pointed to what he'd already noticed. She wore no jewelry. Not even earrings, and he hadn't spotted a necklace either. Not even love beads. Did she not like bangles and stuff like other women? Or had she been too strapped to own any?

The clerk came over, and after introductions, Craig determined Shilo's ring size, and she moved down a bit to look at the wedding bands, giving Jesse a moment to spring his idea on the unsuspecting salesman.

"I doubt you already have anything like this, but wondered about adding some small opals to encircle the diamond. That's her birthstone."

Craig smiled. "I can do you one better. Were you aware that October has two birthstones?"

Jesse shook his head.

"Tourmaline is also an October stone and comes in many colors. I have a specially ordered ring here. The couple broke up before he asked her. We refunded his money, but now we've got this exquisite setting. Shall I show you?"

"Of course." Jesse's excitement grew just thinking of it. When Craig pulled the ring out from beneath and set it on the counter, it was even better than he'd imagined. Pink tourmaline chips played every other with tiny opals all around the diamond. Nothing too showy but tasteful with a three-quarter carat, oval cut in the center. She'd have to admit it wasn't gaudy. "I'll take it. Will you need to size it?"

"Let's have her try it on."

"Shy, I think I've found it. Would you please come check out the size?"

She returned, her friendly smile that even radiated from her eyes leading the way. "You're not going crazy, are you?"

"I promise I'm not."

"Actually, he discovered a sale piece so you can be proud of your fiancé." Craig handed the ring to Jesse.

Why did he do that? Oh. OH. He drew in a breath. Okay then.

Jesse dropped to his knee in front of Shilo. "I get that we've already agreed, but let's make this official. We've known each other and been close friends since we were kids. We're a great team, Shy." He paused. This is where he should tell her "I love you." Even if he did, he couldn't just blurt it this instant, not here. What could he say? "No one has ever known me as deeply as you. Now that you are back in my life, I can't imagine you out of it. Shilo Dawn Anderson, would you do me the incredible honor of becoming my wife?"

"Yes, Jesse. I will."

He rose and slid the ring onto her finger, finding a perfect fit. To his mind it'd been made for her.

She stared at her hand, her eyes turning moist. Then she threw herself at Jesse in a passionate hug.

Stunned, he should've been ready for that. And for Craig's applause.

But then she pulled back, placed her hands on either side of his face, and kissed him full on the mouth.

He might be slow on the uptake, but whoa, this he could do, returning her kiss with more intensity than he knew he possessed. Drawing her close, he deepened the kiss until he heard bells. Little jingly bells. It wasn't Christmas time, or maybe it was, and he was getting the best present of his life.

"Just walking past and saw you two through the window. Wow. Guess you put your money where your mouth is, dude. Or something like that."

Eli.

The last person he ever wanted to see. Especially now.

Shilo pulled back but ran her finger under his bottom lip before turning to the interloper. "Hi, Eli. Check out my ring."

He took a glance. "Nice. If that's the best he can do. Shilo, I would've gotten you at least a three-carat diamond."

"I didn't want that." Shilo held her hand out and gazed at the ring. "This is pushing my boundary a little, but it's so pretty. Plus, Jesse, you remembered. Opal. My birthstone." She wiggled her fingers and kissed his cheek again.

"As long as you're happy, Shilo. That's what counts." Eli turned and left.

Only his comment lingered in Jesse's mind. Was Shilo happy?

Chapter 6
Saturday, May 26, 1973

S hilo stretched and yawned, trying to get her bearings. Right. She was at Aunt Sarah's. Alone.

Aunt Sarah was in the hospital.

Last evening's events rushed back. All her poor aunt had wanted to do was sleep. Bet she ended up wide awake at three this morning.

Shilo hadn't stayed long after she and Jesse returned. He'd taken her to a late lunch at Fenn's, where they used to eat during high school. This brought back a lot of memories. That's where she'd first told him about being chosen as a Breck Girl, and how she needed to leave right after graduation to fly to the Breck corporate headquarters for the professional sitting. A portrait done in pastels to be printed on the backs of women's magazines throughout the country. They'd promised to write to each other, but despite her best efforts that didn't happen.

She believed Jesse never got her letters. Still she couldn't figure out why all of them got lost. *What in the world could have happened to them?*

But there was no opportunity to dwell on the past. First things first. She spent time in her Bible and in prayer. She hadn't started yesterday with her habit, or the day before for that matter, and wondered if her fears had grown from not keeping with her practice. Well, she'd take care of that.

Opening her Bible to Second Timothy she read through chapter one. Verse seven jumped out at her. *For God hath not given us the spirit of fear;*

but of power, and of love, and of a sound mind. She wished she'd seen those words yesterday. But committing the verse to memory, she vowed it would stay close in her heart today.

A bit later she glanced at the alarm clock. Five 'til eight. She climbed out of bed, laid out a pair of jeans and her peasant blouse, and headed for the shower. Good thing she'd done her laundry back on Thursday. Even better, she'd be clothes shopping today. *Wonder if Jesse would be comfortable going through a Goodwill store?*

After she dressed, she fixed herself a bowl of cereal and a glass of juice before calling the nurses' station in charge of her aunt's stay. Aunt Sarah had a quiet night and had just gotten her breakfast. Good. Maybe she'd be up to a quick visit. They'd already planned for Jesse to pick her up at St Joe's.

Driving Aunt Sarah's car was a trip. If Jesse learned she'd let her driver's license expire, he'd flip his gourd. But how else was she to get around? Shilo drove extra careful, mindful of every traffic rule. Aunt Sarah was in no shape to prove Shilo hadn't stolen the car if she got stopped, and the license thing would just make the situation worse.

A parking spot opened up near the front, and Shilo grabbed full advantage of it. See? She could arrive without incident. No need to involve Jesse.

She took the elevator to Aunt Sarah's floor and checked in with the nurses' station before going to the room in case anything had occurred since her call. Nothing had, though, so she headed on over, the scent of disinfectant lingering in the hall.

Aunt Sarah's roommate controlled the TV. *The Brady Kids* were involved in yet another catastrophe solvable in thirty minutes. Shilo heard the theme song before she entered. No wonder Aunt Sarah was awake.

"Good, you're here. I was hoping to see you before your shopping trip." Aunt Sarah reclined in her bed, her smile tired but full of love.

"I told Jesse I needed to come here first. He's to meet me here."

"Oh, then, you better help me. I need my face washed and my hair combed. And my teeth, got to brush my chompers."

Shilo chuckled, gathered everything, and helped get those things done. "Better now?"

Aunt Sarah motioned Shilo closer with a conspiratorial glance toward the curtain separating the two beds. "Some. I'd sleep if it weren't so noisy."

That's what Shilo figured. Now, should she speak to the roommate or just make mention to the nurse? Most people only needed to be aware and would be happy to comply. Still, she shot up a quick prayer for her words to not offend.

Shilo stepped around the curtain. "Hello. I'm Sarah's niece, Shilo. How are you doing today?"

The woman didn't look happy, that's for sure. Her hair splayed against her pillows and in place of a smile, she appeared to have sucked on a lemon way too long. "What do you want? You're interrupting Marcia."

Shilo silenced the Jan Brady voice in her head singing *Marcia, Marcia, Marcia.* "Oh, I'm sorry. I can imagine having something familiar like a TV show you enjoy helps make your recuperation time go easier, Mrs.?"

The woman nodded, still not offering her name. "I guess. I never miss them at home."

Even though it was kids' programming? "My aunt had major surgery yesterday. Is that why you're here?" Now Shilo's inner impatience told her to get on with things, but if going slower, making a connection worked, then all the better.

"Yeah, two days ago. I want out of this place, but the doc says I have to stay."

"Oh, I understand. It's probably just caution on his part."

"That's what I keep telling myself." Though the woman's eyes picked up a tinge of worry.

"Would you like me to pray with you?"

Now the lady stared. "You'd do that? I mean I got no one coming to visit, no preacher or anyone to say stuff. So, yeah. I'd like that. I'm Betty."

Shilo shook Betty's hand and then held on. "Nice to meet you, Betty. And thank you for letting me pray."

"Father, I know You see Betty here and understand what's going on in her body. You know more than the doctors even because You already see tomorrow and next week and next year. So, nothing is a surprise to You. Would You please hold on to Betty's hand, remind her You are with her, that she's not alone, and that You can heal even when doctors don't believe it. Thank You for hanging out with us here. We love You, Father. In Jesus's name, amen."

Betty wiped a tear from her cheek. "Thanks. How is your aunt doing? What's her name again?"

"Sarah. She's tired and sort of hoped to get a nap."

"Want me to turn the volume down? I thought she might want to watch with me, but I get it. I was like that. Takes time for the anesthesia to move out of the system." She used the remote to lower the sound on the TV.

"Thank you. I'm sure she appreciates that. Hope you get out of here soon, Betty, and I'll be praying you experience no more problems." Shilo flashed a smile before returning to the other side of the curtain with her aunt.

Jesse had slipped in while she'd been talking to Betty. He and Aunt Sarah wore big grins, and he shook his head. "Ready to go?"

"I am if Aunt Sarah is okay with my leaving."

Her aunt patted her hand. "You two head out and have fun. I'll be fine. You've planned for others to drop by to visit me. And don't worry about trying to make it back today. I'll catch you after church in the morning. You can tell me all about your big night then."

"You're sure?"

Aunt Sarah nodded, so Shilo kissed her cheek and left holding Jesse's hand.

Once they hit the elevator, he looked like he was about to burst. "How did you do that? Sarah whispered to me about her noisy neighbor, and we listened while you got her to volunteer to turn the volume down. Talk about magic."

"Nah, nothing like that. Just meeting the person where they were and letting them know they have value. Besides, praying for her was an honor for me."

Jesse searched her face for a moment and then shook his head, staying silent the rest of the way out of the building.

She wondered if she should've dressed up a little more since he wore a red OP polo shirt and Wrangler flared chino pants with blue pin stripes. Not his three-piece suit but still fancier than her jeans and top. Well, wasn't that the point? She needed more clothes.

Once in his Ferrari they pulled out onto Jefferson Street. "I'd planned to take you to Indianapolis to shop, but that's not a good idea now. So, how about we go to Golightly's out at Maplecrest? Viv thought that would be a great place. She sort of helped me put a plan together."

"Oh, I remember Golightly's. Sure. Especially if it's Viv approved." She winked at him. They must have some sale items there.

The trip didn't take long, and *The Four Tops* had barely started "Standing in the Shadows of Love" when Jesse parked.

Funny, but when she glanced his way, she understood the title. Now that she'd figured out that she was falling in love with him all over again, a shyness grew. Some things she'd originally imagined they'd talk about, she now wanted to hide from his knowledge.

However, when she opened her door and took Jesse's hand to climb out, the electricity of his touch messed with her head.

Instead of holding her hand, though, he led her with his palm to her lower back. If he figured that was better than the shooting sparks up her arm from his grasp, he needed to think some more. His hand right there made currents charge in all directions. How did her feet keep walking?

Jesse held the door for her. No jingling bells like yesterday, but her new ring helped her remember that event. Like when she'd laid one out on his kisser. Her face heated at the memory. At least he'd kissed her back.

Until they got interrupted.

Jesse hailed a salesclerk and explained about the evening's event and the type of dress needed.

With that, he found a chair where Shilo could model for him and check the three-way mirrors while he commented. At least she hoped he'd comment. She wanted his opinion, valued it in fact. He understood about these social gatherings. It'd been a lot of years since she mingled in a high society crowd.

Oh, she could do it. She knew the right things to say and do. Jesse wouldn't need to worry about her embarrassing him. But she wasn't so up to date with fashions. That stuff didn't pique her interest anymore.

The clerk escorted her to a changing room, promising to bring several dresses for her. True to her word, the girl returned with an armload.

"That's a lot of try-ons."

"I know, but you can weed through and ignore those that don't interest you. I recommend, with your coloring, trying this taupe number. Simple, but elegant." She held the hanger out to Shilo.

The dress was everything the clerk, Susan, said. Spaghetti straps of the same material, the empire-waisted bodice vertically ruched in a matching chiffon, and the full-length skirt covered in the same filmy material with tiny pleats. Shilo shimmied into it. A perfect fit. She slipped out to show Jesse.

"What do you think?" She did a twirl in front of him, making the skirt billow.

"That's lovely. Put it in the yes pile and try another."

"Yes pile?"

"Of course. This won't be the last event we attend. You're going to want a few outfits."

"But I only need one before the wedding, right?"

Jesse shook his head, a half-smile teasing his lips. He got a charge out of all this. Great. Well, she'd keep track of the spending, for sure.

She glanced at the price tag dangling under her arm. A shock raced through her. She should've checked earlier. *Hoo boy.* "What else are you thinking of, Mr. Franklin?" This trip could get super pricey fast.

"We might, or might not, have an engagement party. But you will need pictures for the newspaper. And something to wear to the rehearsal dinner. Viv gave me a list. Plus, what if we go somewhere elegant on our honeymoon?"

"Honeymoon? We're taking a honeymoon?" Her voice squeaked as her nerves churned in her stomach.

"Of course. I've got the perfect one planned."

"B-b-but you said ..." He wouldn't go back on his word, would he? How would she feel if he did? Now her face grew hot.

He stood and captured her by her arms. "Shilo, look at me. Shy, I've got this all set, you don't have to worry. I'll keep my word. I promise."

Yeah, but did she really want him to?

He'd forgotten how much fun they could have. And he enjoyed teasing her. Only, what did her expression mean, the one before she returned to the dressing room?

Being around her again made him feel like he'd crawled out from his hiding place ready to face the world. No one who imagined they knew him would believe his behavior now. But that was Shilo, what she always did to him. The only times in his life where he'd stood up to his grandfather were times he'd talked things over with Shilo, and she encouraged him to stand strong, be bold, take a chance.

Like she'd done with that Breck Girl opportunity.

Not that he'd ever wish anything bad for her, but he would've preferred she hadn't gotten picked. Maybe things might've worked out differently for them. Maybe they wouldn't be looking at a marriage in name only like now.

"How about this one, Jess? I'm not sure." She twirled in front of him in a pale-yellow dress that ended just above her bare feet. The sleeveless top had some kind of metallic trim that rose like straps from the neckline (a neckline with a tiny bit of plunge, not so much to be immodest, but enough to prove she was a woman) and connected in back of her neck. He couldn't tell the material, though as she got closer, he noticed a woven pattern, sort of a brocade thing.

Truth be told, she could be wearing a gunny sack, and her beauty would still knock him out. "It's a nice color on you. It looks...flattering." Yeah, that word. Flattering.

"So, you like it? Better than the first one?"

"Actually, I liked the first one better, but put this with the yes pile too. Why not wear that tannish-pinkish one tonight and save this yellow one for another time." Not that he was an expert in women's fashion. "Or vice versa."

"Jesse, I don't need a lot. I like simple."

"I've figured that out. Just humor me, okay?"

She took one more glance in the mirror, her eyes squinted in critical appraisal. "Fine. So, is this enough?"

"What about daytime dresses? Or pant suits, if you prefer."

"You don't like my jeans skirt?"

How did he diplomatically answer? "Um, it's nice for around the house. Not what you'd wear to appointments or church." Ah-ha, a stroke of brilliance, that last part.

"How did you know I planned to wear that tomorrow?"

His ears grew warm. "I didn't, but it's the dressiest I've seen you since you arrived. Besides, Shy, you only packed for a temporary visit, and now you're moving here. You need more wardrobe. And remember, we have our class reunion this summer as well. You should get something to wear for that too." *Please let that placate her.*

"Fine, I give up. And yes, I want to go to the reunion, but I should have my money by then and can get something myself. Ha!" She headed into the dressing room only to pop out again. "And thank you. I do appreciate this. I'll keep the receipt for my records." She popped back in without giving him a chance to reply.

Fine by him. She wouldn't have liked his answer anyway. He chuckled.

A second later the clerk came out as if on a mission to grab more selections for Shilo. He motioned her over.

"Would you do me a favor and gather some lingerie for my fiancée? I want to surprise her. Any type of undergarment and nightwear she might need."

"Of course. You want her to try that all on as well?"

He shook his head. "Deliver those things. Here's my card." He pulled out the little cardstock rectangle and scribbled his home address on the back. "Send the package here. Can you do that?"

"Oh, yes, sir. I'll get this all together and phone you with the total. She's lucky to have you."

"More like I'm lucky to have her. But thanks, that will work. And please don't say anything. I want to surprise her."

She nodded and took the card to the register before finishing what she'd been doing when he stopped her.

Soon Shilo carried two evening gowns, three dressy daytime outfits, a sundress, and one pantsuit in an earth tone small tweed pattern from the changing room. "We gotta stop, Jesse. This is too much."

"We're almost done, Shy. You still need shoes. And what about nylons? You ought to have a pair of those too, right?" He tried to be matter-of-fact, but heat rose in his cheeks, and he knew he'd turned red-faced. This was so out of his depth.

She must've taken pity on him because she didn't poke fun or fight him. "Fine, let's find the pantyhose first. Where should we get the shoes?"

"How about Raab's?"

Shilo smiled. "I remember that store. Yeah, good choice. Unless I can get by with my Birkenstocks?"

"No Birkenstocks allowed. Hand me your stuff, and I'll start at the checkout while you grab you-know-what."

She laughed at him that time—just like he knew she would—before turning toward the hosiery department.

He took the rest to the cashier, handed her his Master Card, and got her started ringing up the order.

Shilo returned in time to spot the subtotal flash in the register's window. "Oh, Jesse, that's too much."

He swiped the pantyhose package from her and handed it to the cashier. "Add that in too."

She did and returned his card after running it through the machine with a carbon-papered form.

He signed on the line and pocketed his copy of the receipt while the clerk packed up their purchases.

Then they were off to Raab's Shoes.

Shilo found a simple ivory pair that went with most, if not all her new outfits. He wouldn't argue with her, though he encouraged her to choose several pairs. He'd be more than happy to buy them for her. However, he'd rather she be happy, and he knew he'd pushed her far enough.

Considering what potentially waited for them this evening, he wouldn't push more.

Grandfather would not be happy. How much of a scene he'd make had yet to be determined. Jesse figured the real fireworks would start tomorrow.

He drove her back to her aunt's with the plan to pick up Sarah's car when they left from visiting Sarah after church. Shilo'd declined his offer of lunch, saying she needed to do things she'd promised Sarah she'd get done.

Even though he walked her to the door with her packages, she didn't invite him in. Maybe she needed some time alone. He did. Too many thoughts running wild through his brain. But he did brush a kiss to her cheek. "I'll be by around six. Is that long enough?"

She nodded, her smile reflected in her eyes. "Thank you, Jesse. I'm overwhelmed."

"Go get ready. I'll be back soon." He needed to get out of there before he couldn't leave. Somehow, he got his feet to head for his car. But even when he'd closed his driver's side door and checked to make sure she'd gotten in the house, she stood in the doorway and waved to him.

Oh, he never should've made that promise. He'd keep it, but how he had no clue.

What he needed was a shower. A little on the chillier side.

Instead, he climbed upstairs to the bedroom he'd turned into an office. The window set right over the back porch, and he lived for the times he crawled out and sat on the roof, peering out over the copse of trees that hid his home from the road. That had been the selling point when he bought the place. The surroundings gave him the illusion of solitude in the middle of the neighborhood.

He'd snagged his sketchbook and pencils and now leaned against the outer wall of his office, drinking in the greens and blues, the fluffy white clouds. When the firm grew too much, when solutions turned to mist, this place gave him solace, especially this time of year where scents from neighbors' gardens touched his soul. It was similar to the roof he used to share with Shilo, back when they were kids and hanging out at her grandfather's house. Jesse doubted if any of their adults gave a flying fig where they'd gotten off to almost every day. But who cared? On the roof, they shared their secrets and dreams, and made a few schemes and plans. Up there, they were free to be who they were. He closed his eyes as memories flooded of the two of them—Shilo animated, him listening to every word she said, agreeing to every plan she presented.

Would Shilo ever want to join him on this roof? Could he share his sanctuary with her? Very good questions that he couldn't bring himself to speculate about right now. Instead, he sketched the birds and leaves and trees and sky and ... heaven. This is how he pictured it. And if there was a God and a heaven, he hoped this would at least be a part.

Jesse glanced at his watch, shocked to notice the time. He closed his book and climbed back through the window and headed for the shower.

Forty minutes later, he drove to the nearest florist to pick up a wristlet of pink baby roses before heading to get Shilo.

She answered his knock almost before he stopped the motion, pulling the door wide. "Jesse. Come in. I realized I didn't get a purse today, and I doubt you want me to carry my macramé bag. So, I called Aunt Sarah, and she loaned me this clutch. Will it work?"

"I'm sure it's fine. Shy, you look amazing." And she did, with her hair down but little bits from the side pulled to the back in a barrette. Every eye in the place would be on her tonight, she was so dog-gone beautiful. "Oh, this is for you." He held out the florist's box.

As she opened it and slipped the flowers on her wrist, he realized she wore no jewelry but his ring. And yet she glowed. He was about to marry this woman. The notion boggled his mind.

"Jesse?"

"Oh, sorry, I was thinking. What did you say?"

"I said thank you for the flowers. You didn't have to."

"No, but I wanted to. Are you ready?"

At her nod, he led her to the door and pulled it tight while she locked up. Then he escorted her to the Ferrari. A car worthy of her. Man, he had it bad. He made sure she got tucked in, including the hem of her long flowy skirt, and closed the passenger door before climbing in his side.

He ought to prepare her for this shindig, but he had no idea what would be helpful and what was just his general opinion.

Shilo touched his shoulder. "Are you nervous, Jess, or is it something more?"

"No idea. I can guarantee Grandfather will not be pleased. But other than that, I have no clue what to expect."

"Does he dislike me that much?" Her eyes radiated hurt.

Jesse reached for her hand. "He said you were a bad influence on me in high school. After you left, when I didn't hear from you, I stopped fighting for my way with him. I guess I'm more passive aggressive in that I try to do what I want before he has the opportunity to tell me what I should want. And when those moments arise, I tend to let the choice that would tick him off the most have more sway. Not very adult, I know. Just our method of dealing with each other."

"Is that why you offered to marry me? To tick him off?"

His heart seized, and he was glad for the stoplight to give him a chance to look her in the eye. "No, Shy. Absolutely, no. However, I figured out pretty quick he won't like it. I offered because you're my friend, we're good together, and we can help each other." He squeezed her hand as the light changed to green.

"I don't get how I'm helping you, though."

"Lawyers ought to be married. And it takes me off the meat market."

"Meat market?"

Jesse chuckled, though he found no actual humor in it. "Yeah, every one of Grandfather's friends with eligible young daughters or grand-daughters gets thrown at me. Some of them hate it like I do, but too many get man-hungry, and I'm not ready to be consumed as if I'm a plate of steak."

Shilo grinned. "Poor, poor Jesse. Well, I'll be sure to flash my ring around so everyone will be aware you are no longer on the menu."

"Thank you." That's when his conscience nudged him. *Tell her what Grandfather said.*

But she was smiling and happy, and things were going so well. Why mess it up?

Chapter 7

Shilo gazed out her passenger window as the clubhouse came into view, a wiggle of trepidation tickling her gut.

Jesse pulled up in front as a man in a white jacket opened her door and held out a hand. Another twin-dressed assistant met Jesse at the driver's side, greeted him, and gave him a claim ticket.

Jesse had done this before.

Of course he had. This was his life.

Shilo shivered. Would she be a help to him? Or would her love of the simple and uncomplicated bring him and his career down?

"You okay?" Jesse stood at her side, hand at the small of her back.

Of course, she wasn't okay when he did that. She was a nervous wreck that he'd see just how much she cared. But she forced a smile. "I'm fine. Let's do this." *Liar, liar.*

His continued search of her face told her she hadn't sold her white lie, but at least he didn't argue.

They moved toward the doors that were pulled open by two more men in white jackets. She ought to have her head examined so she didn't end up where men in little white coats guarded the exit. White hats, good. White jackets? Depends.

Her hands shook.

"Shy, it's gonna be okay. Stick with me. We might even have a great time. Do you still like to dance?"

She nodded and focused on thoughts of dancing with Jesse. They'd always had fun back in the day. And he'd been pretty smooth for a high school kid. They learned some cool moves. Wonder if he remembered any of them?

Though she didn't say anything, he must've felt her relax a little. He tossed her a wink and led her to a table in the far corner. "We'll have more privacy here. People will wander over, but we won't be stampeded."

That suited Shilo.

However, he'd just held her chair for her and scooted her in when a familiar figure sauntered over.

"Had a premonition you both would be here." Eli took the seat on her right without waiting for an invitation.

"By all means, Shanahan, join us." The level of snark in Jesse's tone was more than Shilo had ever heard.

Eli leveled his gaze at Jesse. "Think I'm going to miss this show tonight? No way."

Shilo glance between the men. "What show?"

"Your honeybunch here didn't prepare you? Hey Franklin, where's your manners? Letting this sweet young thing enter the lion's den like that."

"Shut up, Shanahan. She knows about Grandfather."

This had the makings of another shoot-out at the O.K. Corral. Shilo's nerves kicked into the next gear.

"I'll bet she doesn't. No way you told her everything."

"What haven't you told me, Jesse? Something I should know?" Dread tasted like bile in her throat. Oh, she needed to get somewhere where she could pray and talk with Jesus. *Can You hear my thoughts, Lord? Am I really in the lion's den?*

"Shy, he's making more of things than need be. Remember, we're going to tell Grandfather, and then the rest of the evening is ours. He won't cause a scene here." Jesse sank into the chair on her left and captured her hand. "Don't worry. We wouldn't even be here tonight if he hadn't made me promise to put in an appearance. We have, so once he's aware of that, we're good to go."

The band chose that moment to begin, and their first song was an instrumental version of "The Way You Look Tonight."

Jesse stood. "Dance with me. Let's get this party started."

Temptation tried to lure Shilo to glance at Eli, but she kept her gaze locked with Jesse's and followed him to the dance floor.

Being in his arms with a slower song hadn't been what she'd conjured about dancing with him as they walked in, and as her nerves misfired throughout her system, she understood why. She fit perfectly into his embrace, and he knew exactly what he was doing with the dance.

Was there any chance he felt like she did? She could only pray.

His breath tickled her ear as he whispered the lyrics to her, making her knees weak. Exquisite torture.

The song ended, and they stepped apart to applaud before the next one began.

Shilo peeked up to Jesse's face to find strange thoughts written in his eyes, eyes she thought she'd always be able to read. But not now. Almost a smoldering appeared, but not anger. Overwhelming intensity, but not power. She wanted to label it, understand it, but the moment passed. Another song began.

He pulled her to him as "Strangers in the Night" set the rhythm to their movement.

Shilo leaned her head against his shoulder, taking in strength. If he wasn't afraid, why should she be? More importantly, God remained here with her. Even if Jesse let go of her hand, He never would. Remembering that stilled the fears, though the nervous tingles remained. She had to admit they were pleasant, fun even. God knew. He brought the right peace and allowed her to enjoy Jesse's touch.

He ended with a squeeze as the last notes faded and the dancers clapped again for the live band's abilities. "Want to get something to drink?"

She nodded and followed him to the bar. "I'll have a Coke."

The bartender cocked an eyebrow. Didn't anyone ever order nonalcoholic drinks?

"Make that two." Jesse flashed his smile while the bartender shook his head and poured two cups of Coke over ice cubes.

Jesse handed her the first one before taking the other for himself. "If Mr. Shanahan gave up, maybe we can get our table back." He led her to the far corner where Eli still sat. "Or there's always the terrace."

"It's fine, Jesse. Eli might need some company." She pulled out her chair while both men jumped to hold it for her.

Eli backed off, hands in the air, and returned to his seat.

Jesse scooted close on her left. "So why are you hanging out here, Shanahan? Haven't you got anything better to do?"

"Nope. Figured Shilo might want to dance with someone who knows what he's doing."

"We're all aware of what you're do—"

Shilo covered Jesse's hand. "No thank you, Eli. Tell us about your day. What've you been up to?"

A weird glance passed between the men before Eli answered. "Nothing much. Definitely nowhere near as exciting as with you two kids. Getting all engaged ..." His voice got stronger with the last few words.

Someone cleared his throat. Shilo turned to find an imposing man, white hair, black tux, florid face, the scent of his expensive Cuban cigars preceding him. Despite the past decade, she'd recognize him anywhere. Jesse's grandfather.

"Good evening, sir. How are you tonight?" Eli's grin made Shilo's stomach squeeze.

"Shanahan, go get yourself a drink."

Eli jumped to do his bidding.

"Jesse, you have something you wish to tell me?"

Jesse stood. "Yes, Grandfather. First, you remember Shilo Anderson?"

Shilo stuck her palm out to shake hands. She wasn't sure if this was the correct procedure, but she must be close. And at least the gesture offered friendliness.

It took him a moment, but the elderly man accepted her handshake. "I think Mr. Shanahan wanted me to notice your other hand. If I may?" He reached for Shilo's left hand and examined her fourth finger. "Mighty pretty. I realize I told you, Jesse, it was time you got married, but I never imagined you'd run out and ask the first girl you saw."

Shilo pulled from his grip. Blinking hard, she searched Jesse's face.

It had turned to granite.

"If you remember, sir, Miss Anderson and I have known each other a very long time. I can't imagine anyone I'd rather marry."

"So, that's it? You've got it all worked out?" His eyes bored into Jesse, making Shilo shiver.

"If that is how you choose to put it, yes, sir. We planned to announce our engagement tonight after we told you. Now that you know, we can continue with that plan."

The elder Mr. Franklin pulled Jesse to the side and turned his back on Shilo as if that would keep her from hearing his words. But it didn't. "Why, Jesse? Is this one more way of needling me?"

"Grandfather, sir, I thank you to be polite to my fiancée. For your information, I probably would've married her years ago, if it were possible."

"Fool yourself all you want. I'll be around when you're ready to talk sense." Mr. Franklin stormed off toward the bar.

With his exit, though, Jesse looked like he was about to melt into a puddle.

Shilo stood and pulled out his chair. "Sit. He's gone." She returned to hers. "Jesse, am I making things worse?"

His eyes grew enormous, and he focused on her for the first time since his grandfather left. "No, Shy, no. I rarely stand up to him. Takes so much out of me. But I couldn't let him talk that way about you. You realize you are the best thing that ever happened in my life? I ..." His Adam's apple bobbed as he swallowed. "You're my best friend. Always have been."

Friend. Well, that still called for caring. She'd accept that. "You're not my best friend, Jesse, but you're the best next to Jesus."

"He's a hard act to follow." His grin came slowly but grew. "I can live with that. I think."

"Jess, where are the restrooms? I'd better make a visit."

"Excitement too much for you?"

She chuckled and nodded before he pointed her in the right direction.

Once in the ladies' room, she checked her makeup to see if she needed to freshen her lip gloss. And she did. All that chewing on her bottom lip while Jesse and his grandfather danced like fighters in the ring, throwing verbal jabs, nearly gave her a lip-ectomy.

She'd finished up and headed back out to Jesse when someone stepped in her path. Mr. Franklin.

"May I speak with you a moment, Miss Anderson?"

She wasn't about to say no and cause more problems. But every fiber of her being shouted at her to be wary. Shilo nodded.

"I understand what happened. Your grandfather placed a condition on your inheritance, and I've told Jesse he cannot become a full partner in the firm unless he marries. This situation proved too perfect. But I don't believe this is the best for Jesse. Just as I didn't ten years ago. So, I'll make you an offer."

Something in the words pulled at her, she needed to sort them for a moment. But he wasn't giving her time.

Instead, he continued. "I'll write you a check tonight for one hundred thousand dollars if you will break your engagement. It's for his good. I'm aware that by marrying him, you'll gain a lot more money, but I will also make sure your Aunt Sarah is taken care of. That should relieve you of reason to stay." He paused, as if gauging her reaction.

Only she was too stunned. The man wanted to buy her off.

"I see you drive a hard bargain. I've property in Southern California. I'll put you into your own home, a beachside condo. Can I count on your help to do what's best for Jesse?"

Shilo struggled to make her voice work. Her brain engaged and grew rapidly angrier. "There is no amount of money you could offer, Mr. Franklin. I'd never hurt Jesse that way."

He crossed his arms and blocked her path. "I noticed you never said that you loved him."

She tipped her head. "I noticed you didn't say that either."

"Didn't say what?" Jesse realized two things the moment he spoke. He'd caught the tail end of something important, and he'd startled the speakers. Shilo's eyes grew round, but his grandfather, for the briefest of seconds, looked like he'd been caught doing what he shouldn't.

Then the stone face reappeared. "Go on, my dear. You can tell him."

Tell me what?

Shilo shook her head. "Not here. I'll tell you later."

Jesse saw his grandfather halt Shilo's return and figured he ought to give her some assistance. But now he wondered if the old man had stepped out of line with her. Had he? Did he insult her when Jesse wasn't around? What did he say?

"Let's dance, Jesse." She threaded her arm with his and turned him toward the dance floor.

Like a tension valve releasing pressure.

For the moment he'd go along, but once they left, he expected her to say what she held back. Who was she protecting, anyway? His grandfather? Nothing that man did surprised Jesse.

Maybe he'd told her about how he insisted Jesse get married soon in order to make full partner. That should've come from him, not that old ... *Why couldn't he keep his mouth shut and his nose out of my business?* Jesse's fist curled at Shilo's back. Man, he wanted to punch the ol' buzzard in the face.

"What's wrong?" Shilo gazed into his eyes.

Her sweet caring released the new buildup of tension. "Nothing. But we should talk after we leave."

She nodded and rested her head at his shoulder as the rhythm of George Harrison's "Something" moved them around the dance floor. When the song ended, she glanced up again. "Want to go now?"

"Yes." It didn't matter that they'd miss the rubber chicken dinner or the chance to announce their engagement. He wanted to escape with her.

At the table she retrieved her purse, and they slipped out the doors where he handed the parking ticket to the valet who grinned big. Yeah, the kid would get to drive a new Ferrari for a few yards. Jesse could relate and answered with a knowing grin of his own. A guy thing, and it eased a bit more tension.

By the time he'd tucked Shilo in and climbed behind the wheel, all he wanted to do was drive. Hard and fast. Far from all this mess. Somewhere he could be honest with Shilo and maybe even tell her what grew in his heart.

He let intuition choose the direction. Soon they turned onto US 31 heading north.

"Where are we going?"

"I don't have a destination. Just driving. Want to talk, or should I find a place to pull over?"

"How about somewhere where we can get out and walk while we talk?"

And then he remembered the perfect spot. He took the next exit headed west and kept going to Galveston where he found a small park and pulled the Ferrari into the empty lot.

After helping Shilo from the car and locking up, he laced her fingers with his and started toward the picnic tables. The sky had yet to go full dark. Instead a violet hue outlined the last of the orange setting behind the trees on the west. But to the east, a few stars popped through to remind day it was time to become night.

He pulled out his handkerchief and wiped off the seat for them before Shilo sat and he joined her. Jesse opened his mouth to speak, but so did she.

"Um, I didn't want to say anything at the moment. I got the idea your grandfather wanted to goad me and that's not right."

"No, it's not. And before you tell me, I ought to explain something."

She turned to face him. "That he demanded you get married, or you can't make full partner?"

"He told you. Shy, I'm sorry. I should've been honest with you from the start, but I wanted you to be sure you knew I'm doing this for you. I would've asked you even if he hadn't dangled that edict right before you came to my office. I care about you, and the fact that marrying you meets Grandfather's condition is extra."

Shilo reached for his hand. She wasn't angry at him? "I need to tell you what he said, because I don't think marrying me will help you."

"What did he say?" That came out harsher than he'd planned.

"He said he'd pay me one hundred thousand dollars to break our engagement—"

He shot to his feet. "What?"

She held up her other hand. "Let me finish. He said he'd take care of Aunt Sarah's needs and would buy me a home in Southern California. All I had to do was call things off and leave. I told him I'd never hurt you that way." Now her gaze centered on the dark patch of grass at her feet.

"Shy. I am so sorry. He had no right." He pulled her to him, holding her close. "He had no right."

She drew away and looked deep into his eyes. "I'm so sorry, Jesse."

"You did nothing wrong."

"But you wouldn't be in this fix if I hadn't decided to use the money."

He rubbed his hands up and over her shoulders and back down. "What were you supposed to do? Let your aunt go without when you had access to what would get her what she needs? Shy, you are blameless. I've no idea what I'll do on Monday, but somehow, he needs to understand this is none of his business. If he doesn't want me to make partner, fine. I don't care that much anyway."

"Don't you like being a lawyer?" She linked arms with him, and they strolled.

"Funny, but I do. I shouldn't. Just one more thing he forced on me. But in school, I found I enjoyed the law, the discovery, the debate, the persuasion. It challenged me in ways I never expected. But becoming a full partner? That's more financially motivated. My salary is fine. I rarely spend that much, except for my car—"

"And your fiancée." She giggled.

"Yeah, and you." Twilight gave way to nighttime, and the dark made him braver, so he paused. "I've toyed with the idea of finding a different firm, but I've never had the guts to step out on Grandfather before this. Something about having you here gives me courage. I don't want to appear weak in your eyes."

"I've never considered you weak, Jess. Never." Her arms encircled his waist, and she leaned her head on his chest, just under his chin.

"Do you think ..."

She peeked up at him. "Think what?"

"Nothing. Hey, would you like to see where you'll live after we get married?" It was the first thing he came up with to change the subject instead of asking her what he really wanted to—to make their marriage more than just in name.

"Sure." She pulled away and flashed him with a smile. He needed to get brave enough to tell her how he felt. It might be hard, but holding this inside slowly killed him.

Instead, though, he wove their fingers together and walked her to the car. Bravery was not his strong suit.

A twenty-minute ride later, he parked in his garage and led her into his kitchen.

"This is nice, Jess. I didn't realize Kokomo had places like this where you've got your own private glen."

"That was one selling point. I haven't been here long, about six months, and the decorating is something I keep putting off."

She wandered into his empty living room. "Uh, I can tell." Her chuckle echoed in the void.

"Come upstairs with me." He reached for her hand and figured he should add more. "I want to show you something out a window."

She never hesitated, though. Maybe she trusted him. Or maybe she never saw him as someone who'd love her in that way.

He led her to his office—the lack of furniture other than the desk signaled another place he needed to furnish. At the window, he raised the sash and stepped out onto the porch roof, still holding her hand.

"Jesse, so like when we were kids." She hiked up her skirt enough to get her leg through, then ducked low and came out with him.

"Shouldn't sit in your good clothes, the shingles will snag the material. But yeah, this is where I go when I need thinking space."

"Do you still draw?"

He nodded. "I'm not that great, but it helps me relax."

Shilo surveyed the area from her heightened view. "This is amazing, Jess." She turned and kissed his cheek.

If there was a time to kiss her, to tell her, it was now. Only ... yeah, he'd send them falling off the edge. Without a doubt.

Instead, he squeezed her hand and led her back inside and down the stairs.

In the living room, he caught her gazing around. "Got any ideas for decorating?"

She laughed. "Too many, if I'm honest."

"Then I turn this all over to you. I'll add you to my charge card, and you can start whenever you want."

"Oh, you might not like my style."

"Bet I will. Besides, this will be your house too. And you'll have a lot more time here than me. Make it your own, and I'll enjoy coming home to it."

Her eyes lit up as her grin grew, revealing that bit of gap between her front teeth he thought was so adorable. "This is going to be fun. I promise not to go crazy and to spend responsibly." She held up her hand in the Girl Scout pledge sign.

"I trust you, Shy. I hope you know that."

"I do. And I trust you too." Something he could only describe as a cloud passed through her eyes. But as quick as it did, it vanished, and she smiled.

It'd been a long ten years apart. He realized she had yet to share some personal things. But that never detracted from the girl he placed on the pedestal. That's where she belonged.

"I'd better get you home." He led her to the garage door in the kitchen.

"Are you still planning to take me to church in the morning?"

He'd forgotten about that. "Sure. When should I pick you up?"

"Ten fifteen? That should give us plenty of time to find Viv and get settled."

Right. Viv. "Ten fifteen. Okay then."

He helped her into the car, and then climbed into the driver's seat to start the ignition and push the button to raise the garage door.

This night gave him such hope. And now it was over. No announcement, no sharing his heart. Only more interference from his grandfather, poking his nose into his life like he owned Jesse.

Shilo leaned back into the leather seat with her eyes closed.

He couldn't help but wonder where her musings took her. Was she happy to be staying, or did she miss San Diego? Did she miss someone there?

No, stupid thoughts like that would only lead to irrational jealousy. And that would ruin what little they'd laid claim to.

He pulled up in front of Sarah's place. "We're here, Shy."

"Yeah, I was enjoying the ride." She smiled and glanced out toward the house before turning back to him. "So, tomorrow for church. And yes, I promise to wear one of my new dresses, so you don't have to see my jeans skirt again." She tapped his nose and reached for the door handle.

That made him move. He climbed from his side and raced to hers in time to help her get out and walk her to the porch.

She hugged him tight, and he possessed zero desire to stop her. "Jesse, you are a wonderful friend."

He managed to hold it together until she got inside. But once in his car, all he could do was kick himself for the opportunity he'd let slip. Almost made him wish he believed in God so he could pray for another chance.

Chapter 8
Sunday, May 27, 1973

J esse squirmed next to Shilo, running his finger between his collar and neck. She had a notion more than the heat added to his discomfort. He wore his three-piece suits to work every day.

No, Shilo knew in her spirit that God was dealing with the man, and she sent up a silent prayer as she turned to the next hymn in the book.

She'd gone to church as a child with Aunt Sarah, so it wasn't some foreign thing when she returned after Lonnie and Connie baptized her. What was new was her. The old Shilo had been washed away, replaced by one with a commitment to Jesus.

Since that time, she'd seen people dressed in their finest because they respected the King of kings, and others who came just as they were, not trying to hide anything from their Savior. Both had godly motives. But some arrived in their best Sunday-go-to-meeting clothes because they vied for the approval of those around them more than God's.

The idea broke Shilo's heart. Especially since Jesse seemed to be falling into that camp.

The third verse of "Just As I Am" began, and she glanced again at Jesse who shared her hymnal and quietly sang beside her.

Just as I am, though tossed about
with many a conflict, many a doubt,
fightings and fears within, without,
O Lamb of God, I come, I come.

Could that describe what went on in his soul? Did the words reach his heart? He didn't reveal whether they did or not.

Her morning quiet-time settled on her that she should not press but instead live her faith where he saw it in action. So that's what she did. Along with praying for him. The rest lay in God's hands.

However, the verse about not being unequally yoked raised its head every now and again, making her concerned. Had she missed something in how God led her? But wasn't that the reason they chose a civil ceremony?

She needed to rein in her thoughts and focus on her own attitude before God.

The pastor prayed over the congregation and dismissed them.

Viv, who sat on Jesse's other side, leaned forward. "Do you have plans for lunch?"

"We'll probably grab something at the hospital before we visit with Aunt Sarah." Then, just in case, Shilo turned to Jesse. "That's what you had in mind, right?"

"Sure." He shrugged, but didn't meet her gaze.

"Well, I want you to know I have plenty at my house, and you are more than welcome. My kids have an open invitation, but sometimes they choose to stick closer to their homes after they attend their churches. So, I extend that same invitation to you both. If not today, then another Sunday." Viv's smile seemed a bit lonely, and she never mentioned a husband. Was she widowed?

"Thank you."

Jesse echoed her. "Yeah, thanks, Viv." He stood and reached for Shilo's hand, helping her to her feet. "We ought to get going."

Shilo pulled free so she could hug Vivian. "Thank you so much for recommending this church. I'll be back."

Viv hugged in return and whispered in Shilo's ear. "You are good for him. Hang in there. Don't give up."

Shilo drew away and nodded while swiping a little something from her eye. Then she found Jesse's hand again, and they all slipped from the pew and the church.

Outside brought more quick hugs before she and Jesse headed for his car. After holding her door for her, he shimmied out of his suit coat and vest and pulled his tie free. "Hallelujah! I can breathe."

He tossed all in the backseat and slid in to start the engine.

"It wasn't that bad, was it? I mean you wear a suit to the office all the time."

He shook his head. "Yeah, but I don't sit so close to everyone that I feel like I'm in a straitjacket when I'm at work. Plus, if I won't be seeing anyone, I can either take my coat off or crank down the air conditioner."

"Next time wear shirt sleeves and a tie. It's acceptable. You saw other men dressed like that."

"Nope. I spotted leisure suits too, and I wouldn't be caught dead in one of those. I can suffer through once a week if I have to."

His words wounded. "Not on my account, you don't. I'll go alone."

Jesse must've figured out that he said the wrong thing. "I'm sorry. I didn't mean that as it sounded. No, I want to go with you. I need to understand this God stuff since it's so important to you. I can't promise I'll agree, or even believe, but I do want to understand."

"Thanks, Jesse. I hope you figure things out." All the more, she hoped God would open his heart and mind to Jesus.

He parked in the hospital lot, and they headed for the big glass doors.

Though eager to get to her aunt, she still let Jesse steer her toward the cafeteria. Well, that's what she'd said to Viv, so he must've figured that was her plan.

She chose a pre-made tuna sandwich and a Coke. Jesse ordered a cheeseburger from the grill with fries and a Dr Pepper. More time waiting while his food cooked. *Lord, please cool my jets and help me relax.*

He paid for everything and carried their tray to a quiet table in the back. If only she could get her hands on even a little of the inheritance, she wouldn't have to stand by while he shelled out the bread every place they went.

"Do you mind if I say a prayer for our meal?" Shilo didn't wait for his answer but bowed her head over her folded hands. "Thank You, Father, for this food, thank You for caring for Aunt Sarah, and thank You for the chance to worship You today. Please hang out with us. Amen."

Jesse set down his sandwich. "You say that a lot."

"Say what?"

"Talking to God about hanging out with us."

Shilo studied the triangle of bread and tuna as she tried to figure out how to explain this. "I don't want to ever go anywhere or be anywhere without knowing God is with me. I need Him to know He has an open invitation."

"Do you feel like He is with you?" He asked the questions, but he didn't look at her. Did he want her answers?

"Most of the time, yes. Sometimes I need to check if I've put up any barriers between us."

"What kind of barriers are you talking about?"

Shilo set her sandwich back on the plate. She wasn't that hungry anyway. "Depends on what my motives are, or what I have been doing up until that time. If my faith and my focus weren't on Jesus, why would He feel invited to be with me? I mean, He's always with me. It's my callousness that builds barriers. But if I look to Him first, and I think about what He would have me do, then I can feel his presence with me."

"I see." Jesse took another bite, but never looked her way. Did he really get it?

Shilo put her sandwich on her plate, wrapped it with a napkin, and headed toward the trash. When she returned, she noted the question in Jesse's eyes. "I'm sorry you wasted your money, but I'm too excited to see Aunt Sarah to eat."

"That's not a problem. I'm concerned about you, Shilo. This is a lot on your shoulders. Are you sure you're okay?"

She reached for him and squeezed his hand. "I'm fine. Thank you." Shilo finished her drink and added that to the trash.

Jesse ate about half of his cheeseburger and a quarter of his fries, but he took everything else to the trash and then joined her to walk to the elevators.

At the nurses' station, the child from the other day sat behind the counter coloring on a different picture. She peeked up and smiled shyly at Shilo before returning to her job.

"Looks like you've got a resident artist."

Nurse Beverly wandered closer, her arms crossed. She leaned in and spoke low. "This poor thing has no place to go when she is ready to leave. She's a ward of the court."

"Where are her parents?"

"They're in jail, and they've both given up their parental rights. So now Child Protective Services needs to find her a foster care home, or better yet find her an actual family."

Jesse stepped close. "I ought to remind you, ladies, that since she is a ward of the court, you shouldn't be sharing this information."

Shilo put her hand over her mouth. The last thing she wanted to do was get Nurse Beverly in trouble. However, she still had a lot of questions about the little girl. "Are you able to tell me her name?"

The nurse glanced at Jesse who shrugged and stepped away. Then she leaned close again. "Probably not. But no one can stop her from telling you. Would you like to speak with her?"

"Oh, yes!" Shilo moved to the counter across from where the child worked. "That's a beautiful picture. You do outasight work."

The sweet girl pushed a blonde curl behind her ear and glanced up. "Thank you."

"My name is Shilo." Hopefully the budding artist would respond with her own name. Maybe.

But instead, the child worked harder on her picture. The pink tip of her tongue stuck out between her lips, and her compact fist around the red crayon gripped tighter. She changed colors, and with dark purple she wrote LISA and handed the paper to Shilo.

The printed letters nearly strangled the air in Shilo's throat. "Lisa. What a lovely name." That had been the one she'd picked out. So long ago.

After Lonnie and Connie came into her life, she'd looked up the meaning of the name. Consecrated to God.

That's what she did with her little Lisa.

The emotion rising within her threatened to drown her. So, she wiggled her fingers at the child and left for her aunt's room, still holding the drawn picture. She would put it in her Bible once she got home as a memory and a thank you to God for this moment.

Before entering, she turned to Jesse. "I need to run to the ladies' room. Please tell Aunt Sarah I will be right back." She needed that time to pull herself together. Otherwise, even if Jesse didn't notice, Aunt Sarah would spot something was wrong.

Once alone, her thoughts and emotions rushed to invade. That little Lisa's mother gave her away. Had she been forced? Was she in a situation where she saw no other choice? Or did she not want her child? It was so hard to imagine. Shilo's heart shattered in pieces on the tile floor. The one thing God couldn't fix in her life and now this little one was alone in the world.

The hardest part for her in all of this was Jesse. She might imagine she fooled him with her escape to the restroom, but he'd be wondering what happened and sure to ask when they left for home.

She should tell him. For Pete's sake, they were going to be married. He deserved to know.

But the closer they got, the less she wanted to let him in on things that would bring her down in his estimation. If he ever learned about everything she'd gone through, he wouldn't want to step in and help her. How could he even look at her the same way once he knew the truth?

The fear rumbled inside her, prowling like a roaring lion.

Now where was her faith and trust?

Jesse peered at his watch. What took Shilo so long? But her aunt didn't seem to be too upset.

Just then, he glanced up as Shilo walked into the room. Were her eyes a little brighter? Her cheeks a tad rosier?

He knew she possessed a tender heart. She collected the strays, making friends with people who usually got left out of things.

That didn't explain her friendship with Eli, though. Nothing did. For some reason, she still called that guy a friend.

But it must pummel her tender heart to realize what was going on with the child at the desk.

"There you are, dearheart." Sarah sat a bit straighter in her bed and opened her arms to embrace Shilo.

"Yes, here I am, but I want to know how you are doing."

"Doing pretty good for an old gal. They pulled my drainage tube today, and I'll tell you a secret. It made my toes curl. But it's gone, and I'm better now."

"Makes my toes curl just to think about it. By the way, how is your roommate? She's not in her bed."

"Turns out she has a great niece who came to visit her, only the girl is thirteen, so she's not allowed in the rooms. Not old enough yet. So, a candy striper took Betty in a wheelchair down the way to a little lounge where they could talk. I heard that child rode her bike for a couple miles to get to the hospital to check on her favorite aunt."

"That ought to give Betty a smile. At least she knows someone cares about her."

"She was beside herself with joy. I've never seen the woman so happy. So, tell me, how was church?" Sarah glanced at him.

Jesse had no clue what to say. The entire experience shouted uncomfortable from his extra warm jacket and extra tight tie to the extra close sensation of Viv on one side and Shilo on the other. He wasn't sure he got anything out of the message because his claustrophobia wanted to go wild.

Shilo spoke up. "The pastor talked about how with Jesus, He makes everything new. We have a new beginning. A new chance. He works everything out for our good because He rose and beat death."

Yeah, guess that's what the man said. But it still made little sense to Jesse. Would Shy think he was stupid if he asked her questions after they left? Maybe it was best if he didn't find out.

He chose the easier road and sat back to let the women talk. He couldn't come up with anything to contribute to the conversation anyway. They practically finished each other's sentences.

"Tomorrow is our appointment with The Weather Girls. I'm looking forward to going. It might be fun to look at what they have." Shilo glanced at him a moment, blushed a little, and then turned to her aunt.

What was that about?

Just then, Betty, wheeled into the room. Shilo made a big point of greeting the woman and hugging her. "How are you doing today, Betty? Sounds like you had some special company."

"I did. I can't get over Chrissy riding her bike all this way. I loved visiting with her. Even better to know someone cares." The candy striper helped Betty get back into her bed.

Shilo pulled the curtain from between the roommates. Now everyone could see each other. Betty sure sounded happier than she did the other day. Had that only been yesterday morning? Life had taken off at full speed, and a lot of living happened in the last twenty-four hours.

At least, as far as he was concerned.

Somehow, he needed to let Shilo see he would like to be more than her friend. That he wanted to make this marriage real. But would that scare her? Would she withdraw from him? Truth be told, they both knew she was only marrying him to get the money for her aunt. They walked into that with eyes opened wide.

But nothing changed the fact that he fell more in love with her every day. Her kindness, her empathy, her gentleness—all of that increasingly endeared her to him. He'd never realized how much he'd missed that until she brought it back into his life.

"You're awful quiet, Jess. What's going through that mind of yours?" Shilo tossed him a wink, but he knew she was starting to be concerned.

"Nothing for you to worry about. I'm here hanging out with you ladies. I'll be the dependable driver."

"Oh, that's okay. I've got Aunt Sarah's car. I can drive home, so you don't need to hang out if you have other things you'd rather do." Didn't Shilo want him around?

Sarah tag-teamed in, though she dropped her voice as if to share a secret with him. "Jesse, you've been a godsend. I may not be all excited about why you're getting married, but I love the fact that you're taking good care of my Shilo. So, if you want time to yourself, now's your opportunity. It's fine."

He glanced between the two women attempting to gauge whether they meant it. Or were they trying to get rid of him because he overstayed his welcome? "Really? Are you sure?"

Shilo kissed his jaw. "Really."

He shoved off from the wall and gave Sarah a quick peck on the cheek. Then he squeezed Shilo's hand and drew her toward the exit with him. Outside the door, he brushed her lips with the quickest of kisses. It was the bravest he had been. He took two steps away from her and turned around.

But before he asked again, Shilo pointed toward the elevator. "It's fine, Jess."

Guess he'd better head on out. Jesse rode the elevator to the ground floor and exited out the glass double doors to his car.

In a matter of ten minutes, he pulled into his garage and lowered the door. Why did this place seem so lonely? After he showed Shilo his home, coming back here felt empty.

Okay, so he didn't have a lot of furniture and things on his walls. It never bothered him much before. Now he looked through what he imagined to be Shilo's eyes, and he came up lacking. Did she see him? Truly see him? If she did, why in the world did she stick around?

Because of the money.

Not out of greed, though, but to help someone she loves.

Yet the baseline still came down to money.

Or did it?

Shilo could've taken his grandfather up on his offer. Sarah would've received her treatments, and Shilo wouldn't have to get married. Wouldn't need to stay in Kokomo. Instead, she could be lounging on the beach in San Diego. And she'd have enough money to live a comfortable life, even if it wasn't two million dollars.

And she turned him down. Told his grandfather she couldn't do that. What motivated her? Their friendship? It bloomed and grew as if it hadn't been frozen in place for a whole decade.

Was it out of loyalty? If one looked loyal up in the dictionary, Shilo's picture was bound to be right there.

She'd said she didn't want to hurt him. Shilo never wanted to hurt anyone.

Might she have feelings for him? Was it possible?

Oh, he couldn't allow himself to go there. That would mess everything up.

What could he do?

He did what he always did when questions grew too much. Jesse grabbed a sketchbook, his pencils, and a cushion to keep his dress pants from getting snagged on the shingles, and he went out on the back porch roof.

The weather grew warmer each day. Eventually, he'd only want to come out here in the evenings or early mornings, but for today, this would be a good place. At least he'd thought to turn his stereo on, dropping some old Sam Cooke on the turntable—*Hits of the 50s*—and cuing up "Mona Lisa" on side A. The ballad fit his melancholy mood.

If he were smart, he'd have stopped to change clothes first. But few people ever accused him of being smart.

His pencil tip snapped. A word he seldom even thought hissed past his lips. The sketching didn't flow as naturally as it usually did. Nothing rose to his standard. Oh, he knew he wasn't an artist. Hadn't his eighth-grade art teacher mentioned that? Still, this simply amounted to stress relief. But today the stress was winning, and he found no relief.

Sam moved through his repertoire and had reached the last song on that side— "Unchained Melody"—when the phone rang.

Jesse gathered his things, ready to give up now anyway, and climbed back through the window, reaching the handset by the fourth ring. "Hello?"

"Jesse, it's Shilo." She paused, and he worried that he'd lost her connection.

"Are you all right?"

"Yeah, I guess, but I need help. I'm sorry."

"No, wait, Shilo, what do you need? I'll help you. Is Sarah okay?"

He heard a sniff. Oh, no. Was she crying?

"Aunt Sarah is fine. This is just so embarrassing. I'm awfully sorry."

If she didn't tell him fast, he'd implode. "What do you need, Shy?"

"It's just that, I let my license expire so I've been very, very careful driving Aunt Sarah's car—"

"You've been driving without a license? Why didn't you tell me you needed one? Were you in an accident?"

"Jesse, let me get this out, please. I'm so embarrassed. I've been the model driver, I promise. No accidents. But that police officer who stopped me in the park?"

"Yeah?"

"Uh, he must've figured I was driving too slow. So, he started to write me a ticket for going under the speed limit and impeding traffic. But then he asked for my license, and I tried to explain. Then when he learned that the car isn't mine, well ... Jesse, I've been arrested for stealing Aunt Sarah's car. She's—"

"I'm on my way. Stay put." He hung up and realized what he said. "Stupid, stupid, stupid."

And he'd been planning to surprise her with a car for a wedding present. If that happened, he'd better first make sure she was legal on the streets of Kokomo.

An icy chill slithered down his spine. His grandfather would find out about this. He had no idea how or when, but he realized this little situation wouldn't stay secret for long.

He needed to get to the jail and fast if he had any chance of heading this off.

Chapter 9

S hilo hugged the passenger door of Jesse's Ferrari. The tension grew thick, making her afraid to get too close. If only he'd accept her apology. But he'd been distant and stern ever since yesterday when he picked her up at the police station.

Now they headed for their Weather Girls appointment, and she didn't know what to expect out of him there. Would he be a growly bear? Would he remain silent and frown? Or would he put on a show to keep everyone from suspecting something was wrong? That would be worse than any of the choices.

"Jesse, I just—"

"Don't say anything. I can't deal with it right now." He kept his eyes on the road without a glance her way.

"Can we talk after our appointment?"

He sighed. "I guess. Maybe by then I can."

At least that was something. If they could just hold this charade together until they were finished, then everything might be okay. But it went against all she believed in. Putting up a front when there was no need of it. All he had to do was accept her apology.

He parked at the curb of an old Victorian mansion framed with giant sycamores in the yard. Beautiful peonies and lilies of the valley sprouted at their bases. "We're here."

"Are we going to be able to do this, Jesse? I don't want to feel like I'm lying. If you'd just tell me that we're okay—"

"We are okay, Shilo." At least this time, he reached for her hand and looked her in the eye. "We're okay. But I can't talk about it yet. Let's get inside."

She nodded and gave his hand a squeeze. That felt a little better. She sure would be glad when they could talk this out.

The sign in the door read *open*, so they walked on in.

A pretty blonde met them, holding out her palm. "Hi, I'm Stormy. You must be Shilo and Jesse. Nice to meet you." After shaking hands, she guided them to a group of chairs further into what was once the living room. "Please, have a seat."

Shilo surveyed her surroundings. The interior of this home business stunned, with elegant dark woods and carvings and stained-glass windows. It was obvious the current tenants kept things as close to original as possible.

Jesse waited until both women took their seats, and then he sat. Ever the gentleman.

"So congratulations are in order. Would you like to tell me a bit about yourselves?" Stormy had a pad and pen ready for notes.

Shilo opened her mouth to start, but Jesse jumped in. "We've known each other since we were kids, and it's time we tied the knot."

Not very romantic if you asked her. However, no one had. Or maybe they did, but apparently her voice wasn't supposed to be heard. What got into Jesse? There was no reason they couldn't be honest.

Stormy's slightly narrowed eyes stated she agreed with Shilo. Jesse's answer didn't impress anyone. "I've got a few questions I like to ask couples. It helps them to understand each other's tastes in ways they might not have considered, so they can plan a celebration they both would appreciate. If you're ready, here's the first question. What is your favorite meal of the day?"

Jesse looked her way.

Oh, so he was going to give her a chance to answer something? "I dig breakfast, though I don't eat a large one. I just like the newness of the morning, and if I can eat outside, all the better."

Jessie's turn. He gave Stormy a moment to scratch out her note before he started. "I really don't have a favorite. Sometimes I have breakfast, sometimes I don't. Lunch is often a meeting. Like today, I left work so I could come here. For dinner, well, maybe that's my favorite, because I've not always got business on the brain, and I can relax a little."

Shilo's heart went out to him. She couldn't help it.

"Next question. What is your favorite memory? Jesse, you go first this time."

What? Why did Stormy do that? But something in the woman's gaze told Shilo this was important.

"I'm not sure it's just one moment, but maybe a string of moments captured in a single spot." He glanced at Shilo before continuing. "At Shilo's grandfather's house, there was a window upstairs we climbed out of, and we'd sit on the back porch roof looking out over the neighborhood. We did that so often growing up. That's where we talked and shared and dreamed and we sat silent together. All those moments wrapped into one memory, guess that's my favorite."

Shilo's throat constricted, and she wanted to hug Jesse, though she restrained herself. He'd reverted to the uptight lawyer figure from her first day in town. But to admit that this was his favorite memory when feeling as he did—talk about huge.

Stormy wrote for a moment before stilling her pen and focusing on Shilo. "Your turn."

Shilo wanted to say hers was the same, only it wasn't.

Close, yes, but she had one memory closer to her heart, and Jesse wasn't a part of it. She coughed softly into her fist. "I count the memory Jesse shared as one of my very favorites too. But the very best one, the only one which exceeds that is when I got baptized in the Pacific Ocean. I came up out of the water knowing all my sins had been washed away. God met me where I was and made me new. I thank Jesus every day for that." She felt Jesse's eyes on her but was afraid to peek for fear they'd be filled with hurt because he wasn't first in her heart. Then his hand captured hers and said more than any words could convey.

"That's beautiful, Shilo. Okay, are you ready? Here is the last question. Where do you see yourself in twenty years?" Stormy glanced from Shilo to Jesse, allowing them to choose who answered first.

Shilo followed her lead and gazed at Jesse for a clue as to what he wanted.

He shrugged, so she nodded to him.

"Looks like I get to answer. I haven't thought about it much. Working at Grandfather's firm, I guess I figured that that's where I'd be. Until you came back into my life, Shilo. Now I find myself with dreams I hadn't dared to dream in a decade. But I've learned a lot about myself too. I enjoy being a lawyer. I'm not sure I want to make partner anymore. In fact, I might want to start my own firm or join with someone else and do the type of law I always wanted to do. So, maybe that's it. Having my own firm, being out from under my grandfather's demands, and making a home with you, Shy." He squeezed her hand.

She had no words. The part about being free of his grandfather she knew to be genuine. But still being married in twenty years? Not that she planned to divorce him, but figured he might want out of this deal between now and 1993. Could he really mean what he said?

Shilo swallowed, knowing it was her turn. "I don't often think so far down the road anymore. A few years ago, I nearly died, and ever since I've been grateful for each day God allows me. If I get twenty more years, that is a gift, especially if I can spend them with you, Jess." Maybe he heard her heart clear enough with that.

"I have to say, your answers differ from any other couple I've interviewed." Stormy set her pad and pen aside. "Shilo, you mentioned you want to keep things small and have a justice of the peace preside. My brother-in-law can handle that part."

Shilo nodded and peeked at Jesse for approval. He was wiping something from his cheek.

Stormy clicked her pen. "How small are you thinking?"

Jesse spoke up again. "Mainly immediate family. My grandfather, Shilo's aunt, maybe a few friends, people from my office. We should cap it at twenty-five, maybe?"

Shilo couldn't summon up twenty-five local friends and family to invite. Her number was closer to five.

"Okay, that helps. We have an intimate setting, I'll show you. It had been a parlor originally. Of course, if you'd like a sunset ceremony, we can provide the service out on the balcony of the ballroom." Stormy rose. "How about you follow me? We'll come back and discuss all the particulars after the tour."

Shilo and Jesse stood, and he laced fingers with her. It really was going to be okay.

They followed Stormy to a smaller room off on the far side of where they were. "We use this for modest weddings and to display our cardinal sightings."

"Cardinal sightings?" The question reflected in Jesse's eyes, and furrowed brows mirrored those chanting in Shilo's brain.

Stormy motioned them nearer to the wall of couples photos. "A legend's been handed down for many generations, some believe all the way from the Native American days, concerning the sycamore tree in our backyard and a cardinal. They say if a couple kisses beneath its branches, and a cardinal lights above them, then theirs is a true love destined for a long and happy marriage."

"Sounds like superstition." Jesse's tone hid no disbelief.

"True. And as a believer, I rely on God, not legends. However, who's to say He can't talk to us through nature?"

Hmm. Shilo could accept that. She wasn't one to go looking for signs from God, but she didn't close her mind to how He might want to communicate with her or anyone else. She stepped forward for a closer look at the photos, her finger trailing down a gold frame. "I believe you."

"Shy, you believe a little red bird just happening to land on a tree branch when a couple kisses will ensure them of a happy marriage?"

"No, I don't believe that. But I do believe God can communicate with us through that red bird, and having a little assurance might make a couple work harder on their marriage and not give up so quickly."

He released her grasp and jammed his hands in his pockets. "I don't know."

"It's okay, Jesse. You don't have to believe it. Believing something doesn't make it true. It's true whether anyone believes it or not. Nothing changes the truth." She sort of shrugged at him, and he finally nodded.

"So, let's look at the rest of the house. We'll check out upstairs first." Stormy led them out and up the polished staircase. "The second floor is divided into the living quarters for my sister Sunny and her family on the east side, and the changing/waiting rooms for the bridal parties on the west side." She opened a door to a room obviously used for the bride and her attendants.

"Up one more flight." They returned to following Stormy to the next floor where multiple French doors opened to an enormous ballroom. A petite blonde and a large man on a ladder hung garlands on the walls near the beamed ceiling. "I want you to meet my sister, Windy, and her husband, Kris. Guys, this is Shilo and Jesse, and they're considering a small wedding here."

Windy reached out to shake hands, Kris right behind her. "Nice to meet you. Have Stormy show you the balcony. It's outasight at sunset."

"That's where we're headed now."

When they stepped onto the balcony, something about it took Shilo's mind back to those times on the roof with Jesse. A peace settled into her bones. "Yes, this is the place."

It was hard to miss the smile on Jesse's face, but he still asked, "Are you sure?"

Shilo nodded. There was a lot about this whole marriage thing that knocked her off-kilter like she was in one of California's famous earthquakes. But this location for their ceremony? This was as firm a footing as the sidewalks of Kokomo. "I'm sure."

Jesse agreed with Shilo's choice. Even if he didn't, he still wanted to give her whatever she wished. But knowing they agreed only made it better, melting away some anxiety about having their talk when they left.

Which would not be fun. He shook his head as his grandfather's image blinked in his brain, and he reached for Shilo's hand.

"Let's go back downstairs, and I can show you the rest now that you've made your decision." Stormy led to the ground floor, and this time they toured through the dining room, which had been set up with expensive-looking china and crystal. She explained the room's availability for the rehearsal dinner, cake tasting, and—for intimate weddings—the reception dinner.

Next, they traveled through the modernized kitchen, to the screened-in back porch, and then out to the backyard festooned with flowers—dahlias, hyacinths, peonies, hollyhocks, lilies of the valley, daffodils. And roses. So many roses. The heady floral scent knocked his tension level down another ten degrees.

"We can host the ceremony out here and/or the reception. I understand you want the balcony, but let's make sure you've seen it all." Stormy led down a path to the carriage house and pulled open a barn door. "We also can do what you'd like in here as well. We keep the hues neutral for the season to make it easy to add in the colors you choose." She stepped out of the way so Shilo and Jesse could look around.

This was definitely nice, but nothing would change Shilo's mind about the balcony.

"Last, but not least, let's check out our famous sycamore tree."

That turned out to be a very ancient sycamore with low spreading branches and a painted-white wrought-iron seat surrounding its girth. It didn't look freaky. In fact, the tree stood majestic. He could just imagine the colors come fall.

"Let's go in and figure out how we can help you." Stormy guided them back through the maze of rooms to where they'd started. They all took their original seats.

"I have an album that illustrates the different services we offer. You choose a package deal—there are several price levels—or order à la carte." Stormy handed over a large binder, sectioned off according to cost and packages.

Shilo flipped through the pages while Jesse looked on. "I can get a dress here?"

"Yes. We have several for you to try on. When you find one you like, we'll record your measurements and order it. All alterations are done locally by our friend Thea Carpenter."

"Is it possible to just get a dress off the rack? We're concerned for time. My aunt will be having treatments for her cancer, and we'd like to be married while she is feeling better, before the chemotherapy and radiation make her too run down to attend."

"I'm so sorry to hear about your aunt. I have to tell you, I've been wracking my brain since you walked in. I'm sure I've seen you before. It was at church yesterday, wasn't it? You sat with Vivian Watters, right?"

"Yes, she's my secretary."

Shilo had to ask. "You might know my aunt Sarah, Sarah Flanders?"

Stormy grinned. "I sure do. You say she has cancer? I hadn't heard. We have a telephone prayer chain at church. My grandmother is the head of it. Would you like me to put Sarah on? I won't if you'd prefer to keep this quiet, but the people on the chain know better than to gossip. They simply pass on the information they are given and commit to pray."

"Yes, please. She had surgery on Friday, so we're hoping she can come home this Friday. From what I've been told so far, they want her to heal some before they start the chemotherapy and follow up with radiation. So the window they're giving her to heal is where we need to schedule the wedding."

Stormy pulled out a calendar. "This is our busy season. Everybody dreams of a June wedding these days, well, not everyone or we'd be out of work for the other eleven months." She chuckled. "But if you are willing to have a Friday night ceremony, we can accommodate you on June 8th." She glanced up making eye contact with Shilo and Jesse.

Shilo turned to him. "What about you? Will it give you enough time?"

He squeezed her hand. "Whatever you want. We'll make it work." Then he faced Stormy. "We'll need engagement photos for the newspaper. Do you manage that?"

"Yes. My sister, Windy, who you met upstairs, is our photographer. She has her own dark room here and can get things set up right away. In fact, give me a moment, let me see if she has time now. You both look dressed well enough for the photos." Stormy hurried up the stairs as Shilo turned to him.

Engagement photos? "This is happening quick. I don't want to be scared, Jesse."

"Scared of what?" He tried to read in her eyes if she had second thoughts. Did she worry about being stuck married to him?

"I want to make sure this is what God wants me to do. I was so sure at first. And when you asked me, it was like a weight lifted off, and I felt peace. But now, there doesn't seem to be time to evaluate to make sure we're on the right path."

He didn't know how to respond.

Stormy raced down the stairs, so he squeezed Shilo's hand again.

"She can take them in about ten minutes. That should give you time to pick out your dress and your tux. Will anyone be standing up with you?"

Shilo shook her head while he answered, "No."

"Okay, then." Stormy leaned forward and turned a few pages in the binder. "I can tell you which of the dresses pictured we have on hand in your size. I'm guessing you're an eight? We'll need to make sure it's long enough too, but Thea is fast, so if we do require alterations, she should be able to get it done on time." She picked up a few more pages. "And here we have the tuxes for the men."

"I don't need a tux. I have one."

Shilo looked at him with widened eyes. "You've got your own tux?"

He shrugged, embarrassed as inner heat began to cook his ears. "You never know when you'll need it for one of Grandfather's shindigs."

A giggle escaped from Shilo's lips, and she clapped a hand over her mouth. "Sorry." But then she snorted, and they all laughed.

"Okay, since we have the tux issue settled, let's work on the dress. Oh, we do carry blank invitations you can handwrite on if you want to send any out. They come in boxes of twenty-five." Stormy and Shilo both looked at him.

He had no idea. "Sure. We'll figure out who after this. Let's take one box."

Shilo tipped her head his way. "Think we'll need that many?"

He honestly, *really* had no idea. "We can save the extras for some kind of party in the future. How's that?"

The women nodded and returned to the dresses, giving him a moment to lean back and observe them, or rather watch Shilo.

What about her attracted that cop to keep arresting her? Besides the obvious that she was a natural beauty. Nucum even acknowledged she didn't cause trouble or try to fight him. Shilo wouldn't hurt a flea. Yet the bozo kept finding her and ways to run her in. It'd be comical if not for the fact it gave his grandfather ammunition. And who knew what weapon Alvin Dean Franklin, Esq. would use against her.

He realized Shilo thought he was angry with her. He wasn't, and he needed to make things clear when they left. Instead, he was scared, scared of what his grandfather was capable of. As long as they played nice by those societal rules, or at least skirted along the edges of them, they'd be okay. Probably. But one step from high and mighty Franklin standards, and the fall could be devastating. Jesse didn't want to sever all ties, just the ones that kept him from being who he really was.

The two of them were just discovering their way. And if this meeting with The Weather Girls told him anything, it was that there was a chance they could turn this into a genuine marriage. It might be small, but he clung to that bit of hope.

As long as his grandfather didn't sabotage things.

"Should I show him?"

Jesse brought himself back to the present. "Show me what?"

"The dress I picked out. I'm going to go try it on now."

He had a picture in his mind of Shilo, all in white and lace, walking toward him. "Sure. I'd like to see."

She stood and followed Stormy toward the stairs. "I don't know. It's supposed to be bad luck."

He rose. "Thought you weren't superstitious." Grinning, he knew full well she'd want to show him.

"Fine, but any bad luck is on you." She winked and disappeared up the steps.

Minutes later, she came down dressed in an ivory-colored flowy dress with sheer puffy sleeves and a lacy veil that sat on her head with a wreath of small flowers. She took his breath away.

"Do you like it?"

Stormy giggled. "I'd say that's a yes."

He still couldn't form any words.

She blew him a kiss and went back up.

If she said no to a true marriage, he was a goner.

It didn't take as long to get into her own outfit, one he'd helped pick out before. Back then he still could produce speech even when he thought she looked pretty.

"Let me get those invitations for you." Stormy stepped out of the room for a moment, and Shilo pressed a kiss to his jaw.

"What was that for?"

"A thank you. This will be a wonderful day for us, Jesse. I'm more confident now."

"Good." Actually, whew! He hated her to feel trapped.

Stormy returned with a box and handed it to Shilo. "Should I put you down on the seventh at four o'clock for the rehearsal? That slot is open and since you are keeping it small, it shouldn't take but an hour at the most."

He nodded as Windy came downstairs. "I'm sorry for taking so long. We had a minor crisis, but Kris worked it out. If you'll follow me outside, I'll get those pictures taken for you."

Out under the sycamore, Windy posed them in various ways. Then she paused. "Here's the special one. Jesse, wrap your left arm around her waist and put your right hand at her nape. Shilo, slide your hands up around his neck and kiss like you're about to get married." She grinned.

But Shilo hesitated, glancing up at him as if to ask permission.

That's what he ought to be doing, asking her permission. Instead, he followed instructions—he was good at following those, and at least could enjoy doing what he'd been told to do. Drawing her close, not even caring if his hands were in the right place, he kissed her. He. Kissed. Her. She didn't have to initiate it. He stepped up and deepened the moment with all that he nurtured inside, all he struggled to put into words but longed to show to her.

As he finally broke it off, slowly, gently, he drew away.

Her eyes were closed, and a soft sigh escaped. "Jesse."

"Shilo?"

Her lids popped open, and her face turned crimson, making her freckles stand out. Oh, so lovely.

She stepped away and straightened the hem of her blouse. "Um..."

He dropped a kiss on her pink nose.

"Well, that's it, folks. I'll walk you inside."

Stormy took over again while Windy returned upstairs.

He pulled out his Master Charge and paid for everything, and then led Shilo out to the car where he held the door for her.

"Where are we going now?"

"To the BMV. You need a driver's license so we can get a marriage license."

"Oh!" She leaned back into the seat, but as soon as he climbed in on his side, she grabbed his arm. "Jess, we didn't find out."

"Find out what?" He started the ignition.

"If we got a cardinal. Do you think we did?"

As usual, he had no clue, but for her sake, he sure hoped so.

Chapter 10

Friday, June 8, 1973

Shilo sat in the ready room, her heart pounding. This was her wedding day.

So much had happened in the past couple of weeks. They'd finally gotten Aunt Sarah home and, with some rest, she looked stronger every day. She was even here to witness this ceremony. *Such a blessing, Father. Thank You.*

Both Shilo and Jesse had been waiting for the explosion from Jesse's grandfather that didn't come. Not having it to deal with was worse than getting it over with. She'd imagined all types of schemes—a bigger bribe, saying Jesse could make partner if he called off the wedding—and the more she ruminated on it, the more dire they became. Still, Mr. Franklin remained silent, and she and Jesse could only hope it was because he hadn't learned about her latest arrest.

But she had to stop over-thinking about all that. In a matter of minutes, she'd walk up to the ballroom, cross the floor, and vow to honor Jesse for the rest of her life. Yep, that's what she would do.

She could do that.

Right. That's why her hands shook.

"It's fine, Shilo. You look lovely." Viv volunteered to help her get ready, and Shilo thanked God for her new friend. Especially when it became obvious Aunt Sarah needed to take things easy and couldn't assist as she'd hoped.

"Thank you. That's not what it is." She had to keep from wiping her slick palms on her dress.

"What is it then?"

Should she confide in Viv? She'd understand, but she was also Jesse's secretary.

"Won't go beyond these walls. I promise." Viv sat next to her on the bench.

"I'm concerned for Jesse. I don't want to ruin his life or his relationship with his grandfather."

"The senior Mr. Franklin worked at destroying that relationship long before you came back. I can't comprehend that man." Viv brushed a wrinkle from Shilo's skirt. "I'll never understand either why Jesse's parents allowed the elder Mr. Franklin to raise their child, or why they've stayed out of their son's life so much. None of them did Jesse any favors, and they owe everything to God's provision that he's the kind and loving man he is. Maybe things started because his son remained so out of his reach that he doubled down on Jesse, trying to create him into a younger, better version of himself." Now she shrugged, stood, and pulled Shilo to her feet before moving behind her and fluffing out the skirt of her bridal gown.

Shilo closed her eyes seeing Jesse in her heart and mind. Viv was right. Even her own grandpa had been strict, but nothing compared to Jesse's. And she'd had Aunt Sarah to soften the tough love. Who did Jesse have?

"You love him, don't you." Viv made it a statement, not a question, as she rounded to face Shilo.

As her cheeks warmed, she nodded. "I haven't told him. He's sacrificed his future for me. Unable to marry anyone else, at least for the time being. At odds more than usual with his grandfather. Even his career might be in jeopardy. And still, he wants to do this."

"I wouldn't worry about it. First and foremost, you said you prayed, so trust God to lead you. Besides that, I'd bet my house that Jesse is in love with you too. I can't imagine why he hasn't told you, but understand, I am not a betting person. That should tell you how sure I am about that." Viv held out her hand to Shilo and guided her in front of the full-length antique mirror. "Let's get your veil on you."

I want to believe her, Father. Especially now, right before I vow to be his wife.

As Viv settled the wreath that hosted real rosebuds and baby's breath woven in and draped the blusher over Shilo's face before shaking out the fingertip length veil, Stormy knocked and entered.

"It's time. Are you ready?"

"She is." Viv answered for her.

Shilo stared at Viv as panic rose. How in the world could she be ready? Everything in her wanted to shout, "No, not ready!"

Then Viv took her hand. "Trust. Take a deep breath. You are ready."

After doing what Viv said, Shilo knew to the bottomless depths of her soul this is what she needed to do. God led her to this moment. And He would walk with her down the aisle. She'd lean on her Heavenly Father. "Ready."

A part of her wished she hadn't asked for the justice of the peace. A minister would've added that spiritual bonding to the union. But until Jesse said those words, even if he did promise to love her today by saying, "I do," it wouldn't count. And she'd not utter them to him until he could say them.

At the French doors, Viv slipped inside and found a seat in the small group of chairs focused on the entrance leading to the balcony.

Stormy stayed with Shilo as the music changed and the bridal march began. "Here you go. Just like we practiced last night."

Shilo nodded, grabbed hold of her Heavenly Father's hand, and walked through the open doors straight for the balcony.

Where Jesse waited with Pat Whitcomb, who would conduct the service.

Dressed in his black tux with silk lapels and a baby pink tie that matched her bouquet.

She'd let Jesse choose the flowers. He knew so much about them. He'd told her he picked pink because it represented elegance, grace, joyfulness, and admiration. Besides, he remembered she liked the color.

He was a good man. That she didn't question. If only he really loved her. And that he'd remain in love with her when he learned about her Lisa.

She needed to tell him. With every step closer to the balcony, her hands shook making the flowers in her bouquet bounce, while her conscience chanted that over and over. *You need to tell him. You need to tell him.*

Maybe when they were alone on their honeymoon. Definitely not now, not here. But would he feel tricked?

And she'd arrived. Jesse's chocolate eyes glittered with the light of the setting sun, driving all those thoughts and voices in her head away. She was about to marry her friend and possibly save her aunt. That was enough to make her honestly say, "I do."

Hand in hand, they stood in front of the justice of the peace. It was more than a mere civil ceremony. Pat Whitcomb may not be a man of the cloth, but he was a believer and sprinkled in bits of faith as he welcomed the small group who came to witness the service. More attended than Shilo thought would come, but fewer than Jesse's twenty-five. More like just under twenty. She'd been too in her head to notice who all showed up, except for Aunt Sarah who sat in the first row and beamed at her.

"Friends and family, we're gathered here to witness the union of Shilo Dawn Anderson to Jesse Dean Franklin and on their behalf, I welcome you all. Both Shilo and Jesse told me that they'd like to keep this moment simple but meaningful. I hope you will join me as I speak a brief prayer over them.

"Dear God, please be here as I say the words that make this marriage legal. You are the One Who makes this a spiritual union with Your presence and blessings of which we ask. Amen." Pat paused and glanced at Jesse. He'd asked when they met with him if they wanted to recite their own vows, but Jesse declined, saying that it was private. Apparently, Pat offered a last chance, but Jesse hadn't changed his mind.

Shilo honored him by keeping her personal vows private as well.

"Jesse Dean Franklin, do you take this woman to be your wife, to live together in holy matrimony, to love her, to honor her, to comfort her, and to keep her in sickness and in health, forsaking all others, for as long as you both shall live?"

"I do."

Jesse told her when they'd left Pat's office that they were friends and always would be, and since friends cared about each other, that it was honest to make that vow.

Somehow, it still felt a little like cheating, but in her heart, she loved Jesse as more than a friend. She was in love with him, so when her turn came, she swore to the truth.

"Shilo Dawn Anderson, do you take this man to be your husband, to live together in holy matrimony, to love him, to honor him, to comfort him, and to keep him in sickness and in health, forsaking all others, for as long as you both shall live?"

"I do."

Then Pat turned to Jesse and told him to repeat the following words. "I, Jesse, take you Shilo, to be my wife, to have and to hold from this day forward, for better, for worse, for richer, for poorer, in sickness and in health, to love and to cherish, 'til death do us part."

He did.

Shilo did too when it was her turn.

Next came the rings and "With this ring, I thee wed."

Shilo's hand shook as Jesse gently slid on the band. Even that tiny touch made every nerve ending in her body sing.

"Now, by virtue of the authority vested in me by the state of Indiana, I hereby pronounce you husband and wife. Jesse, you may kiss your bride."

Shilo had waited with great anticipation for this moment. Their kiss under the sycamore spoke peace to her heart that this would be God-blessed. But it also left her wanting more of his focus, more of his touch. And, yes, more of his kiss.

He hadn't kissed her since that day, though she'd hoped and even prayed. But now the ceremony required it. Like a rule. And Jesse was a rule-follower. Mostly.

Her mind flew a million miles per hour, and everyone and everything around them froze in time. What kind of kiss would he give her? Something to meet the letter of the law? Just a peck? Or would he do what she longed for him to do? Speaking hope to her heart when his voice didn't?

He drew her close and lifted her blusher, stroking a finger down her cheek as he gazed into her eyes, and pausing a moment as if memorizing her face.

Then he kissed her.

Not a following-the-rules peck, nor a friendly smooch. One filled with passion, this was a kiss a man gave the woman he loved.

Maybe he did love her.

She returned his kiss with gusto, hoping he heard in it what she held back with her words.

Applause filled the air, and Jesse broke off. When she opened her eyes, he wore a silly grin that matched one of her own.

Pat turned them toward those who came to share their special moment. "Folks, let me introduce to you, for the first time anywhere ..." He winked and smiled. "Mr. and Mrs. Jesse and Shilo Franklin."

More applause followed.

But it wasn't lost on Shilo that Jesse's grandfather, who chose to sit in the back with his arms crossed over his rounded chest, refused to clap with the rest of the guests. At least he'd come. Shilo decided to consider it a gift to Jesse and not a dare to see if they'd really go through with the wedding.

Jesse gripped her hand and led her toward the stairs.

She overheard Pat's voice echo after them. "Folks, if you will follow me downstairs to the garden, we've set up a small reception."

Windy mentioned grabbing a few twilight shots, saying that with the twinkling lights overhead in the garden, it should be lovely. She'd held off getting their engagement photos to them, though she put one into the Kokomo Tribune. That's why Shilo still didn't know if they'd gotten a cardinal or not.

Why it meant so much to her, she couldn't say. Maybe it was some sort of confirmation that she'd heard God right. But with more photos this evening came another chance.

They'd timed their service so that the sun had just started its descent. That left some daylight for the beginning of their reception. In Indiana, the sky stayed light out pretty late. But the shadows and colors coming into the background would make for lovely photographs and memories. Especially if a flash of red appeared on a branch above them.

Windy posed them like before. Since the tree stood adjacent to the garden, the guests watched too.

Sitting, standing, one sitting while the other stood. And then came the last shot. Windy called it the Moneymaker. This is what Shilo had waited for. Yes, Jesse kissed her at the end of their ceremony. But now he'd be kissing her as a married woman. And twice in less than an hour. This might start a habit. Maybe.

Wouldn't that be groovy?

Jesse rubbed his thumb beneath her lips. He wasn't one to take advantage of a woman, but he was more grateful than he could say for this chance to kiss Shilo again. He had no idea what catalysts he might rely on for another opportunity, but this moment was a gift on a plate. "So, wife, are you okay with this?"

Her teeth raked her bottom lip, and she nodded before tipping her face to him.

As he leaned close, her minty breath teasing his nose, a niggling notion hit him as their lips touched. Who did she imagine when she closed her eyes?

That stopped him.

"Jesse?" Now her lids popped open.

"Uh, sorry. Let's try that again." And they did, though the thought still rang in his head, holding back the passion he'd hoped would pave the way to what he wanted to share when they were alone tonight.

When he stepped away, he read in Shilo's eyes she sensed something.

Again, the guests applauded from their garden party seats. At least they were enthusiastic.

Jesse glanced about for his grandfather.

He wasn't there. Of course, he might've slipped out to use the facilities, or be talking with someone inside, but Jesse knew. The old man had gone. Staying only long enough to witness what he declared to be Jesse's biggest, stupidest mistake and then leaving rather than celebrate with them. Fine. If he felt that way, he shouldn't have come.

What started as a day of promise now grew stale and, if he wasn't careful, a real downer.

Why? What was so awful about marrying someone he cared deeply for instead of an Alvin Franklin-approved Stepford wife to help him advance? Had the man ever experienced being in love?

Hold on. Why are you planning a pity party when you should be celebrating this momentous occasion?

The thought turned out to be the kick in the pants Jesse needed. He grabbed Shilo's hand and kissed it before leading her to the cake table.

Windy followed and snapped a few shots of them cutting the bottom tier together. No silliness of shoving the frosted piece in Shilo's face. He could never bring himself to do that. And she only got a rogue bit of icing next to his lip. She dabbed with a napkin while he wanted to melt at her touch.

He'd declined a groom's cake. With so few guests, their small one would be enough. Viv promised to take the top tier home for them until they came back, putting it in their freezer for the first anniversary.

Would they actually have a marriage by then?

They began speaking with each person, going from table to table, while some kids acted as the serving staff, handing out cake to all the guests.

Most of whom were from the office or were Sarah's friends from church, giving support.

Shilo insisted on inviting Eli. He knew it was a mistake when he spotted the dude sitting upstairs in the ballroom. Another person seeming to dare him.

But now they'd arrived at Eli's table. Guess he'd found people who tolerated him since he wasn't alone. Karen Miner must be his date, as both Bill Youst and Tom Hamer sat with their wives. Poor Karen. What did women see in this cretin?

Eli popped up from his chair. "I didn't get a chance to kiss the bride." Before Jesse spoke a word, he pulled Shilo into a dip, practically leering over her.

Just as he was about to lay one on those gorgeous lips of hers—lips that Jesse didn't want to share with anyone, especially Eli Shanahan—a red flutter flew by and dropped something white-ish on Shanahan's head. "Hey!"

"Ew." Shilo pulled away.

Eli raised his hand to his hair and drew it back, white goo dripping from his fingers. His eyes boggled as his face turned beet red.

Tom and Bill cackled, and for the first time Jesse put some credence in the legend.

"I'll go clean up." Eli excused himself and headed for the restroom.

"We shouldn't have laughed." Though Shilo's smile peeked through. He knew she wanted to.

"He's a big boy. He can deal." Jesse enjoyed seeing him get the short end for once.

"I know. But still. I shouldn't have said ew, but I was afraid it would drip on me and my dress. I'm an awful person, Jess."

"No, you're not."

"I only thought of myself."

"That's fine. I was thinking of you too and hesitated to pull him away. That red bird saved us both." He tossed her a wink.

Someone spoke into a mic and called for everyone's attention. "I'm going to start the music, but for the first song, we'd like the new Mr. and Mrs. Franklin to lead off." A song he'd chosen just for this moment began, and he led Shilo out to the dance floor while David Ruffin sang "My Girl." The lyrics said everything he wanted to say without mentioning love. He turned her into his arms. Could Shy hear his heart?

She leaned her head against his shoulder, her soft chuckle rumbling into his chest. "I knew you'd have a Motown song for us."

"What else?" He grinned, catching the humor dancing in her dove gray eyes. They heard each other without words. Why did he worry so much? All they needed to do was let their hearts do the talking. It was safer anyway. At least then he wouldn't stumble over his every syllable or have to practice in front of a mirror. He gave her a little spin.

When she twirled back, her face lit by the twinkling light overhead, all he saw was beauty. Perfection. The gentleness and love he'd always found in her. Tonight was the night. He'd be honest, tell her how he felt, ask if she'd agree to be married not only legally, but really.

Maybe there was a God in heaven. For her to come back into his life like this had to be the work of some loving, all-powerful being. It was as if she helped him remember who he was, who he was supposed to be. She danced in his arms, smiling, seeing into his heart. Could there be anything more perfect than this?

The song ended, and other couples claimed the dance floor. Someone tapped his shoulder.

Eli. Wet hair, like he'd towel-dried and combed it down, but his blond curls all got tightened up.

Ow! Jesse bit his tongue. For real, and not on purpose. The guy witnessed their wedding vows and still was after Shilo? "What?"

"I'd like to cut in, if I may, and have a dance with the bride. I promise to behave." Eli did a quick peek over his shoulder with a flinch in case another kamikaze cardinal lingered nearby.

Shilo giggled and moved toward Eli before Jesse even agreed. Great. Not the place to make a scene.

"Just bring her back."

"Of course." Shanahan glided Shilo away.

Now what? Jesse glanced over and spotted Sarah sitting alone while her table mates danced. That's something he could do. "Guess I can call you my Aunt Sarah after this." He smiled as she grinned at him. "May I have this dance?"

"I'm a little rusty. But if you keep it basic, I shouldn't damage your toes too much."

"I'm willing to take that chance. Let's show them how it's done." Sam Cooke crooned, "Bring It on Home to Me," giving Jesse a slower rhythm for Sarah to follow, though the words only spoke a message for Shilo. After tonight, her home would be with him.

"Jesse? You realize she loves you. You know that, don't you?"

He glanced down at the older, most likely much wiser woman he moved around the dance floor with. "She hasn't said anything."

"I'll bet neither have you. Am I right?"

He nodded, keeping his eye on Eli and Shilo.

"How can you expect her to tell you when you haven't told her? That is unless you don't love her."

Jesse stopped. He wasn't about to say the words to someone else first, favorite aunt status notwithstanding. "You can trust me, Sarah. So can she."

He started their box step again. "That's what I figured. And that's why I didn't cause a fuss about what you were doing. You should've done this years ago. You two belong together. But if my illness brings about what should've happened before, then I'm fine going through all this." She patted Jesse's chest, right over his heart. "Just talk to each other. Always. It'll make the difference, or at least be one thing that will."

"What's another?" He might as well get the inside scoop.

"Putting God first in everything. You need to make it a three-person marriage, and God will help you through the rough patches. And, before you ask, there's gonna be rough patches. It's not all cake and dancing." She winked at him. "But it'll work out, Jesse."

"From your lips to God's ear, Sarah." He gave her a twirl and walked her back to her seat. "Thank you for the dance. Now I'm going to collect my wife."

"Be kind, Jess."

She must've seen his thoughts radiating through his face. "If I have to." He waved and headed for where Eli still commandeered Shilo, but at least the song had a faster tempo, "Dancing in the Street." He heard Shilo's off-key sing-along as he got closer, making him smile. Maybe he could be generous with Shanahan and not break his nose. Okay, he'd save that visual in his head for another time.

Jesse tapped Eli's shoulder. "I'd like my wife back."

"Maybe I'm not ready to give her back."

Shilo reached for Jesse. "All right now, boys, settle down. Thank you for the dance, Eli. I'm glad you could get cleaned up enough to stay."

Jesse danced her away before she could say more. This was time he wanted with her, and he felt antsy to go. He should be concerned about his guests, but he had priorities. Like having this beautiful woman in his arms be in his arms again while alone on their honeymoon. The rolling base chord intro for "Just My Imagination" began. *Please don't let this be my imagination.*

"Jesse?"

"Hmm?"

"When do you think we can slip out of here?"

He pulled her tighter. "Anytime you want."

"When are you going to tell me about our honeymoon?" She raised her head to capture his gaze. If she kept looking at him like that, he'd either give away state secrets or be so tongue tied he'd never speak again.

He closed his eyes and spun her a second to gather his bearings. "I'll give you this much. We've got about a forty-minute drive to get there. You're going to love it. I promise."

"Okay. When this song is over, I'll see what Stormy says we need to do and then go tell Aunt Sarah goodbye."

"Where's your luggage?"

"Oh, you mean the set that got delivered to the house yesterday?" She tried to look stern but busted a grin.

"Good. You won't have to take that backpack along."

"And what's wrong with my backpack?"

"Not a thing. I just want you to have nice stuff. You don't have to count every penny anymore, Shy. I'm here for you."

"I'm paying you back."

"Why? I've put you on my charge cards and checking account. It'll all be in the same place." He caught a funny look in her eyes. "I mean my money is there for you. Your money will go into your account. I don't need it or want it, Shy. You realize that, right?"

She stopped moving and searched his face. "I do, Jess. I do. Now let's get a move on. I want to see my surprise." Shilo tugged on his hand to follow her over to where Stormy spoke with some teens who'd helped.

The gesture, familiar from their old days, gave him hope. Maybe tonight his dream would happen.

And if it did, he'd never be able to deny the existence of God again.

Chapter 11

Bumps in the road jarred Shilo from her dream. She sat straighter in Jesse's passenger seat.

"Sorry about that. Train tracks."

She nodded and yawned. "Didn't mean to fall asleep on you."

"Don't worry about it. I knew you were tired, just never realized how much. We've still got about twenty minutes to go." He glanced her way, the dashboard lights revealing worry lines between his brows.

She shouldn't have made him concerned, but with everything that went on this past week, sleeping hadn't been a priority. Aunt Sarah at home meant she'd listened for any emergencies through the nights. However, her aunt required little to no help, just a lot of rest time.

Shilo had been afraid to leave her side and came close to asking Jesse to cancel any honeymoon plans so she could stay nearby. Aunt Sarah guessed what she had up her sleeve and put the kibosh on that notion. It didn't ease Shilo's mind, though, until she spotted Jesse and her aunt dancing at the reception. And knowing that Viv, as well as Delores Burke and Elsie Brown would be checking in on her, Shilo relaxed. Apparently too much since she fell asleep on her new groom. "What time is it getting to be?"

"Going on eleven. About ten 'til."

"By the way, did you figure out who tied the cans and old shoes to the back of your car?" Jesse had driven around the corner to give the conspirator some satisfaction but cut it all away once they were out of sight of Ferguson House.

"Not yet, but maybe when I can get a good look at the shoes, I'll remember who wore them. Maybe. It's the only idea I've come up with. Had to be someone who knows my car."

"That would be most of the people who came. They were from your firm."

Jesse flipped his turn signal on. "Yeah, but I figure I can rule out the women."

"Why? You don't think a girl would do that?"

"Do you?"

"Sure, if she were ornery enough. But, you're right, it's more likely a man. I wonder who?" Actually, as soon as she spoke, she imagined exactly who. Eli. That'd be just like him to devil Jesse that way. But she didn't dare say anything out loud. "Hey, we're heading toward Mississinewa."

"Wondered when you'd notice. I've rented a cabin on the lake. Thought that would be simple for you and out in nature for me." Though he kept his eyes on the road, Shilo couldn't miss his smile.

"You're right, Jess. That's perfect for us. Thank you. I knew I could trust you."

This time he glanced her way a second. "You can always trust me, Shy. Always."

Her heart agreed with that, but her head could only hope. He didn't know all of her past. Once she told him, everything would be different. Or at least some things. *But Lord, please not all things.*

Soon Jesse turned down a lane that ran between the cabins and the lake, pulling into a drive leading up to a structure a little more house than cabin like. That was okay. He understood her even if he leaned toward the more extravagant of choices.

"Let's get the place unlocked and the lights turned on before I bring up the luggage.

She nodded and opened her car door.

He came around before she climbed out, holding out a hand to her.

Good thing he did. It'd been a while since she'd been this shaky on her legs. She must've been more tired than she realized. She'd changed from her lovely gown to this pantsuit even though it was dressier than the location called for. Plus, Jesse had told her to pack for fun and to bring a swimsuit.

They mounted the steps to the porch where Jesse produced a key and unlocked the front door, pushing it open. But before she stepped inside, he scooped her into his arms.

"What are you doing?"

"It is traditional for the new groom to carry his bride over the threshold." He continued into the living room before setting her down.

"But Jesse, we are anything but traditional."

"You disapprove, Wife?"

She chuckled. "No, Husband, I don't. Thank you for making me feel special."

"You are special, Shy. Never doubt that." He stroked his thumb down her jaw. "I need to get the luggage. Be right back."

She followed him. "I can help."

"No, I'll manage. Just explore. Check out what all we have here."

So she did. The large cabin housed two bedrooms, each with their own bathroom, an eat-in kitchen sporting a long table, and a laundry area in the closed-in back porch. She wandered to the living room as Jesse arrived with the two small suitcases. Since they were heading home on Sunday, neither of them needed a lot.

"Where do you want me to put your things?"

She'd been waiting for that question and knew he'd let her choose her room. Identical but for the color and design, she chose the sunny yellow room and gave him the one done in greens and blues, having left the lights on in them.

Rather than unpack and deal with the awkward moment of going off to her own bedroom, she sat on the couch, taking in the floor-to-ceiling bookcases filled with stories. If she were alone, she'd dive into the first one and read her way through the entire selection.

But she wasn't. She was with her husband. Husband. Definitely a word she had to get used to.

Her alone time with God needed to be something he understood. It was difficult to think even before she'd spent time in prayer. But reading her Bible gave her strength for the coming day and reassurance that God would help her through. That was a line in the sand she'd fight for. There weren't a lot of things she'd go to battle about. For others? Yes. For herself, totally another story—but that bit of morning she held sacred. Jesse would have to understand.

"Are you feeling as awkward as I do?" Jesse plopped on the couch next to her.

"Yeah." This was the moment. Now. She could let him know about Lisa, and her life, and let him choose what he wanted to do. "I need to—"

Only he grabbed her hand and spoke at the same time. "I want to tell you some things." His voice shook, and he stared at her fingers twined with his.

So, this wasn't the right time?

He rubbed his thumb up and down hers. "Shy, there is no one like you. I can't believe you agreed to marry me. Since we were in high school and you asked me to the Autumn Prom, I've wondered why you would ever waste your time on me. Even if he drives me crazy, I get why Eli is so stuck on you. You are amazing, and beautiful, and I don't mean just on the outside. Your inner beauty shines even brighter, and you're plain gorgeous on the outside."

He was making her feel weird, but she smiled in hope that he'd change the subject.

"See? Even your smile is unique, and Eileen Ford ought to get her head examined to think you should get your gap fixed. I lo—" He blushed, from his ears to his nose. "It's one more thing that makes you perfect."

She pulled her hand away. "Oh, Jess, I'm far from perfect. Trust me."

"You think that. You're humble. Never self-centered."

"That's not what I mean." Now telling him the truth seemed urgent, yet the fear of that outcome raged larger than ever. "You don't know a lot about me, Jess. Where I've been, what I've done. There's so much."

"You can tell me, Shy. Nothing you say will change my mind about you."

"That almost sounds like a challenge. Be careful what you dare." Even if she didn't tell him about Lisa, she'd better say something to get him to see her more realistically. "The Kokomo jail is cleaner than the one in LA."

He sat straighter, his mouth open, his eyes round.

"The worst one I've been in was in a little burg outside of Bakersfield." She shook her head at the memory. "I'd been hitching, and the officer accused me of soliciting. I didn't realize that the way they wrote the state law, they used it for prostitution and asking for rides. When I finally saw a judge, he called it time served and let me go. I walked two hours before I put my thumb out again."

"Why, Shy? Why are you telling me this now?"

"Because if you put me on a pedestal, I'm going to disappoint you. I'll do my best to be a good wife to you, Jess. But you have to see me as I really am."

"And what's that?"

"A messed-up chick who God chased down and dragged out of a never-ending spiral. If He hadn't, I can't imagine where I'd be. Or rather I do know. I'd be dead and condemned to hell."

"You believe there's such a place?"

She nodded. "Yeah, Jess, I do. That's why I'm so grateful to Him. Jesus saved my life here and gave me eternity with Him too."

Things got quiet, and she couldn't sense his thoughts, especially since he stared at their broken hand clasp.

Then he raised his head, his eyes glistening with unshed tears. "How did you almost die, Shy?"

God, do I tell him now? I don't think I can.

She swallowed. She never wanted to lie to Jesse, but she couldn't explain about Lisa yet. "It's a hard story. I can't say it all yet, but I promise I'll tell you one day." She stood and paced to the bookcases before facing him. "I'll share this much. I had to have surgery, and it didn't go well. I grew weaker by the hour, and the doctors had pretty much given up, just waiting for me to die. They figured I was out of it most of the time, and I guess I was, but I overheard a lot, so I knew how bad things were. They called it palliative care, just making me comfortable. I laid there alone and scared and wasn't sure I wanted to live anymore, but I feared death."

Shilo came back to the couch and made sure to hold Jesse's gaze. "Lonnie and Connie came by my room at just the right moment because I wasn't always awake, but that time I was. I had no energy, no strength, but then just their conversation seemed to revive me. When they shared about Jesus, I knew I didn't want to die without Him, so I asked Him into my heart. The rest is the miracle He did and keeps doing in my life."

He reached for her hand again, and she didn't pull away. His touch sent delight dancing through her veins.

"What type of surgery, Shy?"

She shook her head. "That's part of the story for later. I ... I can't. Not right now."

He nodded and stood, pulling her up to him. Jesse drew her into his arms, kissed her forehead, then walked her to her room. "I promised. I'm not backing out. You are safe, Shy." He kissed her cheek this time. "Get some sleep. We can have fun tomorrow. Sweet dreams."

Then he stepped away, locked the front door, turned off the living room lights, and went into his room.

She stood watching his every move.

This could've been their actual wedding night, not just in name. But how could she if he couldn't say the words? And even if he did, he didn't love her, he loved his image of her. Their marriage wouldn't be genuine until he saw her, the imperfect but redeemed ragamuffin, now a daughter of the King.

Would that ever happen?

Saturday, June 9, 1973

Jesse threw back the sheet and padded to the bathroom. He might as well be up. He hadn't slept most of the night, so why keep trying?

He had only himself to blame. Pouring out all his thoughts and feelings for her and never saying what he wanted to. He took too long and made her nervous, and she had to try to prove him wrong. But if she could believe God loved her enough to accept her when she was so messed up—her words, not his—why was it so hard to accept Jesse believed the best of her?

Of course, he realized no one was perfect. But he couldn't imagine Shilo Anderson, oops, Shilo Franklin being anything but kind, loving, and thoughtful. He pulled out a pair of jeans, a T-shirt, and his hiking boots and got dressed.

Maybe he could make breakfast for them and start this marriage all over.

He'd paid to have the pantry and fridge stocked. Bacon and eggs would taste great about now. Something in the early morning out away from the city made the first meal of the day sound better. Besides, there was a patio out the back door where they could eat. Shilo would love that.

Jesse pulled out a cast-iron skillet and started the bacon. Then he found an old coffee pot he could heat on the stove and measured out enough Folgers and water to get it going.

On his way to Shilo's room to ask how she liked her eggs, he paused when he heard her voice. Standing outside her door, he spotted her through the cracked opening, on her knees next to her bed.

"And Father, please don't let him be hurt. He's gotta understand that You will always have first place in my heart. Still, the Bible says that You aren't a man, so You can't lie. If you aren't a man, then I can honestly say I love him more than any other man. Right? Help me make that clear."

He moved before he gave himself away. *Make that clear to whom?* Jesse knew she was praying, and intruding on that privacy made his face hot. God being the most important person in her life only made sense once you talked with Shilo. He got that. But who was the him? Was it he? Jesse? Or was she talking about Eli?

Oh, c'mon man. You can't be that thick. She married you. She was talking about you, dummy.

Jesse ran his fingers through his hair, then caught a whiff of the bacon and raced for the stove, burning his hand before he grabbed a towel to pull the pan to a cold burner.

"Thought I smelled something. Oh, you've burned yourself. Here." Shilo turned on the faucet and tugged his hand beneath the cool, running water. "There, that should help. Good, doesn't look like it will blister." She winked at him and gave the kitchen a visual once over. "How about I finish up? You made a great start."

He'd give her anything if she'd flash that perfectly imperfect smile of hers his way. Jesse cleared his throat and found his voice. "Sure. I hadn't gotten the eggs out yet."

"I can handle eggs. How do you like yours?"

"Over easy. With toast to dunk in the yolks." He opened the fridge and handed her the carton. "Two are plenty for me."

"Two it is. Want to sit in here and keep me company or take your coffee out back?" So, she'd noticed the patio. Good.

"I think I'll hang out in here and check out what sort of culinary skills you bring to this joint venture." He winked and pulled out a kitchen chair.

"Okay then." She twirled around and got to work, saving the bacon and starting the eggs. Once they were going, she popped bread in the toaster and poured him a cup of coffee, handing it over before she searched the fridge.

"What are you looking for?"

"Jelly. Don't you want it for your toast?"

"For dunking into the yolks? I don't think so." He made a face at her, and she giggled.

"Fine then. Saves me a step." She closed the refrigerator with her hip and grabbed two plates from the cupboard.

"We're all set here. We'll need forks and napkins out there. Want to take care of that? I'll butter your toast when I dish up."

"Sure." He left his mug on the counter and gathered the utensils and paper napkins, taking them out to the patio umbrella table. When he returned, he accepted his plate from her, swiped up his drink, and waited to follow her out. She still had to pour and doctor her coffee, but a moment later they sat for their first breakfast as husband and wife.

It was a fresh day, and he knew better than to ask questions of depth. He'd keep it light, show her fun, give them both memories to hold on to. That's what he would do.

"What have you planned for today?" She bit off a piece of bacon. When her eyes focused on him, it nearly swiped his breath clean out of his chest.

"Um, how does a hike sound? We can explore the area and after lunch go swimming. Let's bring a picnic, so our time is really our own."

"I like that idea. A lot. Jesse, being here, no pressure, no worries, just us. I can't imagine anything better."

He'd done something right and pleased her. The temptation to try to fix last night waved its hand in his thoughts, but he ignored it. They'd go there later, when it felt safe.

She'd dressed in a pair of jeans that had seen better days, though the patches sewn on the knees and back pocket areas added color. Her top was a tie-dyed T-shirt, and her feet were clad in old tennies that might as well have been sandals because of all of their holes. With her hair braided and over her shoulder, she looked beautiful. Maybe not as stunning as yesterday when she came down the aisle, but this was the real, face-scrubbed Shilo. And he loved her more than he could say. Literally.

She stood and reached for his plate. "Let me wash our dishes. You want to pack up our lunch since I don't know what you planned?"

He knew her thoughts. She added that job in there for him so he wouldn't argue about her cleaning up. Fine. Leave it or do it now, he didn't care as long as they did it together.

"I'll pack lunch, but no complaining if you don't like it." Standing with her, he followed her back inside. While she started the faucet to fill the sink, he pulled out his backpack. She would laugh at him when she saw it. The same one he'd had since high school, though to his mind it had held up better than that battered one she toted.

"Never. As long as it isn't potted meat."

They said, "Ew," at the same time and laughed.

After making peanut butter and jelly sandwiches—the proper use for strawberry jelly—he wrapped them in Saran Wrap and searched for fruit. Green grapes and apples were their choices, so he added both and a few Oreos from the package he found in the pantry. Once Shilo moved on to drying the dishes, he filled a couple canteens he'd brought with water and put in two cans of Coke for their lunch. She liked simple, he'd give her simple.

"All done. Do I need to bring anything?" She dried her hands on the towel before hanging it on the oven handle.

"You're good. I can keep your canteen with mine. Ready?" He slipped the pack straps over his shoulders.

She came close. "Is that ... It is. That's your old backpack. I can't believe you still have that thing."

"Came in handy when bringing things to your house for when we sat on the roof."

Her smile brightened. "Yes, it did. Yep, I'm ready. Lead on, husband."

He chuckled and did.

The air held the right coolness, the sun the right brightness. The shimmers from the lake added a gilding to the morning, and the sounds of nature wrapped around them. Jesse couldn't believe they weren't running into others taking advantage of this stellar day. But he'd not complain about the blessing.

Blessing? He'd started to think in her terms. Did that mean he believed in God?

Well, he didn't disbelieve. Shilo made some good points. Still, all his life had been about what he could see and touch and taste and hear and smell. The evidence. That was real. Reality. Now she talked about—and to—Someone who existed in an invisible realm. How did he find concrete proof God was real?

That's why it's called faith.

Guess he needed more of that because he wasn't ready to declare God's existence in the face of known reality.

With a bit of walking, they connected to the Lost Sister Trail. Occasionally, Shilo pointed out a flower or some small critter scampering up a tree. He shared bits of knowledge he'd filed away about the flora and fauna of central Indiana. And as a boost to his ego, he'd even impressed her a little.

Finally, after a couple hours of taking their time, they wound their way to the picnic area in Frances Slocum State Park and grabbed a table. Jesse laid out their lunch, and Shilo grabbed his hand to pray. Wasn't what he was used to, but it did help remind him to be grateful. That sort of brain adjustment could only help.

Shilo stretched out on the table seat, her knees bent, and her arm flopped across her eyes. "Jesse, do you think we'll always feel like this?"

"Like how?" He knew how he felt, but he could use a clue about how she felt.

"Like God is so close I can feel His breath."

He studied her a moment, trying to understand. "Nature brings us back to the foundations of life. What's important, what's superfluous. It's just when we get surrounded by the rat race, losing ourselves in what's urgent, the gift of the natural world recedes to the background. Is that sort of what you mean?"

"I guess. Only I feel His presence in that rat race. Like when I saw little Lisa drawing a picture, or you dancing with Aunt Sarah. Those things showed me He's still right there. But today, it's not been like a momentary reminder. It's more like being wrapped in His arms while He points out the cool stuff and laughs with us when we laugh." She sat up and captured him with her gaze. "I want to experience that all the time, Jess."

He had no words. This went beyond his understanding, though if God were as real to him as He was to Shilo, then, yeah, he got that. "I hope you always do, Shy." He held on to the visual connection with her as long as he dared. Like a moment of their souls talking to each other.

But then she glanced away and began cleaning up their wrappers and putting the trash into the receptacle. Had she not liked what she saw in him?

He reached for her hand, and they walked with their fingers laced together, taking the trail at a faster pace and arriving back at their cabin in a little more than half the time it took to get to the picnic area.

"Ready for a swim?"

She nodded. "Last one in is a rotten egg."

Ha! No girl—not even his wife—would beat him on that. He'd never changed clothes so fast in his life. But when he ran out to the lake's dock, there she was, in a one-piece swimsuit, ready to jump in.

"You cheated!"

Shilo giggled and dove in, rising to the surface to explain. "Nope, I wore my suit under my clothes. I wanted to be ready for anything."

He cannonballed in, coming up to wrap his arms around her.

She still giggled.

He leaned in to kiss her cheek.

She dunked him, swimming off, her laughter floating on top of the water.

Okay, she wanted fun, he'd give her fun. But later, he hoped for a quiet time together. In fact, he hoped so hard, he almost prayed.

Chapter 12
Friday, June 22, 1973

S hilo padded downstairs to the kitchen. A mug of coffee doctored exactly like she enjoyed it sat on the counter next to a plate of toast. Jesse's open invitation to join him on the roof.

It'd become a way of starting their day ever since they'd come home from their honeymoon. A few quiet minutes together as the sun came up when they didn't have to rush. Afterward, Jesse left for work, and Shilo got busy with whatever project awaited.

Most of her projects had to be small, or something she could continue later because as of last Friday, three days a week she took Aunt Sarah to her chemotherapy appointments.

She climbed the stairs, a triangle of toast between her teeth, and sauntered into Jesse's office that now looked more like an office with the furnishings she'd acquired. Oh, and the large macramé chair she'd made and hung in the room's corner. She'd worked on the contraption every spare moment until she surprised him with it yesterday.

"Ready?"

She nearly jumped from her skin. The hanging chair turned, revealing Jesse sitting in it. How she didn't dump her coffee all over herself, she'd never know.

He chuckled. "This is pretty good. I like it. Maybe all our furniture should hang from the ceiling." He stood and led the way to the window, handing his mug to her before climbing out and then taking both of them so she could join him.

They got comfortable and let the sounds of the morning surround them. God's breath became evident to her whenever they relaxed like this. She felt His presence in their midst and prayed Jesse would come to recognize it too.

Her new husband held her hand at each meal as she gave thanks and sat in church next to her on Sundays. But he didn't bring up the subject when they talked. Sure, he answered when she asked questions, but she cautiously refrained from what might seem like pushing. Simply let God's light shine through her and invite him to join them. That's what the Holy Spirit advised.

"We've got the reunion tomorrow. They're opening up the Sea Shore for the private party. We could skip that part and go to the dinner on Sunday afternoon."

She shook her head. "No, let's go have fun. Wonder if any classmates moved away and need to fly in for the celebration?"

"I doubt there's many. We run into most of them around town every so often. Almost makes the get-together redundant."

"Stop poo-pooing the idea. I want to see what everyone looks like now."

"It's only been a decade. Can't be much different. Now, at our fiftieth reunion, that would be some change." He elbowed her and grinned.

"You're right about that. But I don't want to wait fifty years to catch up. We had a ton of friends."

"You mean you had a ton of friends. Always finding the strays and outcasts and giving them a chance to be included."

She stared at him. Did they remember the same thing? "That's not how I recall."

"Then what's the story?" His gaze challenged her to tell him her version.

"You and me, doing things, meeting lots of people."

"You mean you coerced me to events, left me in the corner while you charmed the room, then dragged me up to your grandfather's roof where you told me all about our wonderful time."

"Jesse. You believed I left you alone to fend for yourself?"

He shrugged and glanced away at his now empty mug. "Maybe it's how I felt. Perspective is a funny thing. Two people can view the same event but give much differing accounts. That's lawyer 101."

Her heart hurt that she'd done that to him. "I'm so sorry, Jesse. I never intended anything like that. I thought we were in it together."

"We were, just not how you imagined. Or maybe I'm the one with the skewed vision. Anyway, I know you are more excited about going than I am. I never joined many of the clubs or went out for sports, so that narrowed things for me too."

"You should've joined the art club."

He sighed. "I did. Only Grandfather made me drop out. He didn't want to feed my enjoyment for fear I'd be distracted from his goals for my life. He pushed for the debate team, but I resisted until I got to college."

"Tell me about university life, Jess."

"In some ways, it brought freedom. The old man wasn't breathing over my shoulder all the time. But then I realized he still did. Telling me what classes to take, what fraternity to pledge, what extra-curricular groups to join. He might as well have lived in my dorm room. And I lacked the strength to fight him for what I wanted. Not alone."

She slipped her hand in his. If only she hadn't won the Breck Girl contest. If only they'd been able to stay together.

But would she have come to know Jesus if that had happened?

Maybe God knew the plan all along, and she fought Him until she almost died.

This morning had turned too introspective.

He gave her hand a squeeze. "So, you have Aunt Sarah's appointment today. What time again?"

"She needs to be at the hospital by nine. We're usually out between eleven and noon. Hope it doesn't run later. It makes her so tired. Praying she's up to lunch today, and she won't fight nausea."

"Think you'll get to see Lisa again?"

"I'm hoping. Wish we could do more for her than visiting or bringing the odd toy." But she knew there wasn't.

Jesse glanced at his watch. "We'd both better start moving if we're going to be where we're supposed to be on time." He dropped a peck on her cheek.

As much as she enjoyed the sweetness, she missed being really kissed by him—thoroughly, completely—with a kiss to set her nerve endings dancing and her toes curling with delight. He could do it and oh, she wanted to experience that again.

He helped her to her feet and held onto the mugs while she climbed back through the window. Then he passed her the cups and climbed in. They'd worked out a great routine that had become almost as important to her as her morning time with God.

Jesse left for the office first, leaving her alone with her continuing thoughts and prayers. Usually, Aunt Sarah called her to make sure she was on her way. But not this morning, which bothered Shilo. She tried not to read anything into it and instead grabbed her purse and headed for the garage to her new Camaro. A gift from Jesse when they came home from their honeymoon. He was too extravagant, and she told him as much. But he said she needed transportation of her own, especially for getting her aunt to and from the appointments, and now, since she laid claim to her own current license, making her street legal, it only made sense.

She couldn't argue. And he'd looked so hopeful. She wished her check would come through soon so she could start repaying him.

After parking out front, Shilo knocked on her aunt's door, but then used her key to enter. "Just me, Aunt Sarah. Are you about ready?" She headed down the hall.

"Don't come back here."

Shilo stopped in her tracks. "Why? What's the matter?" Had something bad happened?

"I don't want you to see me."

"I have to see you to take you to your appointment. Let me help you." Shilo started down the hallway again.

The bathroom door slammed closed. "No. I mean it. No one can see me like this."

Shilo stood outside the door. "Like how?"

She heard sniffles coming from inside the room, then her aunt blew her nose. "I don't think I can handle this, Shilo."

"Handle what?"

"Chemotherapy."

"You said the last time wasn't as bad, that you're getting over the nausea."

"I know, but I didn't realize."

"Realize what?" *Remain patient. Don't let this get to you. Give her room to explain.*

"That when they said ... that, that they meant ..." The bathroom door opened, slowly, only a crack at first, but then all the way, revealing her aunt.

Aunt Sarah was bald.

Mostly.

A few wispy strands feathered out, but for all practical purposes, the woman's hair was gone.

"It's as bad as I feared. You should see your face. I can't go out like this, people will stare at me."

The shock took Shilo by surprise—Aunt Sarah seemed smaller, more fragile and delicate—but she pulled herself together fast. Her aunt needed her. "I wasn't ready. I'm sorry. And I'm sorry you are going through this. But Aunt Sarah, it's only hair and will grow again. Remember what they told you? Even said it would most likely fall out after your third treatment."

"But I never imagined I'd look like this." The tears started all over.

"Oh, don't cry. Hey, do you have a scarf? A couple would be better."

Aunt Sarah sniffed, grabbed a handful of Charmin, and wiped her face before she answered. "In the top right-hand drawer of my dresser."

Shilo raced to find them, choosing two silky multi-colored ones she figured would go together. Back in the bathroom, she lowered the lid on the toilet. "Here, sit. I'll do my magic." She tossed her aunt a wink. "About a year ago I worked in a shop that sold scarves. The manager showed me a few tricks. And what I didn't learn from her, I picked up from roommates over time."

To begin with, she used one to fashion a cap for Aunt Sarah's head with the tails hanging over her shoulder. Then she twisted the second to make a long rope and added it like a headband over the first scarf and tied those ends together right behind her ear so that all the tails dangled down.

"Okay, stand and take a look." She helped her aunt to her feet and positioned her in front of the mirror. "What do you think?"

"I'm afraid to open my eyes."

"You don't trust me?"

Aunt Sarah turned her head. "That's not what I ... oh, it does look nice. Thank you, lovey." She hugged Shilo. "I'm so sorry to cause such a muddle."

"No one blames you. It must've been a shock. But we'd better get a move on to make your appointment."

After they were on their way, Shilo got an idea. "What if, when we're through, we stop by the mall and find you a wig. Would you like that?"

"Aren't they expensive?"

"No clue, but we won't know unless we check."

Shilo escorted her aunt to the therapy room and then excused herself. Knowing that she'd been able to provide a way for Aunt Sarah to get her chemotherapy gave her new hope. That and all the prayers she'd offered on her aunt's behalf. But now she left the chemo room to check out someone else who she longed to help. So far, every time she'd brought Aunt Sarah, she managed to slip away to find Lisa.

Today was no different. The little girl welcomed her with a smile. "Hi, Shilo." She sat at the nurses' station coloring another picture.

It'd be wonderful to take her on a ride in her wheelchair through the various safe places in the hospital, but no one was going to let Shilo be alone with the child.

She hadn't learned any more information about her, but seeing the sweet face light up when their eyes met added a special joy to her day. A part of her wanted to be the one to give this sweetheart the home she deserved. But that was out of the question. They did background checks on people who applied to foster and adopt. *They'd find my record.* Shilo chewed her lip. Sure, all minor things, but that didn't stop the authorities from taking mug shots. She owned enough to start a collection.

No, getting to adopt Lisa remained only a dream, like being able to hold her own little Lisa one more time. She still felt the tiny weight as she lay on her chest. The fuzz of the cotton blanket wrapped around the baby. Then the buzzers, and flashes of sight and sound. *Grab the baby. Grab the baby.*

This wasn't the time for remembering. *Focus on others, show a little kindness.* Here was a chance to add some joy to this child's day, to help her understand she wasn't alone.

And to do the same for Aunt Sarah. Yes, she would add joy to Aunt Sarah's day too.

"Hey, Viv, find out what you can about a child named Lisa, age five, maybe, who's in the hospital as a ward of the court, would you?" Jesse tossed her a grin as he headed into his inner sanctum.

"And good morning to you too, boss. I'll get right on it."

He turned around at the door. "You're right. Good morning, Viv. And thanks."

There was no way to try his plan without all the pertinent details. But Shilo'd fallen hard for the child and would make a wonderful mother. And that little girl stole his heart the first time he laid eyes on her. Last night, while trying to grab some sleep alone in his room, the idea emerged. Still, without knowing what he faced, he couldn't begin.

He'd no sooner gotten his jacket hung up and made it to his desk when someone knocked and didn't wait for the "come in."

Eli. Of course.

Not even his nemesis would ruin things for him today. His life might not be all he hoped for, but it was pretty darned remarkable.

"Just wondered if you planned to go to the festivities tomorrow evening."

Jesse shrugged. No need to commit. "We're talking about it. Why?"

Eli collapsed into the chair in front of Jesse's desk. "I don't know. Part of me thinks sure, why not? The other part doesn't want to bother."

Since when did Jesse become the guy's best friend? "Which part's winning?"

"Don't know. Changes depending on the hour. Honestly, I'm not sure I can handle seeing everyone again."

"What's the big deal? We see most of them around town anyway."

Eli ran his hand through his hair. "I guess it's knowing they've got it altogether, and I'm still trying to figure out how to ... I don't know ... grow up?"

That had to be the most vulnerable statement Shanahan ever muttered aloud in Jesse's presence. Something must be messing with the space-time continuum for Shanahan to take Jesse for some father confessor. "Why are you talking like this? You're the one who always claimed the brass ring. Quarterback on the football team, all-state in track and field, any girl you wanted—"

"Not any girl. I never could compete with you. Shilo pitied me a few times and threw me some crumbs, but that smile of hers lit up around you. Still does. I hope you get just how lucky you are."

This had to be the weirdest conversation he'd ever had with the man. And truthfully? If Eli had any clue about how this marriage came about, he'd be doing his level best to steal Shilo away. "I know, trust me. But I don't get why you're on the fence about going."

Shanahan shook his head. "Forget it. I was just curious." He checked his watch. "I'd better head back. The Drurys are coming in a few minutes to sign the final papers."

"Glad you got that worked out." Jesse flipped through his calendar but stopped and decided to do what Shilo would. "Hey, don't worry about it. You'll have a great time. And, yeah, we'll probably be there. Shy wants to go, so ..."

"Okay." Eli patted the door jamb. "Later."

Viv took his place in the doorway. "I've learned a few things. Here's the number for her case worker." She handed Jesse the slip with the information. Juliet McCleary. "Also, the child's name is Lisa Fonseca. She is five years old. You were right about that. All other information needs to come from Ms. McCleary."

"Got it. Thanks, Viv. When am I due at court?"

"You need to leave in an hour."

That would give him enough time to make that phone call and see what he might learn.

"Oh, one more thing. The check for Shilo came through. You want to take it to her? Or should I mail it?"

"Give it to me. Thanks." She left the envelope on his desk, and he put it into his briefcase so he wouldn't forget.

Once she closed his door, he reached for his phone but pulled his hand back. What if he got Shilo's hopes up over this, and they said no because of her hitchhiking arrests? Officer Nucum had been involved with each of the local nabs, but he'd gone above and beyond the call of duty with bringing Shilo in. Fortunately, in both instances, Jesse managed to get the episode cleaned up and shown for the overzealousness of the arresting officer.

But how many times had she been arrested elsewhere?

At some point, he'd have to tell Shilo what he planned. Maybe then she'd tell him her whole story.

That gave him courage to reach for the phone again, and this time he dialed.

"Juliet McCleary here."

"Ms. McCleary, my name is Jesse Franklin, I'm with *Hamilton, Franklin, and Reynolds* and hoped you might have a moment to talk with me about one of your cases. Lisa Fonseca?"

"I'm acquainted with your firm, Mr. Franklin. You realize I'm limited on what I can say?"

Boy, was he aware of that. "Yes, I am. But I might have a family who'd be interested in fostering with the hope of adopting. Can you share why Lisa is living at the hospital?"

"You don't know?"

"No, the hospital liaison gave me your number."

She paused. "Her father nearly killed her in a drunken rage while her mother looked on. Both have lost all parental rights. They broke Lisa's legs and she's having to learn to walk again. She'll be having physical therapy for some time and will always have a pronounced limp."

The fury erupting inside Jesse at the notion of what the child endured frightened him. He'd never been so livid in his life. Then something dripped onto his desk blotter. Again. He touched his face to find it wet. Now he couldn't breathe.

"Mr. Franklin, are you still there?"

He worked to clear his throat, so she'd hear sound. Then he shoved out a "yes."

"I understand. It's horrific that she went through that, but the good news is that those monsters are out of her life. We hope that the adoptive family will be patient with her. She has a hard time with men."

"I see. Ah, well, thank you for this information. What is the next step for the family? Do you have forms to start with?"

"I do. Should I send them to you?"

"Yes." He gave her his office address and phone number. "Appreciate your help, Ms. McCleary. I'll get back with you once the paperwork is ready."

They hung up.

Jesse could only sit behind his desk as the conversation repeated in his head. Of course, the child would fear men. How would Shilo take this news? That he knew. Getting her to let the process work would be the hardest thing.

No, that's wrong. Learning that she'd been disqualified because of her record—that would be the hardest thing.

Did he protect her and not start something that might blow up in their faces? Or did he move forward and stand up for her, fight for her, make sure Child Protective Services viewed Shy the way he did?

Someone knocked, and Viv peeked in. "Better leave for court if you want to make it on time."

"Okay, but when I come back, I'm bringing you lunch and we're having a talk."

Viv's face paled.

"Oh, stop worrying. I just need your opinion. Maybe even your prayers."

"That I can do. Now get going before you're held in contempt for being late."

Jesse saluted her and headed out. Fortunately, he had only an informal hearing in the judge's chambers. He arrived on time and left by eleven thirty. With takeout from China Clipper, he returned to the office and called Viv into his so they wouldn't be overheard.

He sat out the food while she set the table over by the back wall. Soon they were in the chairs sharing Chow Mein. Jesse even bowed his head while Viv asked the blessing.

"So why do you need to talk with me?" Viv didn't wrestle with the chopsticks but ate with her fork.

"I need your advice. There's a little girl at the hospital."

"The one I called about this morning? Lisa?"

Jesse nodded and wiped his mouth. If Viv didn't attempt the chopsticks, why had he? He never could get them to work. He switched out to a fork too. "Yeah, Lisa. She's a sweet little thing, and Shilo is getting attached to her. So, I called her case worker to find out about the procedure for becoming foster parents with the hope of adoption."

Viv's fork clattered on her plate. "Without talking things over with Shilo?"

"I only asked for information and first steps so we can discuss things. But I learned more than I expected."

"What's that?"

He took another bite to allow time for the words to form in his head. "Her father beat the child while her mother looked on. They're in prison now and stripped of their parental rights. That little girl is learning to walk again and may always have a noticeable limp."

"That poor baby."

Jesse paused and got around to the question that brewed in his mind ever since he hung up the phone. "How can the God you and Shilo worship allow that to happen?"

"Oh, Jesse. God didn't do that or just allow it to happen. We live in a fallen world. Bad things happen to good people all the time and not because God is flawed or vindictive. He's allowed each one of us to decide for ourselves whether to accept his gift of salvation or not. If we do, bad things can still happen because sin is in this world. But those of us who know His grace also know that there's more to life than the years we have on Earth. All He asks is that we continue to show His love and offer His grace to those around until He calls us home." Viv reached for his hand. "Do you believe, Jesse?"

"I don't know, Viv. I want to. I really do. I'm thinking about it."

"How about this: today's Friday, your schedule is pretty empty, and I can clear anything that's left. You go home and spend time with that bride of yours. You might've gotten into this to help Shilo help her aunt, but I can't miss the love blooming in your eyes whenever you speak of her."

"Finish your lunch first, and then I'll take you up on your brilliant plan." Jesse winked at her and forked another bite.

Twenty minutes later he was in his Ferrari headed for home. Where Shilo waited. Maybe when he sat her down and told her about his idea for Lisa, he'd also mention how much he'd fallen in love with her. Considering that part of the checking by the state would be to send someone to their house, a good plan would be for Shilo to move into his bedroom by then—and to make that happen, he needed to tell her that this was more than him helping her, more than mere friendship. This was his heart saying over and over that he'd fallen in love with his wife and wanted an actual marriage and that he'd wait until she was ready, but that was his goal.

He practiced the words all the way home, drilling them into his brain. He could do this. Sure, he could.

After lowering the garage door, he slipped into the kitchen without her noticing. She'd cranked the radio volume up loud.

Shy stood at the sink, her back to him, singing "Tie a Yellow Ribbon 'Round the Old Oak Tree," just enough off key to make him smile. She had her hair done up in a scarf, and her hips swayed side to side. He tried to simply watch for a moment, but he couldn't resist.

Tiptoeing behind her, he tugged on the silken dangles hanging down her back.

The scarf fell away as Shilo spun toward him, clutching her head.

Her bald head.

Bald. Head.

His wife was bald.

Chapter 13

This was so not the way Shilo wanted to tell Jesse. She'd known he'd flip, lose his mind, and come crashing down into his uptight lawyer mode.

And she saw it happening right before her eyes. "Jesse, hang on a sec. Remember, it's just hair."

"Just hair? Are you kidding?" He looked around at anything but her.

Shilo pulled out a kitchen chair for him. "Sit." She guided him until he did, snatching her scarf back from his fingers where he'd been twisting the material.

"How could you do this?"

She took the chair next to him and scooted knees to knees and held his hands. "Listen. Aunt Sarah's hair all fell out during the night. It freaked her out. Big time. I couldn't let her feel so alone."

"But your hair ..."

"Jesse, I know you figure I did this impulsive thing. But really, I thought about it. I did. After Aunt Sarah's therapy, we drove to the mall and I bought her a wig—" She held her hand up, keeping both of his caught with her other. "No arguments about this. I had to use your charge card, but I have the receipt and will pay you back as soon as my money comes in—and while they helped her, I found one that resembled my hair. So, I got it too. Want to see it?" She squeezed his fingers to get him to respond, though he still looked like a sky diver without a parachute bracing for impact.

Finally, he nodded.

So she hopped up and ran upstairs to her bedroom. Quickly, she slipped on her wig cap. Then, opening the box, she pulled out her wig, shook it as they'd shown her in the store, and placed her replacement hair on her head. Not perfect, but so close she doubted most people would notice. She whispered a quick prayer. *Here's hoping Jesse agrees.*

Back downstairs, Jesse still sat in his chair, frozen in the same position as she'd left him. He must have heard her, though, because he slowly raised his face, and tension ebbed away. Even the touch of a smile appeared. "I thought it was true. But you didn't. I was hallucinating."

"Jess, I did shave my head. This is the wig I bought."

The light that began to glow in his eyes now dimmed. "Oh."

"Don't you get it? Aunt Sarah is more important to me than my hair. And it'll grow back, like hers will." How could she help him understand? She sat in her chair again and reached for his hands.

At least he didn't fight her. Now if she could only say the right thing. But what he wanted to hear was that she pulled an April Fools' joke in the middle of the summer. And that was a lie. She wasn't going to lie to him.

"It'll be all right, Jess. You and Aunt Sarah and I are the only ones who'll know."

"Sarah let you do this?"

He had to grab hold of that, didn't he? Not the rest of what she said, but the one thing she'd hoped to slip past him. "Well, she will. I had to come home to shave, so she hasn't seen me yet."

Jesse pulled his hands away and cradled his head in them. "No, this is so bad, so, so very bad."

"Why, Jess? What are you afraid of?"

He froze. "What if Grandfather gets wind of this?"

"What if he does? I won't live my life to please him. Neither should you. This is none of his business. Our home, our lives. Not his."

Jesse raised his eyes and caught her gaze. "You really believe that, don't you? I can say I do, but as soon as something happens, I feel his condemnation. I can't get him out of my head."

Shilo pulled him into an embrace and began praying for him. "Oh, Father, You understand exactly what Jesse is saying, how he feels, and what he needs to do. Please speak to his heart and mind. Reveal what You want him to do. Help him let go of the past and grab hold of the future You have for him. In Jesus's name, amen."

Softly, she heard him echo, "Amen."

"I promise to always wear my wig out in public. And I'll get so good at putting it on, no one's gonna figure out the difference. Okay?"

He nodded.

She started to tell him about her appointment with The Weather Girls to pick up all their wedding and engagement photos tomorrow, but she wasn't sure if telling him would send him into another freak out.

So instead, she finished dinner. They ate on the back patio. Or rather, she ate. Jesse picked at his pasta primavera.

After she cleaned up from their meal, she found him on the roof. But when she started to join him, he shook his head. "Shy, I just need some time alone. I'm sorry."

She backed out, stung. But if that's what he needed. She'd messed with his mind, and hadn't figured everything through as well as she thought. Still, she couldn't imagine doing anything different.

So, with a sigh, she spent the evening working on macramé plant hangers for the back patio before going to bed early, telling herself Jesse needed to process, and he'd be better by morning.

When she woke and finished her quiet time, Jesse had already gone, leaving a note on the table.

Need to get away. I'll be back to get ready for the reunion. Don't worry. We're good. It's just me.

Her chest hurt. Not for herself, but for him. He had to be wrestling with something big. Maybe it had nothing to do with her and her missing hair, so she started praying for him to hear God's voice clearer than anything else.

After her trip to Ferguson House to get the photos, she made a second stop at the Ben Franklin to buy a picture frame and an album for the rest of the shots. Maybe this would prove to Jesse that everything would work out.

She took extra time finding just the right spot to put the frame—it held two photos. Extra special photos with a tiny red visitor. One from their engagement photo shoot and the other from the wedding. She decided on the living room's new sparsely filled bookcase. It gave them space to grow with their reading choices, knickknacks, and keepsakes. She stepped back to check her work. Perfect.

She'd almost made a stop by Aunt Sarah's, but after Jesse's reaction, Shilo wasn't ready to let her aunt know about her gesture of solidarity.

So, she pulled out her clothes for this evening. A part of her wanted to wear her jeans skirt with a white peasant blouse and her Birkenstocks. But she'd freaked Jesse out enough for the time being. Instead, she stayed with the cotton blouse but chose a pretty skirt Jesse bought her. That should please him and still let her feel like herself.

Shilo had just returned to her bedroom after her shower when his footsteps sounded up the stairs. He'd kept his word. If she'd been wearing her wig, she'd have peeked out at him, but no, not at this time.

However, he knocked on her door. "Shy, I'm back. I'll be ready to go in a bit."

"Okay. Did you get everything worked out?"

"Some. Maybe. It's gonna take time." His stride continued down the hall, and she knew he didn't want more conversation. He had to work this out in his head. That was Jesse. Always had been, and she wasn't out to change him. She only wanted him to see himself as God saw him and to embrace all the possibilities that opened.

Thirty minutes later, he tapped on her door again. "I'll meet you downstairs."

She'd nearly finished, but wanted to give him a moment to see what she'd left for him in the living room.

When she got down there, Jesse stood in the kitchen staring out the back door.

"Ready. How do I look?" She needed his approval more than she wanted to admit.

"Beautiful as always. And your hair is nice. You're not going swimming, right?" Yet, instead of smiling, his eyes dimmed with worry as he spoke.

"No, Jess, I'm not. No bathing suit under my clothes." She reached out, but he turned.

"Let's go."

He guided her out to the Ferrari and held her door before he raised the garage's. Then he backed out and closed the garage again.

Shilo waited for him to start a conversation, and all the while the voice in her brain reminded her that she'd have to do it. When he retreated inside, chatting debilitated him, so she chose her words with care.

"Any idea who is coming?"

He shook his head. "No. Eli's the only person who said anything to me. And he's a definite maybe."

"Oh." Perhaps most people thought like Jesse and figured they saw each other enough in the daily workings of living in Kokomo.

So, when they pulled into the parking area of the Sea Shore, it surprised her to find so many cars. In a good way. It was the great picker-upper she needed. "Looks like people decided to come. This should be fun." If only her excitement were contagious and he caught a big case of it.

They entered the block building that had been built in the 1930s as part of FDR's New Deal. For a long time, this municipal pool claimed the title of the largest in the state of Indiana. Shilo spent many a spring earning money or fulfilling activities that enabled her to get a season pass, and until she was in high school, she hung out all those hot summer days at the Sea Shore. When she got old enough, she'd earned her spot as a lifeguard and sat perched on the tower chair or on the center structure, keeping kids safe. Just being back here opened up wonderful memories making all the reunion chats extra fun.

"Saw you two tied the knot. Congratulations!" Sally Jerrot sat at the check-in desk handing out *Hi, My Name Is* labels and markers.

Shilo slipped her hand in at Jesse's elbow and smiled. "Thanks, Sally."

"Oh, yeah!" Fred Milkins joined in. "Gotta say, it's about time. Figured you two would've been hitched right out of college if not high school."

"Well, we waited until things worked out." Shilo paused for Jesse to add something, but he stayed silent. At least he nodded and smiled when he handed over the marker.

As they meandered out to the pool deck, they ran into others who offered congratulations. Finally, Jesse loosened up and added a few words.

Things filtered back to Shilo. The sensation of having to do all the talking. Worries that Jesse wasn't comfortable.

Now she remembered. How could she do this to him? He'd never be the extrovert she was.

"Would you like something to drink, Shy?" He startled her back.

"What? Uh, yes, please. A Coke is fine."

He gave her hand a squeeze before leaving her to go to the refreshment stand.

That allowed her to scan the crowd, putting names to faces, and enjoying how so many showed up.

Then she spotted him. Eli, deep in shadow and behaving strangely. Or maybe not strangely after what she'd seen in California. But for him here in Kokomo? Strange was the word.

She wandered closer. Though his back remained to her, she caught movement that made her hope against hope that she wasn't seeing what she feared she did. She angled her approach to get a better view.

He sat at a table, alone. One away from everyone, completely shadowed. Something in his hand made a tiny chopping motion.

The closer she got, the more she observed. White powder on a small mirror. That's what he'd been chopping. Now formed into a thin, straight line.

He laid aside what looked like a credit card, picked up a dollar bill, and began rolling it into a cylinder.

"Eli?"

He jumped, the money floating to the table. Glancing at her with huge eyes and then back at his stuff as if to make sure the white powder hadn't disappeared, he shrugged. "Shilo. Hey. I'll catch you later."

"Eli, I know what you're doing. I know cocaine when I see it."

His demeanor changed. "I'd share, but I didn't bring enough. Sorry." He rerolled the dollar and lifted the homemade tube to his nose.

"Eli, don't. Please don't."

Eli raised his eyes to her, and she thought she'd gotten through. Then all at once, he snorted the line.

Shilo scurried away.

Jesse returned to where he'd left Shilo only to spot her charging his direction. And she didn't look happy.

"What's the matter?"

She shook her head. "I'll tell you on the way home. Not here."

"Okay." That was weird. Must be something pretty bad.

She linked her arm with his and stepped close. "You still haven't mentioned about what I did in the living room." An obvious change of topic tactic.

"I didn't notice anything. Never even stepped in there."

"Oh." She grew quiet.

"I'll check it out when we get home."

She nodded just in time for another old schoolmate to congratulate them. Maybe they should've invited a few more people to their wedding.

Someone got the music going. "Moon River" had been the theme for their Autumn Prom. Girls asked the guys to that one. Having Shilo ask him made him wonder if he'd been dreaming. But no, it happened. The best night of his entire life, at least until she walked back into it again.

"Wanna dance?" Her eyes said she remembered too.

Jesse spun her in his arms. He should've told Shilo what filled his mind today. After her stating that his grandfather had no say so in their affairs, he realized two things. First, she was right. Dead right. And second, if he stayed at the firm, it didn't matter how right she was. They'd never get him out of their business.

So, he'd contacted Pat Whitcomb, who officiated at their wedding. He'd made the phone call as soon as it was reasonable this morning, and Pat invited him over to talk. Really talk, as things turned out. Pat understood, having come from a similar situation. Not necessarily abusive, but having the awareness of no control over his own life.

The way it panned out for Pat wouldn't, couldn't be the same for Jesse. Pat told his dad he'd work for a year and get loose ends tied up. Afterward, he moved from Indianapolis to Kokomo to start his own practice.

Giving Grandfather a set time frame wouldn't make life easier. The better way would be a clean break. However, that would put him out of a job just when he needed to have one to prove to Child Protective Services his capability to provide for Lisa.

That's when the miracle occurred. Pat said his practice was growing, and he could use a partner. Definitely something to think about, and he told Pat he would. In fact, the stereo in his brain replayed that phrase over and over like the needle got stuck in the groove.

In order to go with Pat, he'd have to make the break, though. And as much as he wanted to, everything in his avoidance nature began ducking and running.

He needed to talk this over with Shilo first, too. Oh, and he still had to give her the check.

Now Chubby Checkers crooned "The Twist" followed by Little Eva with "The Loco-Motion." It was hard to play catch-up conversations with old acquaintances or even come up with answers to Shilo's whispered questions when his thoughts kept running back to this morning. And he needed to share this with her before he came to a decision. She was his check and balance. His hand slid down her arm to her hand and he locked fingers with her, leading her away from the dancers.

She glanced down at their hands and up to his face.

He tried to send her a message in his grin and when she smiled back, he knew she'd received it.

Even if her smile didn't beam as big as he'd hoped.

But that might have to do with what she needed to talk to him about after they left.

They wandered from group to group, Al Hirt's rendition of "Alley Cat" playing over the voices, making a complete circle of the pool when a scream came from the far end.

Jesse glanced up to spot Sueanne Brinegar getting plopped, fully clothed, into the water. The splash drenched the deck area a yard and a half or more out and thoroughly doused all who stood close.

Some yelled, some laughed. He couldn't tell the major reaction, but then another woman, this time Betsy Aaron, got tossed in the air and landed in the water.

People scattered at that point, and Jesse spotted the instigator.

Eli Shanahan.

Of course. Why wasn't he surprised?

But then he realized the lunatic stormed their way.

"Where's Shilo?" The man shoved the crowd aside, doing his best steamroller impersonation.

Shanahan would never lay a finger on Shilo, not in that condition and not while she couldn't go in the water. Jesse moved Shilo behind him. "I'm warning you, Eli."

"What about? A little splashy-poo? You afraid your sweet thang might melt? Trust me, she's not sugar." Eli's eyes squinted, and he tipped his head as if trying to see past Jesse.

"Leave her alone. In fact, go home. Sleep it off, Shanahan."

"Still acting like you're the boss. I'm done with doing what you say. Besides, the night is young. This party's just getting started." As he finished, he reached around, attempting to get to Shilo.

Jesse moved her farther behind him and smacked at Eli's arm. "Go. Stop trying to bother her."

"I knew we'd come to this, Franklin."

But Jesse spotted the fist coming in time and blocked, following up with a right cross of his own, white-hot rage filling his veins.

Only someone held his arm. He jerked his elbow free as Eli nailed him. Jesse stumbled backwards into that somebody.

"Oh!" *Shilo!*

She hit the water.

Only she didn't come up like the others who'd been tossed in.

Jesse knelt at the pool's edge.

Shilo's wig settled on the bottom. With her eyes closed, blood oozed from a wound on her head.

Someone else, a guy in the pool on her other side, lifted her toward Jesse. Had she swallowed any water?

Open your eyes, Shy.

A woman yelled, "Call for an ambulance."

Jesse settled Shilo on his lap, checking to make sure she still breathed. She did.

He rolled her so if she had swallowed any water, she'd be able to cough it out.

But she wouldn't open her eyes, and the gash on her head scared him.

Her white top clung to her body revealing she already had a major scar. From below her waistband to her chest.

"Should we drive her to the hospital instead of waiting?" Voices around him called out ideas.

"Wake up, Shy, please. I'm so sorry. I didn't mean to hurt you." Jesse rubbed her back.

"No!"

Jesse raised his head to see where the shout came from.

Eli crouched, his fingers raking his hair, his eyes wild with fear.

Something inside crushed the rage that wanted to destroy Eli Shanahan and covered it with ... empathy? "She's not dead, Eli." *God, don't let her die.*

Eli jumped to his feet and raced away.

But Jesse wouldn't leave Shilo no matter what she whispered to him in his head. *Go after him, Jesse. Help him.* She couldn't ask him to do that.

Instead, she began to sputter, then cough.

When she stopped, her eyes opened.

"Oh, Shy." He pulled her close, and she allowed him.

"Let the ambulance workers through!"

And then they appeared. Two guys in white coats with a gurney. "We'll take her from here, mister."

"She's my wife." Their job was to help, but Jesse couldn't let go.

"It's fine. But we ought to get her to the hospital. Follow us if you want. We'll head for St. Joe's."

They wouldn't let him ride with her in the ambulance? But somehow, he understood what he had to do and released her.

The men gently lifted her from Jesse's lap, placed her on the rolling bed, and wheeled her to the parking lot.

Jesse followed as closely as he could. "Tell her I'm coming. Even if her eyes are closed, tell her."

"We will, mister." One guy jumped in the back with her, and the other went around to the driver's side and climbed in.

"Jesse, hold on a sec." Dave Kingsley held him by his shoulder. "I'll go with you. You shouldn't drive alone."

"I'm fine. I just need to get there." Jesse took another step then turned back. "Thanks anyway. I appreciate it." That was the best he could do, but he had to credit Shilo with even coming up with those words.

He raced to his car and tore out of the parking lot, managing the roadways and avoiding any stops if he could help it. That was a bonus of knowing your hometown, being aware of all the back streets and shortcuts. Jesse beat the ambulance and waited in the bay while they unloaded Shilo.

She spotted him and held out her hand, the one not hooked up to an IV.

They'd put a pressure bandage on her head over the gash. When her hair grew out, nobody would see it. But then, she wouldn't have cared if it was on her face. Looks held no importance to her; she didn't have a vain bone in her body.

In Emergency they tried to keep Jesse from going in with Shilo to where they would stitch her up, but they were no match for his wife. She wanted him with her, and what she wanted, he'd make sure she got.

They gave her forty stitches in four layers to seal up the gash.

Then the doctor pulled Jesse aside for a moment. "We noticed your wife's head. Is she a cancer patient? It has bearing on how we treat her."

"No. Her Aunt Sarah is, and she didn't want her aunt to feel alone."

"So, she shaved her head?" The doctor stared as if he didn't understand English.

Jesse nodded. "My wife is very compassionate."

"I see. Well, good. We worried about other complications. We'd still like to have her stay overnight to make sure she's not dealing with a concussion."

"I understand. May I go back in now?" The longer he was away from her, the more his tension grew. Seeing her open-eyed, watching for him, made everything right with the world.

"Sure. Someone will be here directly to move her to a room."

He didn't wait for more and charged back into the cubicle.

Her lids closed again, but she smiled as he came close. "Jesse. Guess everyone knows about the wig. I'm sorry."

"Are you kidding me? Shy, I knocked you into the pool. I nearly killed you. You could've drowned."

"But I didn't. I'm here, Jess. I shouldn't have grabbed your arm. I just hated for either of you to hurt the other." The first tear slipped down her cheek and dropped in her ear.

"You'll get your brains all wet if you keep crying like that—they'll fall in your ear and into your head." He tried to give her a smile while he wiped her face with his fingertips.

"Only you would say that." She smiled for him. "How is Eli? Is he okay?"

Jesse pulled back. Eli Shanahan was the last person he wanted to discuss. "He freaked, sure you were dead until I told him you weren't. Then he ran for the hills. I've no idea where he went, and I used up all my generosity for him by not hunting him down."

"You would've done that?"

"I wouldn't leave you. And, okay, this will sound hokey, but I sort of heard you in my head telling me to be kind. So, I told him you were alive, and I didn't have anyone grab him for me." He brought her hand to his lips and kissed each finger. The fact that he could still do that, could still talk with her, still have her in his life made him very grateful. Maybe to God. He needed to figure that out, but with all that went on tonight, it'd be awhile before he did.

"Jess, stay with me, please."

He rubbed the back of her hand against his cheek and smiled. "Try to pry me away."

Chapter 14

S hilo relaxed now that Jesse would stay with her. Of course, her Heavenly Father would never leave her either, but Jesse here was a bonus.

"Looks like you'll be with us overnight. We're going to move you up to the second floor." The nurse nodded to the aide who'd followed her into the ER cubicle before pulling back the curtain that separated Shilo from the hallway. "Ready to roll?"

Jesse leaned close, still holding her hand. "Don't worry, I'll come too."

"Sir, you need to take the visitors' elevator. We'll meet you there. Her room is 217." Apparently, the nurse had practice because her tone brooked no argument. Zero. Zip. Nada. Shilo wasn't up to fighting.

Jesse squeezed her hand. "Guess I'll see you up there. It'll only be a minute." He kissed her forehead and with one more hand-squeeze he left the room.

Shilo only experienced loss like that two other times in her life. The first when her parents died in the car accident. The second, when Lisa … no, she was too vulnerable to be going down that path now. The only good thing was Jesse would be waiting for her upstairs. She'd hang on for those few minutes.

They wheeled her to the employees-only elevator and, after a brief ride, to her room. Looked like she had a roommate. An older woman.

Jesse'd arrived already, and as they brought her in, he smiled at the roommate before pulling the dividing curtain out that separated the two beds. When the nurse and her aide left, he scooted the visitor chair close to her and spoke in a soft voice. "We don't need a third-party listening in. This is just us. I can't give you the back porch roof here, but I'll make things as private for you as possible."

Funny, but he offered what he would want. Normally she'd be happy for interaction, but tonight she preferred Jesse's way. Maybe he read her heart. If so, did he have any clue just how much she loved him? She reached to brush his hair off his forehead. If he could get a load of himself now, he'd be all bent because he looked rumpled and tired. Made her smile that he'd get messy for her.

"Shy, can you tell me something?"

She'd tell him anything he asked. Even be the first one to brave an I love you, if that's what he needed. She bit her bottom lip and nodded. Ow! Her hands braced her head. Just that slight movement set her brain throbbing.

"Stay still. Just talk to me, as long as nothing hurts." He recaptured her hand.

"Okay. What do you want me to tell you?"

He stared at the bed and picked at some non-existent lint. "Um, how did you get that scar?"

Panic began its climb from her toes, kicking in a desire to flee. "What scar?" As if she didn't know.

"The one that goes from here to here." He traced her scar over the hospital blanket with the index finger of his free hand.

This was the moment. She'd swore she'd never lie to him. And he asked. She could say she wasn't ready to talk about it, but it was time he knew. That she let him know. So, she focused on a dent in the footrest of her bed. That way, she didn't have to watch his face as she shared her darkest memories with him. "In 1969 I was deep in the drug culture. I don't think I even knew who I was, just living on emotion and sensation. I ended up pregnant. Couldn't tell you who the father was. Never saw a doctor, but at least I cut back on the drugs. Only some pot now and then.

"One night, something started to hurt really bad. Friends took me to the hospital. They did an emergency C-section. I had a little girl. Lisa."

Jesse's grip stiffened, but if he'd noted the year, he realized the Lisa here in Kokomo couldn't be the same one.

"But then there were more problems. They gave me a complete hysterectomy, hoping to save my life. I only held Lisa—" Her air hitched. "—in the delivery room for a short few minutes." Shilo ran her free wrist under her nose and sucked in a ragged breath. "I later learned I started crashing, and they got the baby away so I couldn't drop her." She still heard the voices. *Grab the baby, grab the baby.* Shilo shuddered but pressed on. "They put me under, and when I came to, the doctor explained he'd nearly lost me twice on the operating table. He also mentioned he hoped my affairs were in order because it'd take a miracle for me to pull through. He said that before it became too late, I should give my baby up for adoption." Jesse's hand held on tighter to hers, giving her strength to finish.

"I believed him and signed the paperwork. I don't know how long I teetered between awake and unconsciousness. Until Lonnie Frisbee and his wife came into my room and prayed for me. My life was saved, but I lost my Lisa and any chance of having children." She couldn't say more. The sobs choked her air.

Jesse leaned in and held her to him. "I'm so sorry, Shy. So, so sorry."

He didn't run away as she feared. But she knew for a fact that she no longer sat on that pedestal he'd perched her on.

She sniffed. "Told you I wasn't perfect."

He said nothing.

She pulled back, unable to fight the curiosity of what ran through his mind. Any emotion pumping through him should be written all over his face. And it was. Compassion. His eyes gazed at her tenderly, filled with moisture.

"It's going to be all right, Shy. I promise."

How could he promise such things?

He opened his mouth when the nurse came in. "Sir, visiting hours are over. You can come back to see her tomorrow at ten."

She didn't give him a chance for anything private but stood guard to make certain he left.

Jesse brushed a soft peck against her lips, so fast she wasn't sure but that she'd imagined it. "I'll be back tomorrow. And you'll be released. It's gonna work out, Shy. Sweet dreams." He blew her a kiss from the doorway and sauntered off.

"Wondered if I was going to be able to chase that man of yours out of here. Rules are rules, but I tell you, he wanted to stay. Must love you a whole lot." The nurse straightened Shilo's bedding, did a vitals check, and flipped off the lights before leaving and closing the door.

Shilo considered starting a conversation with her roommate, but soft snores filtered through the curtain divider.

She could talk with her Heavenly Father. There was an idea. And so many needs. As a rule, she prayed aloud, but rather than wake the other woman, she mouthed the words with a soft whisper. "Oh, Father. What's going to happen? I've embarrassed Jesse with everyone seeing me without my wig. I didn't stop Eli and now he's off somewhere. I never told Jesse that he tripped on cocaine. He wouldn't have done all that if he hadn't been high, and I should've been able to keep him from snorting. Should I have knocked the mirror away? I kept wondering if I ought to say something, but he had to make the decision. And when he did, and it was the wrong one, all I saw was that if I'd just shoved everything off the table into the dirt, none of this would've happened. That means I'm to blame. I'm so sorry, Lord. I tried to do the right thing."

She fisted the edge of her bedding. "And, yes, I've needed to tell Jesse the full story, but now I'm afraid that as he mulls over things, he'll decide he doesn't want me if I can't live on his pedestal. That since he sees more of the real me, he'll realize he only loved an image he'd created in his mind."

That brought the tears back, making her head pound more than ever. She couldn't find a comfortable position, and every move added a wave of pain. Physically, emotionally, even spiritually, this was the most she'd suffered in a very long while. She only hoped that God would bring her through like He did the last time.

"I need to take your temperature."

Shilo blinked against the light streaming in from the window. She'd fallen asleep. *Thank You, Father.* She opened her mouth for the thermometer as the nurse shook down the mercury.

Moments later, the nurse smiled. "Normal." She shook the glass tube again. "They'll be in with your breakfast in a few minutes." And she left.

Shilo glanced around and spotted the big round clock high on the wall facing her bed. Eight twenty-five. A little more than an hour and a half and Jesse would be back for her. A part of her hated that he'd miss church, but selfish or not, she wanted him here with her.

About that time, her room turned into Grand Central Station. If the professional person wasn't here for Shilo, they came for her roommate who she never did meet because of all the interruptions. Breakfast, doctors, evaluations, and discharge orders. Finally, an aide came in offering to help her wash up.

Jesse hadn't arrived with clean clothes, but she hoped she could shake out what she had. Everything got soaked, so someone had hung it all up in the tiny bathroom shower. *Wonder if they also made sure to rinse out any blood stains?* She hated for the skirt Jesse bought her to be ruined.

Where was he, anyway? Oh, it wasn't ten yet.

A knock sounded. Shilo glanced over to find a rumpled Eli in the doorway. Looked like he hadn't slept, and his crash had been brutal.

"May I come in?" He sounded so pitiful, her heart went out to him.

"Of course, get in here. Are you all right?" She pointed to the chair Jesse had used.

"I should be asking you that. How bad is your head?" He pulled the seat closer and sat.

Her fingers patted the gauze-wrapped cap she wore and smiled. "I got some sleep, so I'm better today. Last night it hurt to move at all. Now I'm ready to get out of here." She waggled her eyebrows and pulled a small smile out of him.

"I'm so sorry, Shilo. I should've listened to you."

"Why, Eli? Why didn't you?"

He squirmed a bit. "I used to do weed back when we were in high school. When I got drafted, I found other stuff. Figured I'd have to jump on the wagon in college, but it was so easy to get on campus. When old man Franklin started taking an interest in me, letting me know what classes to take, giving me an internship until I finished and passed the bar, and hiring me afterward, I knew I had to stop. So, I did. Been clean ever since." Eli grimaced.

"Then what happened?" Shilo really wanted to understand.

"I was supposed to be the big success. The quarterback, Autumn Prom Rex, even had a decent GPA. But I've barely started my career, and I worried I'd be seen as a loser."

"Eli, you got drafted. Of course it took longer to get things done. And you've already joined a firm."

"Yeah, old man Franklin's been watching out for me. Guess he made a promise or two."

"What do you mean?"

"*Hamilton, Franklin, and Reynolds* came together through three college friends. Hamilton's kids and grandkids had no interest in the law. Your husband is the only hope for the Franklin line. Then there's my family. My great uncle Abner Reynolds had only one sister, and my dad, her son, wasn't the least bit interested. But then we were about to graduate from high school, and my draft number got called. Old man Franklin learned from Uncle Abner that Senator Bayh could wrangle an exemption, and he jumped on that for Jesse before my uncle could do anything. Once Uncle Abner got ahold of the Senator, it was too late.

"Uncle Abner'd grown ill by this time, and he swore old man Franklin's trick shortened his life. Anyway, I wasn't supposed to know this, but my mom shared the dirty little secret with me. Uncle Abner made Franklin swear he'd help me through college and law school and give me a position. Guilted him into it. I'd planned to throw it all in the old man's face, but then I decided to take him for all he's worth."

She reached out and squeezed his hand.

"But you wanted to understand about last night. I'd been bought, manipulated, and passively went along with it. I didn't want to feel that anymore. So, I tried for life of the party and grabbed some courage to do it."

"Eli, you are worth more than that."

He shook his head. "Nah."

"Yes, you are. You are a child of God, and He loves you more than you can know."

He raised his gaze to hers, his eyes glinting with tears ready to drop. "Do you love me, Shilo?"

"Of course. I love you, Eli."

Jesse froze. Had he heard correctly?

But there they were, Eli hugging Shilo.

How much of a masochist did he plan to be? Just standing around, watching and listening. His insides twisted so hard he could hurl.

Still, Shilo didn't look up.

Jesse had to escape. Then he remembered what he carried in his hands. Somehow, he got his feet to move to the nurses' station. "Um, would you take these to Shilo Ander...I mean Shilo Franklin? I have to leave."

"Yes. I'll make sure she gets it." The nurse took the bag of clothes from him, giving him the freedom to race for the elevator.

He needed to get out of there. By the time he reached the glass exit doors, he sprinted all the way to the parking lot. He couldn't unlock his car fast enough.

Then he had to figure out where to go. And he had no idea.

Instead, he pounded the steering wheel as the urge to cry ravaged its path through his body, his heart, his head, his face. Tears streamed his cheeks. Sobs wracked his soul.

Shilo loved Eli. Not him. Eli. She said the words. He heard it.

His wife loved another man.

All he wanted was for her to tell him she loved him. He'd convinced himself that she did, that all he lacked were her words.

But she gave those to Eli Shanahan. The man who wanted to take her from him. He'd succeeded.

God, if You're real, why? Why would You do this?

Someone tapped on his window.

He ran his hand over his face and turned to see Viv.

She tapped again, so he rolled down the glass.

"Jesse, what's wrong?"

He cleared his throat. "Viv, what are you doing here?"

"I just wanted to check in on Shilo before I leave for church. Did something happen?"

He shook his head. How could he explain to her?

"Unlock the door. I'm getting in." She hustled around to the passenger side and tapped her manicured nail right above the lock.

It was useless to argue. He reached across and popped the lock for her.

Viv slipped in and turned in her seat. "Drive around and start talking."

"I can't, Viv."

"Yes, you can. I'm already praying for you. Now tell me what more I need to pray about."

He rubbed his hand over his face again, started the ignition, and pulled out of the lot. Maybe some useless driving would help.

Her silent waiting for him to start got the better of him. "Um, I've never been able to say ... certain words. I struggle to let my feelings out."

"Tell me something I don't know."

He chuckled a little, because of course this came as no surprise. She knew him better than his own mother. Someone he never heard utter the words to him. "Once, when my parents were home on furlough, my mom spent time with me, teaching me about the flowers and plants that grew around here."

"That's where you get that."

He nodded. "Yeah. It was the best day I'd ever had with her. And I had this urge to tell her that I loved her. But just as I grew brave enough to force out the words, my father called her away. She apologized for having to stop, but they had to go. I never experienced that moment again, nor had anyone I wanted to say that to until Shilo. I arranged a special evening for us right before graduation. And then we got the news that she'd won the Breck Girl ad campaign, so I held back. We'd planned to write to each other, but no letters arrived from her. She said she wrote. I don't know what happened, but I'd put everything behind me until her grandfather asked me to make out his will."

"Guess I tried not to get my hopes up, but when she came back for the money to help her aunt, I couldn't let her marry Eli Shanahan."

She gave him the look, one that told him he'd officially arrived at crazy.

"Anyway, every moment with her only brought more uncovered feelings. And each time I've tried to tell her, something has gone wrong. I thought today was the day until I walked into her room and heard her tell Shanahan that she loved him."

"Oh, no, Jesse. I'm so sorry. Are you sure you didn't misunderstand something? She said she was in love with Eli?" Viv gripped his hand.

"She said, and I quote, 'Of course. I love you, Eli.' Pretty clear, doncha think?"

Viv withdrew her hand and shook her head. "No. I don't."

"What do you mean?" Hadn't he spoken English? How could she not reach the same conclusion?

"Shilo is a loving person. She didn't say she was in love with Eli, just that she loved him. Bet she's told her aunt that she loves her too."

Could that be true? He drove in silence and realized he'd made his way back to the hospital. He spotted Viv's car and pulled up next to it. "Maybe you're right. Hey, how did you learn about her accident?"

"You have been busy. *The Tribune* ran an article this morning. That's why I hustled to get ready for church and left early to come by here. I knew I couldn't stay long, but wanted to check. I'd called your house, but no one answered."

He nodded. "I took the phone off the hook. Everyone from the reunion phoned to check how she was. A lot of people love Shilo. But I needed the quiet. Guess I forgot to hang it back up." He glanced at his watch. "You're going to be late for church."

"That's okay. God understands. Jesse, would you let me pray for you?" She didn't wait for his approval but put her hand on his shoulder. "God, please bring comfort to Jesse's heart. Give him hope and direction. And bring him peace. In Jesus's name, amen."

Then she hugged him.

Funny how he didn't feel himself go all stiff, though his return hug proved a little awkward.

"Jesse, before I get out, I want to tell you something. You are like a son to me, and you are the only reason I stay at the firm. I love you. I think you needed to hear that."

His throat tightened so much he wasn't sure he could breathe. No one had ever said those words to him. Okay, they were part of the wedding vows they repeated, but he'd told Shilo they'd say it as friends. But aside from that, those words were golden, special. He absolutely needed to hear that. "Yeah, me too, Viv." He hoped she understood him. Shilo had to be the first one to hear him say it, but once she did, he'd make certain to let the woman who'd been a surrogate mother to him know he loved her too.

Viv climbed out.

He watched as she got into her Ford Torino and started the ignition before driving home. After getting his car in the garage and the door pulled in place, he went into the house. The emptiness echoed worse than last night.

He should've just gone up to her at the hospital right then when he dropped Viv off, but he still needed that time to process. He wandered into the living room and at once spotted what Shilo added. There, on the new bookcase, sat a large double frame. One side showed them kissing for their engagement photos. The other had them kissing again after their wedding. And in both pictures, a bright red cardinal hovered on the branch overhead.

They'd gotten their cardinal. Twice.

Shilo swore she wasn't superstitious but believed God could use nature to get His point across. Maybe Jesse was thickheaded enough that it took two cardinals.

That made him smile and go to the phone. Hopefully, Shilo would accept his apology and be waiting for him to bring her home.

He dialed and asked for her room. The line rang several times before someone picked up. "Nurses' Station."

"I was trying to reach my wife in 217. Can you connect me please?"

"Mr. Franklin, I'm afraid she's not here. She left an hour ago."

He never even said goodbye. Just hung up as a cold fist squeezed out the bit of hope he'd found.

The doorbell rang. Maybe Shilo came home, and she didn't have her keys. He raced to the door and yanked it open. "What are you doing here?"

Eli didn't bother to be invited, just barged right in. "Are you a complete imbecile?"

"You wedge yourself between me and my wife, charge into my house, and now you insult me? The only thing keeping you from getting your butt kicked is Shilo doesn't want you hurt."

"But you can hurt her, though. Right? She's your wife, so you're allowed to treat her like dirt."

Jesse growled, deep in his throat. It'd take all he had to not smash that pretty boy's face. "Get out."

"I will. But you better understand something. You've broken your wife's heart. She waited for you to come pick her up, and then some nurse delivers her things and said you dropped them off for her and left. Look, I'm smart enough to get you love her, you have since high school. I get it. I've been in love with her too. But you won. Was that all there was to it? Just beating me?"

"Now who's the idiot? I was there. I heard her. She told you she loves you."

"Yeah. Like a brother. You stopped listening too soon or you would've known that. Wait ... you mean that's what happened? You thought she was in love with me, so you walked away? Didn't even fight for her?"

Jesse's knees grew weak, and he dropped to the closest chair. "Oh, no. Oh, no, what have I done?"

"I don't know, man, but you better come up with something before you lose that very fine lady."

"Did you drive her someplace?"

Eli shook his head. "No, I offered, but she called a taxi. Checked herself out and sat at the curb until it arrived. I stayed with her. She kept trying to get me to leave, but I refused to until I knew she was on her way to where she wanted to go."

"I don't think she has her purse with her. I'm not even sure where it is, so she wouldn't have any money. She had to go to her aunt's house.

It's the only place since she didn't come here." Jesse was halfway to the phone as he talked out his deduction.

"Want me to stay and help you look for her?"

Jesse stopped dialing long enough to glance up at Eli. "No. Uh, thank you, man. I'm sorry."

"Don't tell me, tell her. And, on that topic, I'm sorry too. I told her the whole story. I can't go through it again. But I am sorry."

Jesse gave him a nod, and they held their gaze. Somehow, he knew they both understood.

Eli headed for the front door as Jesse finished dialing Sarah's number. After several rings, Shilo's aunt picked up. "Hello?"

"Sarah, it's Jesse. Is Shilo there?"

The speaker got muffled, but he heard a voice, though he couldn't make anything out. Finally, Sarah spoke again. "Jesse, she doesn't want to come to the phone. I don't know what happened between you two, but I'm praying you work it out. In the meantime, she's asking you to let her think. She said you asked that of her, now she needs you to do her the same favor."

That icy fist roared back into his chest. Every time he got an ounce of hope, it showed up to snatch it. "Thanks, Sarah. Tell her I'll honor her request for a short while, but I need to see her soon."

"I'll tell her." They said goodbye, and he hung up.

Now, what did he do?

Chapter 15

"What did he say?" Shilo needed to know now.

Aunt Sarah set the handset back in the cradle and turned to her. "He said he would honor your request for a little while, but that he needs to talk with you."

"A little while? How long is that?" Shilo needed to pace her aunt's front room, but with her headache the way it was, sitting still was her best bet. "What if he comes looking for me and I'm not ready?"

Aunt Sarah sat on the couch next to her. "C'mon. Tell me what's going through your head. You aren't afraid of him, and we both know he's not out to hurt you. So why are you ducking him?"

Shilo sighed and obeyed. She might as well explain. "Jesse placed me on a pedestal. I keep trying to tell him that I'm just me, a flawed, messed-up chick who God saved. So, I told him the dark stuff that happened in LA." She didn't want to explain everything to her aunt. Yes, it was a part of her past that Jesus forgave her about, but revealing it all to Aunt Sarah would hurt the woman. And Shilo would do anything to not cause her pain.

"You realize that whatever happened, God forgave you, and you are not the same person. Right?"

"I know. And He has given me hope and a new future. I just figured it would be with Jesse. I prayed so hard and hoped that was what God had in mind for me, for us. But if Jess can't accept me now that I'm off his pedestal, I'm lost. What do I do? I hated to be up there, but I still want to be loved by him." Shilo leaned her head against the sofa back and closed her eyes, hoping to lessen the pounding in her brain. This was such a mess. Maybe she shouldn't have even come to Kokomo.

But if she hadn't, Aunt Sarah wouldn't have gotten the chemotherapy.

And if she left, since they were all waiting for her to get the inheritance that she now wouldn't receive, would they stop the treatments?

It was way too much to consider when her head hurt from her concussion. Thinking was plain hard.

"You're looking pale, sweetie. Why don't you go lie down?"

Shilo sat up and met her aunt's gaze. "You're the one who needs rest."

"We both do. When we get up, maybe you can tell me the actual story of what happened to your hair. I'm sure your stitches didn't require all that."

Oops. What made Shilo imagine her aunt wouldn't notice? She knew the gauze head wrap didn't look like it hid her long hair. Well, she'd use this bit of respite to figure out how to tell her. "Okay. After our naps. I'm definitely ready for one."

The women stood, hugged, and Shilo slowly wandered off to the guest room.

After shutting the door, she stretched out on the bed, closing her eyes, waiting for sleep to come. She needed it. The emotion of Jesse walking away from her hurt so deeply. An abandonment that tore at the center of her heart. Just letting the memory play again set the tears to flowing.

You're going to get your brain wet.

Jesse had no right dropping little phrases in her mind. Not after turning his back on her. She'd been so sure things would work out, that he'd begun falling in love with her, the real Shilo. But see what a new day brought?

She used to look forward to a new morning, a chance for a fresh start. But today blindsided her. Nothing went as she'd hoped.

Right now, she should be curled up in Jesse's arms. He'd be taking care of her and showing her he loved her. Because she'd pretty much given up on him speaking the words. But God said to watch his actions. They'd say more.

They sure had.

She rolled to her side and pulled her knees up, wrapping her arms around them to hold herself tight. "God, I need a hug from You."

Sleep drifted in, and soon Shilo woke from a dream where she'd been a child, lifted onto Jesus's lap, and hugged and comforted. Exactly what her battered heart needed.

She still had no answers. Instead, a peace that even this would be worked out for her good settled over her like a comfy blanket.

Shilo rose and wandered to the kitchen to find paper and a pen. She needed to come up with a plan. The idea of heading back to California grew strong. But if she did, she'd have to make arrangements, like calls to ensure Aunt Sarah got to her appointments. That would be hard, leaving her aunt and not being close by.

She'd also need to go to Jesse's house and get her things and leave what she hadn't brought. Maybe she ought to write him a note too. She wasn't sure about that.

It would require hitchhiking again. No way would she drive her car.

And since she hadn't gotten her check yet, they could send the money back to the executor. Somehow, she'd figure out a means to earn the money to pay for the chemotherapy treatments. She still didn't know how but counted on God to show her. Tomorrow was Monday, a treatment day. She found Delores Burke's number and asked her to take her aunt to her therapy appointment.

Shilo reread her list. Yeah, the hardest part would be telling Aunt Sarah. She started on dinner, and soon her aunt joined her. Together they made Manhattans—roast beef open-faced sandwiches cut in two, with mashed potatoes in between and gravy overall. Plus a garden salad on the side.

Their naps seemed to have mellowed them both, for there wasn't a lot of conversation, but the vibe remained gentle and pleasant. They even hummed together, which made Shilo's heart lighter. "All to Jesus."

However, once they were seated at the table and the food blessed, Aunt Sarah focused on Shilo so intently she squirmed.

"How about you tell me what happened to your hair now."

"Okay." Shilo forked one more bite, buying time, and swallowed. "I realized losing your hair bothered you. And even with caps and wigs and knowing it would grow back, you still felt alone. I just didn't want you to feel that way."

"So you shaved your head?"

Shilo gave a small nod and took another bite.

"What were you thinking? I mean, yes, that's an enormously compassionate gesture, even for you, and you are the most compassionate person I know. Didn't Jesse get upset?"

Memories of his face when he first saw her flashed through her brain. "You might say that."

"What happened?"

"Before I could tell him, he'd come home, and I didn't hear him. He thought it'd be funny to tug the scarf off my head. Then he nearly had a heart attack." His expression still etched in her brain.

"I can imagine. Shilo Dawn, what possessed you to do something like that? When you are married, you need to discuss things. Appearance is important to Jesse. I know, and I'm getting the message into my brain that it's just hair. And hair will grow. But you can't make those kinds of decisions alone and assume he'll change who he is in order to accept it."

"But he did. Last night. When I landed in the pool, I must have lost my wig because I didn't have it at the hospital, and it wasn't with my things. My purse wasn't either, for that matter. So, I'm guessing it came off and everyone saw me. I apologized to him. He told me that was the least of what was on his mind." Though something changed.

They cleaned the kitchen together and watched evening television until Shilo begged off and headed for bed. She wasn't all that tired, but the light from the TV screen hurt her eyes. Besides, she wanted to go over her list again to figure out when to leave Aunt Sarah's so she'd arrive home after Jesse left for work.

Home. That's how she thought of it. But now she needed to remember the house belonged to Jesse, and she couldn't call it hers anymore.

Sleep finally came, and then the morning. Shilo headed out to the kitchen. She'd need to leave Aunt Sarah a note about Delores picking her up. If she'd mentioned her plan last night, there would've been a row.

Shilo slipped out the door and slowly started out before her aunt woke up. One hurdle down. The walk would also stretch her tired muscles that missed moving while she recuperated from the accident, though her head needed her to take it easy and not rush too fast. She walked a good twenty minutes, but arrived in time to see the garage door go up. Stepping behind a nearby maple tree, she kept out of Jesse's sight until he'd driven away.

Then she realized she didn't have her keys because her purse hadn't been returned. How would she get inside?

With a resolute decision and a prayer she wouldn't fall, Shilo worked her way to the backyard and scooted the patio table out to where the back porch roof sloped the lowest. Then she used a chair to step onto the surface of the table before pulling it up with her and stacking it on the tabletop to gain more height. After a couple tries where she had to stop to keep the hammer in her brain from cracking her skull, she hoisted herself up over the edge of the roof and dragged her body until all of her lay on the rough shingles. They scratched her legs, but at least she'd gotten up. The roof's angle proved shallow, which made walking on it easier. However, now her head officially hated her.

She tried the window, finding it open. *Thank You, Lord.* Ducking through, she breathed a sigh of relief and headed for her bedroom.

Jesse would be at work for some time, so she took a few minutes to lie down on her bed, long enough to get some control back with her headache.

Twenty minutes later she was ready to try again. She found her backpack and placed all her possessions that she'd brought with her inside and took a second to change from her new clothes to her jeans skirt and a T-shirt. Bringing anything Jesse bought her would be wrong, besides being a constant reminder of how life could've been.

As she wrote him a note to explain, she spotted her wedding rings. Did she leave them too? Yes, though it hurt like a knife thrust to her chest as she pulled them off.

She wiped her palms over her eyes and tiptoed down the stairs, heading to the kitchen. The next part of her plan had her phoning Vivian for help with Aunt Sarah's transportation needs. Her call went through faster than she expected.

"Jesse Franklin's office, how may I help you?"

"Viv, it's Shilo—"

"Shilo! Wait a sec. Jesse got called to his grandfather's office. I know he'll want to talk with you."

She couldn't let that happen. "No, Viv. I only wanted to tell you that I'm glad we met. I'm leaving for California and am asking you to do two things for me, please. Aunt Sarah has therapy appointments and will need to be driven to them. She's too shaky afterward to drive herself. Could you arrange that? Delores Burke is managing today for me." She heard scratches, like pen on paper.

"Okay, what else can I do? I'm already praying."

That returned the blanket of comfort around Shilo's shoulders. "Would you please take care of Jesse? He's not going to be happy about this. He wants to do what's right, but this is for the best."

"I'm not sure I agree, Shilo, but I will gladly watch over him. He's one special man."

"Yes, he is. That's why I can't keep hurting him anymore. Bye, Viv." Shilo hung up before her friend talked her out of her plan.

She picked up her backpack and sauntered to the living room, taking in the place she'd started to call home. She'd miss every inch, but more she'd miss what could've been. Her glance fell on the double frame. She pulled the wedding photo out and tucked it with her other possessions.

She had no money for this trip, but God provided on her way out. He would again, she was confident.

With one last look around, she slipped out the door and turned her steps toward US 31. "Heavenly Father, please pick out the perfect ride for me, and keep me safe in Your protection."

Monday, June 25, 1973

Jesse had hoped to wait until he had his things moved, or ready to move from his office—and found a moment to tell Viv—before he announced to his grandfather that he planned to leave the firm. However, the summons from the great Alvin Dean Franklin, Esq. changed his timetable. So, with a cleansing breath, he opened Grandfather's office door.

His secretary spoke on the phone but pointed with her pencil toward the inner office.

Jesse nodded and gave her a smile. It must be brutal working for the old man.

Once inside, his grandfather kept doing what he was doing at his desk, knowing full well Jesse stood waiting to be acknowledged. Fear of disturbing him or saying the wrong thing held Jesse in bondage for as long as he could remember. But no more. He and God talked way into the night. Becoming totally sold out to Him hadn't happened. Yet. But something did. Something that gave him the peace to do this. Today.

He cleared his throat.

Grandfather raised his gaze. "Have a seat, boy. I'll be with you in a moment."

Jesse chose to stand as a man, not a child. But he did move to where the visitor chairs faced the desk.

Finally, Grandfather put his pages down. "I want you to see the type of woman you married. I had a private detective do a thorough search of her life ever since she left here. You sure picked a winner, boy. Soliciting charges, drug charges. Here, get a load of what she is underneath." He shoved a paper toward Jesse.

A photo, a mug shot, to be precise. And Shilo looked nothing like herself. Instead of feeling upset at her, though, his ire mounted at the old man who gloated as if he'd won the war. "You don't know the entire story."

"And I suppose you do? Look, I have done my best to keep you two apart. Why you had to oversee her grandfather's will, I'll never understand."

"What do you mean you did your best to keep us apart? What did you do?" Jesse flexed his fists at his side.

"You don't think she won that beauty contest on her own, do you? And once I moved her out of the way, keeping her letters from reaching you was the simple part. She doesn't belong in our family. You will get this marriage annulled. I've got the paperwork right here. You only need to sign your name. I'll make sure she gets her signature on here, and then you two are through. No more, do you hear me?"

Jesse closed his eyes and breathed in. *You can do this.* "No. I am not signing that or anything else to end my marriage. And please hear me, I said My Marriage. Not yours, not the family's. Shilo has more integrity and compassion in her little finger than you've shown in your whole life. I came today to inform you that I am leaving the firm. You just severed all lingering doubts." He strode to the door.

"You get back here. We're not through."

Jesse paused before exiting. "Goodbye, Grandfather."

And then he left, his grandfather's rants echoing after.

When he returned to his office, Viv was hanging up the phone.

"Hey, just wanted you to know I no longer work here. I'll be starting with Pat Whitcomb and his practice in the very near future. If you want to come along, say the word."

She stood and grabbed his arm. "Absolutely, boss. But I need to tell you something. Shilo called."

"Shilo? Where is she? What did she want?"

"She's leaving for California. I think she called from your house. I tried to call her back at her aunt's, and Sarah said Shilo already left a good hour ago. I'm not sure, but if you hurry you might catch her."

Jesse pulled his keys from his pocket before he even pressed for the elevator. Had this behemoth of a contraption always been this slow? He should've just taken the stairs, but now the doors opened.

He pushed the basement floor button five times and fairly danced waiting to arrive. Jesse tore out to where he'd parked in the parking garage and shattered the speed laws into pieces heading for his house. He pulled in the drive and raced in the front door. "Shy? You here?"

No answer, so he hustled up the stairs to her room. All her clothes still hung in the closet. But just as he started to breathe about that, he realized her backpack, her jean skirt, and her Bible were gone. Then he spotted the note on her nightstand.

Jesse,

I'm sorry about everything. I told you I'm not the perfect girl you keep on the pedestal. I'd thought that maybe you could deal with the real me, but I'm not going to make you try. I do hope you can shake free from your grandfather one day and I wish you a long and happy life, hopefully with Jesus as your Savior.

Thank you for letting me be your wife. I promise to pay you back all the money.

Love,

Shilo

Her rings lay underneath.

No. No way he'd allow this to happen. He'd been an idiot to not see she loved him, and he'd been the one to screw this all up. So, he had to fix it.

God, I could use some help here.

He raced down the stairs and just as he headed for the front door, he spotted the empty photo frame. He paused and stared, the message clear. She wanted to remember. He knew that as well as he knew he loved her and had to tell her. There was still hope.

What if she took her car?

Jesse realized without having to look that if she left everything he'd given her, she wouldn't take the Camaro. That meant she'd be walking.

Or hitchhiking.

He threw himself into his Ferrari and screeched from his driveway. Then he burned rubber tearing out to Lincoln Road and headed east toward the highway.

She wasn't walking alongside Lincoln, so she had to have reached the 31. He turned south at the light and about fifty yards ahead, he spotted her.

And a police patrol car parking a little ways in front of her.

Oh, great.

Jesse skidded to a stop beside her and jumped out. "Shilo, hey, Shy."

She stopped and faced him. "What do you want?"

"You know what I want."

The officer walking toward her paused, his hand hovering near the butt of his gun.

"C'mon, Shy. Get in. Let's talk."

Shilo glanced toward the officer and stepped to the Ferrari. When she slid in where he held the door for her, she pointed her finger at him. "You realize I'm only doing this because I don't want to talk with Officer Nucum anymore."

"Whatever works." Jesse shut her door and climbed in his side. "Look, Shilo, I was stupid. I overheard you tell Eli that you loved him, and I lost my mind." Words now came in a rush, most likely from the pressure of the officer heading their way. "I've wanted to tell you, in fact I'd planned to—"

"Where did you get this?" Shilo held up her mug shot that he hadn't dropped until he climbed in his car.

Stupid, he should've gotten rid of it. "Grandfather called me in today to give me that and tell me we were getting an annulment."

"Maybe he's right, Jess. Now that you know I don't belong on any pedestal—"

"If God can see you as someone clean and beautiful, why can't I?"

She didn't answer, so he continued. "I told Grandfather no, that our marriage was none of his business. Then I quit the fir—"

"You did what?"

"I quit the firm. You were right. He doesn't have any business dictating our lives."

"But what about your job?"

"Shy, I'd do anything for you. Don't you get it? I—"

Tap, tap. Officer Nucum's face peered in his driver's side window.

Could he not catch one break?

Jesse lowered the glass. "Yes, Officer?"

"Is everything okay? I was about to talk with the young lady about the perils of hitchhiking when you accosted her."

"She's my wife, and I need to speak with her. So, if you don't mind."

"I gotta hear it from you, miss."

Jesse erupted. "That's Mrs. I just told you she's my wife. Now if you'll get out of here, I can finally tell her I'm in love with her an—"

"You love me?"

Jesse groaned. Nothing had gone as he'd wanted. "Yeah, but please forget I said it. Just for a minute?"

Officer Nucum tapped again. "Um, so, are you sure you are okay, ma'am? I noticed your bandage." He made a little circle in the air while pointing at her head.

Shilo grinned. "I'm wonderful, officer. And if you will excuse us, I believe my husband wants to say something again."

The cop glanced between Shilo and Jesse, shrugged, putting his ticket pad away as he headed for his patrol car.

"So, as you were saying, Jess …"

He reached for her, gliding his fingers over the softness of her cheek.

She leaned into his hand, making him cradle her face, and closed her eyes. "You say an awful lot with your actions, Mr. Franklin. But may I hear the words again, please?"

"I love you, Shilo Franklin. I have for as long as I can remember. I want our marriage to be real. Complete. Will you please be my wife, my partner, my best friend, for better or worse, for richer or poorer, in sickness and in health, until death separates us?"

She kissed his palm. "Yes, Jesse Franklin. I love you too and want a genuine marriage with you. A complete one."

He hated to bring it up, but he'd better. "I do need to let you in on a couple things, maybe three."

Her eyes opened. "Like what?"

"Like, Saturday morning when I left, I went to talk with Pat Whitcomb. I wanted someone who'd worked for family and had survived that to listen. He did more than listen, he offered me a position, a partnership at his practice. I need to call and update him, but I might ask for a week to spend with my wife."

"I like that idea. What are the other things?"

"Your check came. I had it with me on Friday, but with everything that happened since... It's at the house.

"And I did some investigating about Lisa, the one at the hospital. Even with what you went through in California, we should be able to at least foster if not adopt her. Her case worker and I had a long talk, and she's sending the paperwork to me to get started. Oh, no!" He slapped his forehead. "I need to call her to have her resend it to the house." Then he caught Shilo's gaze.

Tears threatened to stream her cheeks. "You did that for her?"

"And for us. There's a lot to her story, but maybe we should go home first." He used his thumbs to wipe away her tears.

"Okay, but before we do, we need to address something else."

"Anything. What?" He'd do whatever she asked.

She grinned. "Do you know, Mr. Franklin, that you have not kissed me since our wedding day? I don't think I can wait to get home for that."

"My pleasure, Mrs. Franklin." And he pulled her as close as the console between them allowed, kissing her still damp cheeks, the tip of her nose, and then gently placing his lips to hers, the surrender and release making the kiss go deeper—soul deep.

He didn't want to break it off, but he'd do a much better job once they were in their house. "Let's go home, Mrs. Franklin."

She wove her hand at his elbow and leaned back in the seat. "Yes, Mr. Franklin, let's go home. The sooner the better."

Epilogue

Thursday, June 27, 1974

Shilo held Lisa on her lap as they sat outside the courtroom. She hoped her own nerves didn't get through to the little girl she loved as her own.

Fortunately, back when her birth parents got called before the judge and lost their parental rights, the child hadn't been able to attend. The jury relied on photos to see the damage those monsters did to their daughter.

Shilo wondered if Lisa would make a connection and be afraid of the courthouse, but once she and Jesse explained everything, she was happy and excited to go. She and Shilo shopped for matching dresses just for the occasion.

Jesse paced. He understood more about how the law worked and had figured out all the potential outcomes. He might imagine he played it cool, but she could see this meant the world to him too.

In fact, Jesse took to fatherhood like nobody's business. He'd told her he worried that since he'd never had much of a role model that he'd make a bunch of mistakes. But that giant heart of his couldn't be missed.

He'd explained to Shilo before Lisa came to live with them that she had problems with men, for good reason. Somehow, the child figured out that he was safe and took to him quickly. They were the best of pals. For instance, when her kindergarten class held a Daddy-Daughter Dance, they attended and had a blast. Though walking now, she still limped, but Jesse showed her how to stand on his feet as he twirled her around. It worked perfectly.

Now that he'd joined Pat Whitcomb, they'd renamed the practice Whitcomb and Franklin. Viv kept them both in line because Pat's secretary had been ready for maternity leave and decided to stay home with her newborn.

So much good came since last June. Even Aunt Sarah, who adored Lisa, was getting back to her old self with a new pixie cut hairdo. Her hair grew in thicker and finer than before, and she looked stunning.

Shilo wore a similar style.

"Mr. and Mrs. Franklin, would you please come in?" The court clerk held open the door for them.

Shilo stood, helping Lisa to stand.

Jesse took the child's other hand, and together they walked into the courtroom.

The judge wore his black robe and a friendly smile while he sat high behind his bench.

"I want to welcome you, Mr. Franklin, Mrs. Franklin, and Lisa. I understand you're all here to officially become a family. What do you have to say about that Miss Lisa?"

The little girl glanced at Shilo, growing quiet.

"It's okay, honey. The nice man wants to make sure this is what you want and not just what Jesse and I want. Can you tell him?"

Lisa nodded. "I want us to be a family, please."

Even though they'd discussed it a bajillion times, hearing Lisa speak the words to the judge filled Shilo's heart to bursting. She glanced over the child's head and caught Jesse's gaze, telegraphing the same sensation.

"Then I think that is what we'll do. Miss Lisa, your name is currently Lisa Mae Fonseca. What would you like it to be?"

The child turned to Shilo again. "I can change my name?"

"Yeah, honey. We're sort of used to calling you Lisa, but you can change any or all of it. What would you like?"

Lisa closed her eyes, squinching them tight. Then she smiled and opened them. "Please, can I be Lisa Dawn Franklin?"

"Absolutely." The judge smiled. "I'll make a note here that her new birth certificate will be made out for Lisa Dawn Franklin. A very pretty name."

Shilo wiped the tear from her cheek and hoped she could keep her voice from wavering. "It's perfect."

Then there was a tug on her hand. Lisa tried to stand on her tiptoes.

Shilo stooped down so she wouldn't have to. "What is it?"

Lisa cupped her palm to her mouth and whispered into Shilo's ear. "Does this mean I can call you Mom and Dad?"

"Yes, sweet girl. Yes, you can."

Jesse had a questioning look, eleven lines forming between his brows.

Shilo grinned at him, and then whispered back to Lisa. "How about you tell Jesse?"

Lisa's face bloomed with a smile, and she turned to him. "I can call you my dad now."

Jesse's eyes grew moist, and he blinked and swallowed. "Yes, you can, daughter."

"Here is your paperwork. And I am so glad to have met you today. My best wishes for the Franklin family." The judge handed the page to his clerk and stood.

Lisa pulled free of Shilo and Jesse and limped to the steps leading to the judge.

Jesse started to follow, but Shilo shook her head. They watched as their new daughter managed the stairs and went straight to the man in black robes.

"Thank you for making us a family." She wrapped his legs in a bear hug.

"Come with me, Miss Lisa." The judge scooped her up in his arms, hugged her, and then carried her back to Shilo and Jesse. "This is the best part of my job. You two take mighty good care of this precious one." He tousled the child's blonde curls.

"We will. Thank you." Shilo took Lisa's right hand and Jesse held her left.

"Mom, Dad, can we go out to eat?"

Jesse chuckled. "Well, sort of. There's a party waiting for you that Miss Vivian put together over in the backyard next to my office. Should be a few more kids to play with. We want to celebrate becoming a family. Does that sound like a good idea?"

"Yes!"

They piled into Jesse's new Monte Carlo. The Ferrari wasn't a dad car, and he was determined to do everything to be a good father.

Once at Ferguson House, they climbed out and headed for the backyard. The Weather Girls, along with Viv's help, put together a pleasant lunch out in the garden.

"Don't forget, we want pictures of this new beautiful family." Windy's reminder wasn't needed. Shilo counted on photos to mark today.

Then she paused. "Maybe we should do this now before anyone spills."

"Good idea. Let's head over to the sycamore." Windy set up several poses. For the last one, she put Lisa standing on the white bench with Shilo and Jesse on each side of her, placing kisses on the child's cheeks.

"Oh, you are not going to believe this." Windy lowered her camera.

While Jesse helped Lisa down, Shilo stepped over to Windy. "Won't believe what?"

"Well, if there was any doubt about you all becoming a family, you can forget about it now. You got a cardinal."

"What? I thought that was only for couples." Shilo scanned the sycamore's branches.

"First time I've ever seen it, but you got one."

She turned to Jesse and Lisa and pulled them both into an enormous hug.

Then Jesse echoed what her heart sang out. "Thank you, Lord. Amen."

The End

Acknowledgements:

Abba Father, You are teaching me to rely on You more and more and this book is a prime example. Thank You for Your faithfulness and love.

Thank you to the ladies of 20BooksGals who have advised and brainstormed with me. You all hold a wealth of information and are so willing to share. Our two Julies, Robin, Jen, Diana, Sibella, Ang, Cynthia, Katy, and Kristin—I thank you all.

Stephanie with Alt 19 Creative, another wonderful cover. The collection is stunning with all the special details and this book fits in perfectly. Thank you!

My Beta Readers and Street Team, you are such a huge support. Thank you! And extra thanks to Katherine Karrol, Diana Lesire Brandmeyer, and Jennifer Crosswhite who keep that bar high.

To Robin Merrill, my editor and friend, you jumped in when the crisis hit! I can't thank you enough for your wonderful edits and encouragement. You are amazing, kiddo. Hugs!

My amazing family, I love you all—Phil, Jaime, Jonathan, Alyssa, Juan, Natalia, Meg, Mat, Owen, Kami, Amy, Rick, Rusty, Sandi, Aunt Kay, Sheilia, Dardie, Vicki, Jo, Suzy, Linda, and all my extended loved ones. I couldn't do this without you all.

And, Mom and E.B. I miss you.

Author Notes

I can't tell you specifically when the idea of Shilo presented herself. I do know that I thought Neil Diamond's song was about a girl only to learn it was his invisible male playmate from when he was a child (Insert face palm here). However, his interpretation would not work with this story. So, with my own twist, here ya go.

There are a few things that happen in the story that I pulled from my own life. Like the homecoming dance my senior year. I was excited to go since I was a new student and a popular boy had asked me. But he claimed to not feel well pretty early into the dance and said he needed to take me home. I learned the next day he'd invited me to get his old girlfriend jealous and it worked. He went back after dropping me off and made up with her.

Back in Kokomo, my bedroom window looked out over the front porch. I climbed out there and sat more times than I can count.

Also, my mom had breast cancer surgery when I was in the sixth grade, before chemotherapy was standard practice. I got frustrated one day that people weren't giving me the answers I needed, so I hopped on my bike and rode to the hospital. I wasn't old enough to visit in her room but they allowed me to go to a small lobby on her floor and then they wheeled her out in a wheelchair. She told me they'd taken her drainage tube out that morning and it "made her toes curl." I mixed parts of my experience into both Sarah and Betty's stories.

And for Shilo's act of compassion, I got that from my friend Heather Farrah. I ran into her one Sunday morning at church and she was wearing a scarf on her head. It was obvious she didn't have her hair. I said I hadn't heard that she had cancer and she promptly replied she didn't. But a friend did and she didn't want her friend to feel all alone, so she shaved her head. Less than two years later, Heather had cancer herself and the chemo took her hair again. She survived that attack, but when it returned, we lost a very kind lady. Shilo and Heather look nothing alike, but they both have that kind, compassionate character inside.

Oh, and Shilo's stitches? Yeah, I still have the scar from when I got them on my forehead—forty stitches done in four layers. But I moved her wound so that her hair, when it grew again, would cover up the scar.

I hope you enjoyed getting to know Jesse and Shilo. I have a confession. I really like Eli so look for him in a future book— *Walk Away, Rene*. Right now I'm finishing up with *Bernadette* (Her first chapter follows this note) and then I'll write *Pieces of April*. After that, it will be Eli and Rene's turn.

So, if you are ready, turn the page and check out *Bernadette*. She's a spitfire, that's for sure.

And until we meet again in the next book,

Abundant blessings!

Sneak Peek of Bernadette: A Sweet, Quirky, Romantic Twist

Book Eight of the Weather Girls Wedding Shoppe and Venue series

Bernadette Chapter 1
June 12, 1973 Kokomo, Indiana

"**B**ernadette!"

Bernie slid lower in her seat trying to figure out how to slide under the lunchroom table and sink into the linoleum floor. The last thing she wanted to do on this break was talk with her stepmother. But the clack of heels on concrete echoed through the garage and told her this woman was on a mission.

"There you are." Roberta Sawrey rounded the corner, coming through the doorway in all her glory. As usual, she was dressed to the nines, not a hair out of place in her gorgeous, highlighted gypsy shag. And her makeup had been done to perfection.

Which only made Bernie feel drabbier in her work clothes. But what in the world should she wear when she was either crawling under cars or leaning over their engines to find the mystery problem, and she didn't for sure want to go out in the tow truck dressed as a glamor puss. Despite that, the contrast glared.

Bernie sighed. "Yep, you found me. What is it, Roberta?"

"Could we talk, please? It really is important."

What should she say? Especially when her dad's new bride had that look in her eye. No wonder he seemed to do whatever Roberta wanted. "Sure. I've got a few minutes. Have a seat."

Roberta pulled out a chair at Bernie's table, grabbed a napkin, and wiped it off before sitting. Her smile appeared a little nervous. Must be something big. "So, how are you doing today? Are you having a good day?"

"You didn't come all the way down here to ask me that. What do you need, Roberta?"

Her stepmother leaned closer, her hands folded in front of her. Could she be praying? "So, you know I've been working with the City Council. Right?"

Bernie nodded, hoping she'd just get on with it.

"Well, I followed up some of my connections, and now we have a film company coming to Kokomo to use it as the backdrop for their latest movie. They want to film lots of things in this location. But here's the big thing." She paused as if trying to build up anticipation. But all she built was irritation.

Bernie glanced at her watch, hoping she'd get the message.

Apparently, she did because now her hands looked more like she was pleading rather than praying. "You know the actor, Garrett Lomas?"

Who didn't? The guy was a hunk, too good to be real, and what really got to Bernie was the way he could drive. Well, she assumed it was him driving. Could just be part of her daydream, but it wouldn't help to let her stepmother know about her secret. "Go on."

"This will be one of his movies. And the executives and I have been talking. We've come up with an idea that I think you're going to love."

Just the way she said that convinced Bernie's stomach to tighten into little, itty-bitty knots. There was no way she was going to love this.

"We decided he needs to escort a local girl around town to all the publicity events. We thought—"

"Whoa there. Hold your horses. There's no way. You cannot convince me to do this. Don't try. Don't even say it." Bernie would melt into a puddle right on the spot if she got forced into doing that.

Only now Roberta looked like she was a puppy who had just been kicked, making Bernie's steel-toed boots into the bad guy. Those big eyes of hers could make anyone feel so sorry.

However, Bernie was not going to fall for it this time. She would not give in. She was not going to be some kind of experiment like out of *My Fair Lady*.

"Fine, then. Had to ask. Like I said, it really is very important to a lot of people." Roberta pushed away from the table and stood. "I'm sorry I bothered you."

Oh, great. "Wait, Roberta. I'm sure you can find someone else. I guess it does sound like a good idea, and I am very honored that you thought of me. It's just not going to work. You can see that, right? I'm not cut out for wearing mod clothes and hanging on some movie star's arm."

Her stepmother turned at the doorway. "I think you underestimate yourself, Bernadette. Really, you are very attractive. Besides, this is the kind of thing you could tell your kids and grandkids about in the years to come."

She just didn't get it. There was nothing in common between the two of them outside of Bernie's dad. It was obvious that Roberta loved him. Bernie loved him more than she could say. However, that was where the commonalities ended. "Roberta, I don't see any kids or grandkids in my future. There's no man. And to be honest, I'm not looking. I'm perfectly content right here where I belong. Again, thank you for thinking of me."

"That's your final answer?"

Before Bernie could assure her it was, the phone rang in the office adjacent to the lunchroom. She held up a finger to Roberta as she grabbed the receiver. "Sawrey's Garage. How can I help you?" She slid a pad of paper closer and wrote down the pertinent info from the caller. When she hung up, she looked back at the doorway.

Roberta had left.

Bernie couldn't help but feel she had been saved by the bell. Or rather this time the telephone's jingle.

What could her stepmother be thinking even asking Bernie to do that? There was no way she could walk around Kokomo all dressed up, holding onto the arm of some movie star, and not fall flat on her face or do something equally embarrassing. And besides that, it wasn't just a movie star, it was Garrett Lomas. Garrett. Lomas. The guy who starred in her dreams. Oh yes, he was so pretty to look at, and he said his lines so well, but when he got behind the wheel of a car and drove in those races, Bernie just wanted to fan herself. That was hot. My, oh my. She needed to get a hold of herself.

The message. Oh yeah, she needed to take the message in.

"Hey Lenny, you got a second?"

A skinny, blond, thirty-something looked up from where he was checking spark plugs on a Chevelle. "Sure, Bernie. What's up?"

Bernie waved the note in her hand. "Looks like you made an impression on those people you did the work for on that Caddy yesterday. They want to bring in a '65 Charger for you to give it a once over. They bought it for their son for his sixteenth birthday, and they want to make sure everything's in top running order."

Lenny grinned around his chewing tobacco. "That sounds like fun. I really like those folks. Glad to do it for them." He took the note, glanced over it, and stuffed it in his pocket. "I'll make sure to be free this afternoon for just for them."

The phone rang again, so Bernie gave him a quick wave and headed back to the office. "Sawrey's garage. How can I help you?"

"We've got a flat, and the spare is in no shape to help. We're going to need a tow truck to pull us in. I'm calling from a farmhouse out on

County Road F." The caller gave some more information, and Bernie wrote it down. These folks were way out of town, it would take a while to get there.

"Hang on, and we'll have someone to you as soon as possible. They'll be leaving right away."

"Thanks so much." Whoever the guy was, there was something about his voice that did funny things to Bernie's stomach. Tiny little flutters. Probably just leftover insecurities from her talk with Roberta.

She stepped out of the office and looked for her dad.

He was rolled under a Ford pickup.

"Hey dad, I need to take the tow truck out. Got someone with a flat and a messed up spare."

"Make sure you dress right." He pulled himself from beneath and sat up. "You be careful, you hear?"

"Aren't I always?" Bernie leaned over and kissed his smudged cheek. "I'll be back in a bit. And I promise to do just what you've told me."

Bernie went around to the side of the building where they kept the tow truck shaded underneath a canopied tarp, unlocked the door, and pulled herself in. She might as well get busy now dressing in her costume.

If it weren't for that guy who tried to make a pass at her, none of this would be important. But it put her dad's mind at rest. And hers too, she could admit to herself.

Before starting the truck, she slipped the faded blue overalls over her feet and pulled them up, wiggling and squiggling until she got her arms into the sleeves. Then she zipped it up to her collar, thankful Dad had added an air conditioning unit to the truck. This summer was turning out hotter than blazes.

Next, she pulled out her red Farmall ball cap, making sure all of her short brown hair got tucked beneath. Then she added the aviator sunglasses and fake mustache that her father insisted on. Like anyone believed a five-foot man drove this tow truck. However, no one outside the garage would believe a five-foot nothing female could drive it either. But Bernie could. And as cockeyed as this disguise looked, at least it was something.

The drive out to the country didn't take long, especially with WLS playing good music on the radio. Dad's garage was located on the north side of town, so it was easy to slip up to where all anyone could see for miles around were cornfields.

The man had mentioned that someone let him make the call from their house. Even that close to town it probably would've ended up being a long-distance call. That was some real neighborliness in action. Wonder if it cost the guy anything?

Bernie followed the directions the caller had given and soon spotted the brand a new Rolls-Royce at the side of the road. She slowed while her heart stopped in her throat. Boy, she hoped they could fix that spare at the garage, because ordering a new wheel would take weeks and she had a feeling that the caller wasn't going to be the patient kind.

Everything for that car had to be special ordered.

Wow.

Just as she coasted to a stop, she spotted a guy walking up to the driver side of the rolls, opening the door to climb in.

Bernie shook her head. There was no way. It couldn't be.

Except Roberta told her just an hour ago that he was going to be here in town. Now Bernie's palms started to sweat. If she had known that he was the driver, she would've talked her dad into making this trip. Or any one of the guys in the shop. Anyone but her.

But then they would've asked why.

And she would've had to explain.

There was no justice in the world. Could Roberta have arranged this? Nah. It was just her stupid luck. Like always.

Bernie should've known why his voice sounded familiar, but never in a million years would she have guessed this pick up was for Garrett Lomas.

Gabe Lomas sank into the leather driver seat of the studio's rolls he'd borrowed. Stupid. That's what he was. Spending so much time in LA checking on the cars to be used in the film, it never occurred to him to check over this behemoth. Gotta ride in style, they said. Take the rolls, they said. "They" were going to get a piece of his mind when they ever got back. If they ever got back.

"Guess you got through to someone." His brother Gary had slipped down in his seat with his cowboy hat covering his face. "They nearly beat you back."

"I thought they might. I think I walked forever. Finally spotted a farmhouse and took a chance. The lady was kind and let me use her phone, though I think she might've recognized me, or rather you."

Gary didn't even move his hat. "It really doesn't matter if they recognize one of us. For all of this," he waved his hand in the air, "we are basically the same."

"Try telling that to Debbie. I bet she'd notice a definite difference." Gary's girlfriend and leading lady, soon to be fiancé, he was sure was not happy with all of Gary's female fans.

"She better not have any way of comparing." This time, Gary peered at his brother.

Outside of their family, the world pretty much merged the two of them together as Garrett Lomas, the movie star. But their family was well aware these were identical twin brothers, who looked amazingly alike on the outside, but were very different on the inside.

"That driver is taking a while to get out. Wonder if he needs some help." Not that Gabe really wanted to return to the humid summer heat, but the sooner they got the rolls to the garage where it could get fixed the better. What was left of his Coke was just a brown melted ice puddle in the bottom of his paper cup from the Dog 'N' Suds. Lunch had been a while ago, though the look on the chick's face when she skated out to a shiny new Rolls Royce with their orders would be indelibly printed on his brain for a long time to come.

The tow truckdriver finally started climbing from the truck and walked to the rolls's driver's side. Actually, he moved more like a dawdle or a really slow stroll. It was obvious the guy had nothing to do and all day to do it. That was not going to work in this situation.

Gabe opened his door, but then the guy really moved. Practically ran.

"Stay in the vehicle." The guy's hand emphasized his words. Still, he repeated, "Stay in your vehicle."

There was something funny about this guy. Even his voice was strange. Gabe climbed back in and closed the door. "Gary, move the hat and take a look. There's something weird going on."

Gary sat up, put his hat on his knee, and looked where Gabe tried to point without being seen pointing. "What? So the guy is short. He obviously can do the job. Not everyone has to be six-foot tall, ya know." He slid back into position and settled his hat on his face again.

His brother was right. The dude hooked things up as if he had done this his whole life. And as Gabe watched the movements, he could tell this guy did things the correct way. He shook his head. "I don't know.

Guess I was wrong. There for a minute I could've sworn that dude was a chick."

Gary snorted but didn't say anything.

It wasn't long before the rolls got pulled up onto the truck bed. Gabe waited for an invitation for him and Gary to ride along with the tow truck driver, but it never came. Guess they were really to stay in the vehicle. Yeah, that made him feel very safe. Ha!

Just when he was sure this driver was going to break all the safety rules, he headed back towards the rolls and waved them out to join him in the tow truck. Shouldn't he have done that before they hooked the car up onto the flatbed?

"Come on lazybones, we've just been informed we're riding with the driver."

Gary adjusted his hat and slid his sunglasses back into place. "Shouldn't we have climbed out first?"

"That's what I was thinking. Should we say anything, or should we just keep our mouths shut and hope he doesn't like your movies?"

"That's totally on you, big brother. This is where that ten minutes older counts. I'm disguised enough, though, so if anyone is going to get the fan treatment, it's going to be you." Gary touched the brim of his hat as he laughed.

That's what Gabe got for trying to run interference for his brother. If that's the way he wanted to play it, Gary could ride in the middle. It would serve him right.

They both jumped down from the truck bed and headed for its passenger side. Once inside, the driver never glanced their way but silently shifted into first and started the tow.

Thankfully, the ride was not that long because much more of the lack of conversation would have been mind-numbing. The driver had the radio turned up, and occasionally his fingers tapped the steering wheel. Again, it was one more thing that made Gabe wonder if maybe this driver was a girl. But then how did she grow a mustache?

Once back at the garage, Gabe hopped out and Gary followed.

Their driver seemed to disappear, but an older man with iron colored hair and a grease streak down his right cheek soon called them to the office. The guy shook their hands, but didn't seem to fawn on them. "Sorry about the snag to your day. We'll do the best we can to get the spare fixed so you can get out of here. If we can't, then we'll need to order some parts."

Gary at least spoke up now. "We're with the studio that's going to be filming here in town. They've got a lot of car stuff, a roster of mechanics, but most of that crew hasn't arrived yet. If it looks like it's going to take some time, maybe we can get the car to them and let them handle it?"

The older guy nodded. "Yeah, that makes sense. Well, give me a few minutes, and I'll let you know about your spare." He pointed out some chairs in a tiny waiting room and left to keep his word.

Gabe sat where he'd indicated and settled in, expecting a longer wait.

Gary picked up one of the *Popular Mechanics* magazines from a shelf and began combing through it before setting it back. "I need to talk you into something."

"Well, when you put it that way." Gabe didn't know whether to laugh or be scared.

"I am just being up front with you. It's kind of important. The studio execs came to me a couple hours ago. They have this publicity plan, and I have to tell you it really isn't all that bad except Debbie hates it. So, I'm kind of asking you to do what we did in high school."

Gabe had an inkling that he was going to like this as much as he did back in good ol' Hawthorne High when Gary talked him into things, a lot of things. Which made it difficult to guess what activity his twin referred to. He couldn't imagine what it could be. "I'm still paying with our parents for what you talked me into. So, this better not be something to get me into more hot water with them, or anyone else for that matter."

Gary chuckled, even if it was a little nervously. "Well, you know that Debbie and I are serious. In fact, I plan to ask her to marry me as soon as I can get the right moment."

There was no surprise in that for Gabe. He knew his brother would be doing that. The only surprise was that it hadn't happened as of yet. But he would play along. "Congratulations, and what do you want me to do?"

Gary remained silent a little too long, so Gabe punched him on the arm. "Fine. This is it. It's not a big deal. Except to Debbie. The studio wants me to go out with a local girl to a few places and drum up some publicity. It's all very up and up. From what I understand, the chick is really nice. It should be easy because her mom or some relative is setting up all of the events for while we're here. It's as simple as that. You just go out a few times with the girl."

This was not what Gabe expected. And it hit him like a ton of bricks. "You want me to go on a blind date?"

"It would only be for the first date. After that you would have met, so it wouldn't be a blind date."

"And that makes it okay? Where? How? What in the world made you think I would agree to this?"

"Actually I'm saving you, big brother. Debbie is the one who wanted to talk you into this. And I think you would've been steamrolled by what she can do. So, I'd take it as a personal favor for you to insure my love life here. No one says you have to do anything romantic with this chick.

There is nothing about love scenes or even holding hands. All you have to do is be a gentleman and escort her to the events."

Gabe rubbed the bridge of his nose. He had a headache coming on and he was ready to give his brother one too. "How many events are we talking?"

"I don't know. Just for however long we're here in town shooting. It's goodwill with the city."

"Please point out to Debbie that I am already driving your car to keep you safe."

"And she appreciates that, big brother." Gary slid his glasses down and peered at Gabe. There must be a lot of words flashing across his face—words he would've gotten in trouble for using back when they were kids.

Gabe was not the actor in the family. He was the stunt double. However, that was a recent development. He hadn't realized he would be signing on to be a full double. Still, even their mom occasionally checked Gabe's right jaw to spot the telltale mole that Gary didn't have—Gary's was on his left. So, technically, this could work, and no one would know it wasn't the great Garret Lomas doing the escorting.

He shook his head, mystified he would even consider doing this. But he would. For his brother. "Don't count on a wedding present from me. I think I've given you enough gifts. Tell Debbie fine. But I may be calling for a favor in return. So just beware."

About the Author

 Historical Christian Romance author, Jennifer Lynn Cary, likes to say you can take the girl out of Indiana, but you can't take the Hoosier out of the girl. Now transplanted to the Arizona desert, this direct descendant of Davy Crockett and her husband of forty plus years enjoy time with family where she shares tales of her small-town heritage and family legacies with their grandchildren.

You can contact Jennifer via her website www.jenniferlynncary.com Or use this QR code.

Also By Jennifer Lynn Cary

The Forgotten Gratitude Journal

Cheryl's Going Home (A Weather Girls Novel)

The Weather Girls Wedding Shoppe and Venue Series:
Judy in Disguise (Book One)
Sylvia's Mother (Book Two)
Runaround Sue (Book Three)
Cracklin' Rosie (Book Four)
Ronnie (Book Five)
Tracy (Book Six)

Nonfiction:
When God Holds Your Hand

Or use this:

QR code for Amazon Author page

Made in the USA
Monee, IL
29 December 2025